Bianca's Joy

Rose Island Book 3

By Kristin Noel Fischer

www.KristinNoel.com

Cover by Lyndsey Lewellen

Formatting by Paul Salvette

ISBN-13: 978-0-9997856-9-0

ISBN-10: 0-9997856-9-9

Chapter 1

Bianca Morgan

18 Years Ago
South Carolina

TEARS FILLED MY eyes as I entered the hospital nursery to say good-bye to my newborn daughter. Last night, I'd given birth to a beautiful baby girl. Today, I would be signing away my parental rights. Was I doing the right thing? I hoped so.

"She's wide awake," the nurse said, wrapping my baby in a blanket before lifting her out of the bassinet. "Have a seat in the rocking chair and I'll bring her to you."

Wincing, I lowered myself to the chair, careful not to sit directly on my stitches. Giving birth had been more painful than I'd imagined, but it was the soreness afterward that surprised me. For some reason, I thought there wouldn't be any pain once the baby was out. How naive I'd been.

Smiling, the nurse placed the baby in my arms. As I gazed down at my daughter, a rush of love and wonder filled me. How in the world had someone like me produced such a beautiful baby? Everything about her was amazing from her tiny fingers to her long eyelashes.

"She's beautiful," the nurse said. "What are you going to name her?"

The question hit me hard. Maybe insisting on holding my daughter one last time had been a mistake. "I'm not keeping her, so I didn't name her."

"You're giving her up for adoption?"

I nodded. "I'm too young to raise a baby on my own."

"What a brave thing for you to do." The nurse's tone was accepting and nonjudgmental, something I sincerely appreciated and needed at that moment.

I gently stroked my daughter's cheek. I'd never considered my decision as being brave. If I was truly brave, wouldn't I be keeping her like I wanted to?

Then again, my dad was probably right. I couldn't exactly give her a very good life.

I wasn't ready to be a mother. Well, not a real mother anyway. No, I was just one of those girls who'd gotten knocked up by a worthless boy at a drunken high school party on the beach last summer.

Stop being negative, I told myself. My time for

motherhood would come. Right now, I was simply making the best of a difficult situation by giving my baby to a couple unable to have children of their own. At least, that's what I kept telling myself.

"Do you know anything about the family adopting your baby?" the nurse asked, surprising me by sinking into the chair opposite me.

I shook my head "no" and explained that I'd agreed to a closed adoption. "I just hope they'll love her as much as I do. And I hope when she's old enough I'll be allowed to see her again."

The nurse absently stroked her thumb over the ragged scar that ran from the corner of her eye down to her mouth. What in the world happened to cause such a visible scar?

"I just met my birth mother," she said.

"You did? How was it?"

She hesitated a moment before smiling. "It was wonderful. She looks just like me."

"Wow." I gazed down at my baby. Did she look like me? I couldn't see any resemblance now, but maybe she'd eventually have my auburn hair and brown eyes.

"How was your delivery?" the nurse asked.

I cringed. "It was awful."

"What happened?"

Because she seemed genuinely interested, and I was

incredibly lonely, I told her everything. Not just about the birth, but about keeping the pregnancy a secret, being sent from my home on Rose Island, and now feeling my heart pulled out of my chest at the thought of leaving my daughter and never seeing her again.

"I just want her to be happy and have a good life. I want . . ." I choked back tears. "I'm sorry. Thank you for listening to me. My aunt has been kind, and my mother has been supportive, but—"

The nurse reached out and squeezed my hand. "I understand. Sometimes you just need another mother to talk to."

"You're a mother?"

She nodded. "I have a newborn daughter, so I understand. You just want what's best for her even if that means sacrificing your own happiness."

Wiping my eyes, I smiled and glanced at the nurse's name tag. Tiffany Jackson. "Thank you for saying that, Tiffany. I do want what's best for her."

Behind me, the door opened. Tiffany looked up and glared at the person who'd entered. "Yes? What is it?"

"I wanted to hold my baby," said a young woman with an accent I couldn't quite place.

"She's sleeping." Tiffany spoke in a harsh voice, and her facial scar seemed to turn red with anger. This other mother had obviously done something wrong.

"Can I not hold my baby when she's sleeping?" the other mother asked.

As though responding to the tension in the nursery, the other baby began to cry. Nurse Tiffany rubbed the scar along her face a little harder. When she saw me watching, she gave an exasperated sigh. "It's my mark to remind me that the gods despise me."

I frowned, not understanding why she'd say something like that. Then, she rose and left me.

Looking down at my daughter, I blinked back tears. It was time for me to go. Time for me to say my last good-bye and walk away.

Please take care of my baby, Lord. Give her good parents who love her and understand what a gift she is. I know she wasn't conceived under the greatest of circumstances, but I also know that every child is loved by you. Bless her life, always let her know I love her, and when she's older, bring us back together again.

A flash of light interrupted my silent prayer. Glancing up, I saw Tiffany holding one of those instant cameras I hadn't seen in a long time. The picture slid out, and she handed it to me. "This is for you, so you'll have a way to remember your daughter."

I took the photo, incredibly grateful. I hadn't thought to bring a camera or ask for a picture of my baby. A camera had been on the list of things to bring to the hospital, but I hadn't thought it'd applied to me. Plus, neither my aunt nor my mother had encouraged any photos.

I stared at the dark picture, watching it slowly come to life. "Thank you, Tiffany. Thank you so much."

She gave a curt nod. "Well, are you ready?" She held out her arms for my baby as though knowing the sooner I left, the sooner I could start to heal.

Gathering all my strength, I nodded and surrendered my child. Then, without looking back, I left the nursery, clutching the picture and praying I'd done the right thing.

Chapter 2

Bianca

Rose Island, Texas
Present day

RIDING MY BIKE across Rose Island before work was one of my most favorite things to do. I loved the peacefulness of this early March morning. Loved cruising through our quiet town to the paved bike trail that ran along the water. Giddy with happiness for today, I pedaled past the Pelican Pub, past The Blue Crab, and out to the country club.

From there, I raced down Blackberry Lane, where my sister Jillian lived with her husband and their three kids. Because Jillian wasn't sitting on the front porch drinking coffee, I figured she must've had a rough night with the baby. My newborn niece had her nights and days mixed up, and nothing Jillian did seemed to help.

Had my own daughter kept her parents up like that when she was a baby? Maybe I'd find out today. Or maybe I'd have to wait a little longer.

Regardless, today was my daughter's eighteenth birthday. She was now a legal adult who could decide for herself whether or not she wanted to see me.

Ever since signing away my parental rights, I'd hoped one day to be reunited with her. In a heartfelt letter I'd sent through the adoption agency, I'd introduced myself and told her about my family and life on Rose Island. I'd also expressed my deep desire to meet her. Or rather, to meet her again.

Hopefully, she'd receive my letter and be just as eager to meet me. Maybe she'd been wondering about me like I'd been wondering about her all these years.

In order not to get my hopes up, I'd convinced myself she wouldn't call until tomorrow or later in the week. I imagined she'd be too busy celebrating this momentous birthday with friends and family. Still, I planned on keeping my phone with me all day just in case she did call.

Cutting down Fourth Street, I passed the church and headed home. Today was also the day I'd finally tell Anna and my sisters about having a baby when I'd been in high school.

Throughout the years, there'd been so many times I'd wanted to reveal my secret. I worried, however, that admitting I'd given away my daughter would make living without her impossible.

So, I'd remained silent, something I usually wasn't very good at. Today, my silence would end, and everyone would know that eighteen years ago I'd given birth to a beautiful baby girl.

Turning left onto Main Street, I pedaled past the courthouse until I saw the sign for my hair salon, The Last Tangle. Owning the salon and living in the apartment above was a dream come true for me. I was proud of all I'd accomplished, and for the most part, I loved my life on the island.

Of course, I wished I wasn't several pounds overweight, but time in counseling with an eating disorder therapist was helping me learn to honor my body instead of mistreat it. Yadira, my therapist, had been the one to suggest my early morning bike ride, not as a way to lose weight but as a way to enjoy the body God had given me.

At first, I'd resisted. Now, exercising in the morning had become a habit. While I would never have the figure of a supermodel, I was strong and blessed with a beautiful life. Best not to squander it away feeling sorry for myself just because I loved my sweets.

Inhaling the heavenly scent of freshly baked bread from my sister's bakery, I circled around to the back of the building, parked my bike, and stepped inside our hodgepodge foyer. From there, I had three choices—the salon, the bakery, or the stairs leading up to the apartments.

I chose the stairs. In my apartment, I walked around the uninstalled granite countertops that'd been leaning against the living room wall for the past month. The contractor I'd hired to update my kitchen had disappeared after I'd given him an advance so he could pay off his hardware bill before beginning my job.

I know, I know. I shouldn't have done that, but I did.

I needed to own up to my mistake and find someone else to finish the job. A girl could only live so long with uninstalled granite countertops in her living room.

After showering, I got ready for church, carefully applying my makeup and styling my hair. Then, I finished dressing and pulled on my new designer boots. The boots had been expensive, but they felt amazing, and I'd instantly fallen in love with them at the store.

Looking in the mirror now, I cringed at my appearance. My makeup looked okay, but . . . was I too fat to wear these boots?

I turned to the side and studied my profile. Yep, too fat. I'd have to change my whole outfit.

Before I could, there was a pounding at my door. Without bothering to wait for an invitation, my bossy little sister barged into my apartment. "Bianca? Are you ready?"

"Almost," I shouted from the bedroom.

"We're going to be late."

I glanced at the clock on my phone. Vicki was right. If we didn't leave this instant, we'd be late again.

"*Bianca.*"

"I'm coming," I said, accepting the fact that I had no choice but to wear the boots.

Quickly, I opened my nightstand drawer and removed the photo the nurse had taken of my daughter and me. I'd had it framed years ago, and it was by far my most valued possession.

Smiling, I thought about that precious moment I'd held my baby in the nursery. *Happy birthday, sweetheart. May God bless you today. Call me soon, please. Don't make me wait.*

"Bianca, seriously." Vicki stomped down the hall. "Stop looking in the mirror and let's go. Your lipstick is fine."

"Okay, okay." I stuck the framed photo into my handbag and headed out the door, determined not to be disappointed if the day didn't unfold exactly as I wanted.

After all, I had my health, my family, and a successful business. God willing, I'd soon have a relationship with my daughter.

⟡

DESPITE THE COLD temperature, the sun was shining as Vicki and I walked to church. When we entered the sanctuary, I spotted Daniel Serrano kneeling in prayer. His head was bowed, and my heart did its usual jumpy thing it always did at the sight of him.

As though reading my mind, Daniel looked up, brushed back his dark hair, and smiled right at me with those chocolate-brown eyes of his. Then, he gave a little wave, causing my knees to knock. I waved back and kept walking forward, reminding myself he was just being nice. A smile and a wave didn't mean anything.

Daniel Serrano was gorgeous after all. I'd been secretly in love with him ever since he came to the island with his daughter four years ago. He really was the perfect man for me. There was just one problem. Guys like Daniel never went for girls like me. The sooner I accepted that, the better.

"You're drooling," Vicki said.

"No, I'm not."

"Yeah, you are." She looped her arm through mine as I wiped my mouth, which was perfectly dry.

"When are you going to do something about that?" she asked.

"Something about what?"

"Something about that massive torch you're carrying for Daniel. You're not getting any younger, you know."

"Ha, you're one to talk. Last time I checked, you were closer to forty than thirty."

"Hush." She pinched my arm before pulling away.

As the youngest Morgan sister, Vicki had always been the *cute* one. In my opinion, she was still cute with her short blond hair, petite figure, and understated elegance. In my opinion, the only reason she couldn't find Mr. Right was because of her unreasonably high expectations.

Me, on the other hand . . . well, I was interested in lots of guys. The guys I liked just never seemed to be interested in me the same way.

For the most part, that was okay. There was a lot of me to love after all. Not every guy could handle loving a larger woman like me.

Sometimes, however, Daniel Serrano looked at me with all that smoldering Latin appeal, and I'd think . . . *maybe*. Maybe he'd like to try to love me. Keeping his eyes on me, he'd run a hand over his short cropped hair or stroke his scruffy beard, and then . . .

Then, the moment would pass, and he'd look away or make an excuse about needing to check on his daughter or return a phone call for work. Was he just being shy or did he honestly feel nothing for me?

As Vicki and I joined our parents and the rest of our family in the front pew, I told myself not to look back at Daniel. No need to appear obvious, especially not in church where I was supposed to be concentrating on more important matters.

Then, because self-control had never been my strength, I did glance back. At first, I didn't see him. Had he left? Had seeing me this morning made Daniel finally realize that I was the woman for him and he needed to run out right this minute to buy me an engagement ring?

No, he was still there. I hadn't seen him because my view was blocked by single mom and PTA president, Kate Tate. Ever the opportunist, Kate had slid into the pew in front of Daniel and was flirting with him. In church. In front of her kids no less.

Seriously, Kate? Do you think church is an appropriate place to flirt with my future husband? Hands off, lady.

Pushing away thoughts of Kate and Daniel and future husbands, I knelt beside my mother and prayed for my daughter as I often did. I also prayed that things would go well when I made my big announcement at family brunch in a few hours.

While my mother had understood my desire to meet my daughter, my father had insisted I was making a big mistake. I'd tried talking to him about it, but the stubborn man had refused to listen.

When I finished praying, I slid back beside my mother. At the far end of the pew, Jillian's husband, Keith, shot me a sympathetic smile. Keith was a recovering alcoholic, and we'd talked extensively how binge eating was similar to alcohol abuse.

We both believed prayer was a powerful tool in combating one's addiction, so he probably thought overeating was the reason for my fervent prayer today. Well, he and everyone else would find out soon enough what was on my mind.

Chapter 3

Bianca

*A*FTER CHURCH, VICKI and I drove to our family's small hobby ranch situated on the south side of the mountain. Technically, the mountain was a large hill in the center of the island, but locals had been calling it *the mountain* for years.

In addition to organic farms and free-range ranches, the mountain boasted several farm-to-table restaurants surrounded by fields of wildflowers. This time of year, the winter roses were still in bloom, but in a few weeks, they would be replaced by daisies, bluebonnets, and hundreds of other breathtaking wildflowers.

As Vicki and I drove down the gravel driveway toward the house, I took in the familiar sight of chickens, cows, horses, and goats grazing in the fields. Usually, the dogs sounded the alarm with their barking, but they must've been out in the barn with my dad because I didn't see them.

At dinner, I sat between my nephews, waiting for the perfect opportunity to share my news. Once dessert was served, I took a deep breath and opened my mouth to speak.

Before I could say anything, Jillian's youngest son, fourteen-year-old Drew, interrupted me. "Aunt Bianca, can you please pass the caramel sauce?"

"Of course." I slid the little plate containing the mason jar of homemade caramel to Drew and watched as he dumped it on his gingerbread cake.

Jillian's oldest son, Matt, groaned. "Save some for the rest of us, why don't you?"

"I did."

"No, you didn't."

Jillian shot both boys a warning look. Then she glanced at her husband who was too busy arguing with my dad about some political issue to notice her plea for help.

Not that Jillian needed Keith's help. Like all Morgan women, she was strong, independent, and capable of standing up for herself. Since the birth of her daughter a few weeks ago, however, she seemed tired, which she probably was.

"Matthew," my mother said, shifting Jillian's baby in her arms, "there's more caramel sauce in the refrigerator if you'd like to get it."

"I'll get it." Drew jumped to his feet and headed to the kitchen.

As soon as he left, Matt reached across me to steal a forkful of his little brother's cake.

"Oh, you're going to get in trouble for that," I said, teasing him.

"Get in trouble for what?" He smiled at me innocently.

Laughing, I shook my head. For the most part, my nephews were sweet boys, but like most siblings, they bickered and gave each other a hard time. One thing they never argued about, however, was their darling baby sister, Linda Faith. Although my new niece was a little on the fussy side, her brothers adored her as did the rest of us.

I glanced at my mother, holding the baby. Had my own daughter been fortunate enough to have aunts, uncles, cousins, and grandparents in her life? Had she read my letter yet? What did she think? What if she was trying to call me right now?

I snuck a quick peek at my phone, disappointed to see no new messages. Matt nudged me with his elbow. "No phones at the table, Aunt Bianca. You know the rule."

I rolled my eyes and stuck my phone back into my pocket. "Thanks for the reminder, Matt."

We grinned at each other, and I was struck by how much he and his brother had grown in the past year. I was lucky to live so close to them. I missed my other nieces and nephews who currently lived abroad. It'd been almost a year since we last saw them. Hopefully, Nick and Anna would receive orders to come back to the States soon.

When Drew returned from the kitchen, I decided it was now or never. Clinking my spoon against my glass to get everyone's attention, I came to my feet. "Sorry for the interruption, but I have an announcement to make."

"An announcement?" Drew shoved a bite of cake into his mouth. "What is it?"

I looked at my father who was staring down at his plate, avoiding my gaze. "Well, it's just that . . ." I hesitated, second-guessing myself. After keeping the secret for so long, I was suddenly nervous.

"Please don't tell me you're moving out of your apartment," Vicki said. "Do you know how long it took me to train you to be a good neighbor? I really don't want to have to break in someone else."

"You're moving?" Jillian said.

I smiled. "No, I'm not moving. I . . . well, do you remember how I went to South Carolina my last year of high school?"

"No," Drew said, completely serious.

Matt flicked his little brother's arm. "Of course, you don't remember. You weren't even alive back then."

"Oh yeah."

"*Oh yeah*," Matt repeated, sarcastically.

Ignoring them both, I continued, wanting to get this over with. "Well, I left Rose Island because I was pregnant."

"What?" Vicki's perfectly plucked brow lifted.

"I was pregnant," I repeated. "I had a baby and gave her up for adoption. She was a little girl."

Jillian shot a quick glance at Keith, but Vicki and my nephews just stared at me as if waiting for the punch line. I often joked around, so they probably thought I was kidding.

"Well, that's it. That's my big announcement." Sitting back down, I nodded. "My daughter is eighteen today. I always told myself I'd contact her when she turned eighteen. That's why I'm telling you this. I sent a letter through the adoption agency. She's supposed to receive it this morning. They said they'd deliver it via private courier since the post office is closed today, so hopefully, she'll get it."

Picking up my phone, I looked at Matt. "That's why I've been checking my cell. I'm hoping she'll receive my letter, read it, and call."

Stunned silence dominated the room. All eyes, except my father's, focused on me.

"You're serious?" Vicki said.

"I am."

Jillian brushed back her long honey-brown hair. "I always wondered, but you never wanted to talk about that year you were gone."

"I know," I said.

"So, when do we get to meet her?" Drew asked.

"I don't know." I refrained from checking my phone again. "I guess it will depend on whether or not she wants to meet me."

"Why wouldn't she want to meet you?" Drew asked. "You're awesome, Aunt Bianca."

"Thanks, honey." My heart lifted at his loyalty. Then doubt crept in as I thought of all the reasons why my daughter might not want to meet me.

Maybe she resented being adopted. Maybe her parents had never told her she was adopted, so she didn't even know about me.

Or maybe . . . my stomach twisted at this last horrible thought. Maybe, like my younger brother, this child of mine was no longer living. I pushed away the morbid idea. Surely, the adoption agency would've contacted me if that were the case.

"Well," Drew said, a mischievous tone in his voice, "if she's eighteen, I guess that means Matt's not the oldest cousin anymore."

Matt shrugged and dished up another piece of cake. I was so nervous that I wanted another piece of cake, too. *You can't solve this problem with food*, I reminded myself.

Drew took a sip of his drink. "Who's the baby's father?"

"*Drew*," Jillian chastised.

"What? I'm just curious."

"It's not an appropriate question," Keith said.

"Oh, sorry."

"That's okay," I said.

My dad pushed away from the table and came to his feet. "Please excuse me. I need to check on the dogs. Lady pulled a muscle in her leg, and . . ." He gave my mother a nod before turning and leaving the dining room without further explanation.

My stomach twisted. Having him walk away like that nearly killed me. Why did he have to be so stubborn and unsupportive? There wasn't anything wrong with Lady. He was just using her as an excuse.

Keith offered a sympathetic smile before addressing his boys. "Come on, guys. Let's clear the table and start on the dishes so the ladies can talk."

"But I want to hear more about Aunt Bianca's baby," Drew said.

"Later." Keith stacked several plates, setting the silverware on top. His boys did the same, clearing everything in one trip.

"Thanks, babe," Jillian said.

Keith winked at his wife. "You're welcome."

My mom, Vicki, and I thanked him as well, then my mother said she was going to check on our father. "I'm sure Lady will be fine, but you know how your father gets. He loves his dogs."

No kidding, I thought.

"Do you want to leave the baby with me?" Jillian asked.

"No, I've got her." Propping the infant on her shoulder, my mother left the room.

For a few moments, my sisters and I sat in silence. Then, Vicki winked at me. "You always were great at finding an excuse to get out of doing the dishes."

I laughed. "You're one to talk."

Jillian shook her head. "You both were always disappearing, leaving me to clean the kitchen by myself."

I lifted my chin. "Well, we can't all be the responsible, oldest child. Avoiding chores is my superpower as the forgotten middle child."

They both groaned, making me relieved they weren't upset I'd kept this secret from them. I considered Vicki and Jillian two of my closest friends, and I didn't want anything to come between us.

"There were rumors you were pregnant when you left Rose Island," Vicki began. "Somehow, Marcus convinced me you'd gone away for weight loss."

"Weight loss?"

She nodded. "You did come back a lot thinner."

"I did, but that's because I lost a ton of weight after the baby was born. I can't believe this whole time you thought I was at fat camp."

"I knew that rumor wasn't true," Jillian said. "Mom told me you needed to get away from the crowd you were hanging out with. I thought you were having an issue with drugs or alcohol."

"Wow," I said sardonically. "I don't know which I prefer—fat camp, secret pregnancy, or rehab. Such great choices." I laughed at the absurdity of it all, and my sisters both smiled.

Vicki peeked over her shoulder, before looking back at us. "Dad's not taking it well, I see."

I shrugged, wishing his behavior didn't hurt so much. "He says I'm making a mistake by contacting her. He thinks I'm going to ruin her life or something."

"He'll be okay." Jillian spoke in her oldest-sister-knows-best voice. "Sometimes, it just takes him a while to process things."

Vicki nodded. "That's true. Remember how he

didn't think we should buy the building downtown? In the end, he helped us negotiate terms for the mortgage as well as helped with the renovations."

"You're right." I took a sip of my iced tea. "I just hate disappointing him."

"Don't we all," Jillian said, even though she was Dad's favorite and had never disappointed him.

Me, on the other hand . . . I'd been one disappointment after another. At least, that's how it felt sometimes.

Vicki brushed an invisible crumb off her silk blouse. "Was it horrible being away your senior year? You gave birth in March, but you didn't come home until that summer."

"I wanted to finish school out there, and no, it wasn't horrible. Aunt Wynona was good to me. I made friends with a retired librarian who lived next door. She kindled my love of reading, introducing me to all sorts of books I'd never heard of before. Saying good-bye to the baby and wondering about her was the hardest part. Well, that and not telling anyone."

"Does Anna know?" Jillian asked, referring to our sister-in-law who'd once been married to our deceased brother, Marcus. Anna now lived in Germany with her new husband, Nick Peterson, and their four kids.

I shook my head. "No. I'll tell her tonight when we

talk on the phone."

"Why didn't you tell us before now?" Vicki asked.

I shrugged. "Mom and Dad encouraged me not to. They thought it'd be easier to get on with my life if I wasn't thinking about the baby all the time."

"Was it?" Jillian asked, her arms looking empty without her own baby.

I glanced out the window at my mother's large organic garden surrounded by pecan trees. "I've had a good life, but not a day has passed without me thinking about her. I guess I've always worried she might've gotten more of her father's genes than mine."

Vicki lowered her voice. "Chad?"

I nodded. "How'd you know?"

"Just a hunch."

Not wanting to think about Chad or how he'd reacted when I told him about the pregnancy, I reached into my purse and withdrew the framed photo. "In the hospital nursery, when I was saying good-bye to my baby, one of the nurses took this photo."

Jillian reached for the photo and smiled. "Oh, Bianca, she's beautiful. She looks exactly like Linda Faith, doesn't she?"

Even though I'd spent hours staring at the picture, I leaned closer to get a better look. "You think so?"

"Yes. Our daughters have the same eyes."

My heart warmed at my sister's words.

"I don't know," Vicki said. "People are always trying to find familiar characteristics in newborns, but I think all babies look alike."

"That's because you're not a mother yet." Jillian placed a hand on Vicki's shoulder. "Once you have your own baby, you'll be able to see those slight differences."

Our youngest sister made a scoffing sound. "Like having my own baby is ever going to happen. I can't even find a decent man."

"Well, it's not going to happen with that attitude," Jillian said.

Vicki sighed. "I know. It's just discouraging. While I'm happy that you and Anna have dropped out of the Morgan Sister Spinsters' Club—"

"You're jealous," I said, speaking more for myself than Vicki.

Vicki nodded. "Yes, I guess I am a little jealous. It's not like I've stopped trying. I just haven't found anyone I can imagine spending the rest of my life with."

"What about Seth Watson?" Jillian said, referring to our neighbor who'd been in love with Vicki since the beginning of time.

"Seth? No. He's too young," Vicki said.

"He's just five years younger than you," I pointed out.

Vicki shrugged. "I know, but he was Marcus's friend, and it just feels a little weird."

I raised my brow. "You obviously haven't seen the man in his turnout gear. Maybe before discounting him, you should consider taking some blueberry muffins to the fire station."

She batted a hand through the air. "I know he's cute—"

"Cute?" I said. "Have you seen those dimples?"

Vicki groaned. "If you're so in love with him, why don't you date him?"

I shrugged. "He's not really my type."

"Well, I don't think he's really my type either."

"I guess we'll just stay single forever, then."

"Don't say that," Jillian scolded. "You're both beautiful women. If God's plan for you includes marriage, He'll make it happen."

Vicki sighed. "I hope so."

I nodded. "Me, too."

But at that moment, I realized I could easily live without finding Mr. Right as long as God's plan included meeting my daughter.

Chapter 4

Claudia

Kansas

SITTING ON HER bed, Claudia stared down at the letter from her birth mom. Thank goodness the courier had come when her parents were at the grocery store this morning.

She didn't want Mom and Dad dealing with this. Not now. Not today on what was supposed to be a celebration for both her eighteenth birthday and her father's recovery from prostate cancer.

It'd been a rough year. This time last spring, her father had undergone surgery. Months of chemotherapy had followed. Thankfully, doctors now expected Dad to survive.

Over the sounds of her little brothers wrestling in the hallway, the doorbell rang. Claudia sighed with relief.

Leland.

Standing, she folded the letter in half and stuck it in her back pocket. Eager to talk to her boyfriend, she ran out of her bedroom just in time to see seven-year-old Clark pin six-year-old Clay to the floor.

"Who's the boss of you now?" Clark asked.

"Let me go," Clay shouted, kicking his legs as he twisted back and forth.

"Aren't you two supposed to be cleaning up for my party?" Claudia asked in a voice that was half serious and half teasing.

"What do you think we've been doing for the past ten hours?" Clark asked.

"Yeah, right." Claudia groaned. Despite what her parents thought, her little brothers were worthless when it came to cleaning. As usual, she'd probably have to do their chores in addition to her own. "Mom and Dad will be home in ten minutes, so you'd better finish up."

"Or what?" they both asked.

The doorbell rang again, and not bothering to reply to her brothers' question, she headed downstairs. As soon as she peeked through the glass door and saw Leland standing on the front porch, her tension eased. Not all of it, of course, but most of it.

Happy to see him, she flung open the door. They'd only been dating since the beginning of college last fall, but already they were extremely close and told each other everything. Although they were both freshmen, Claudia was actually a year younger since she'd been homeschooled and had graduated early from high school.

"Hey, birthday girl." Leland smiled down at her, the depth of his green eyes looking right into hers.

Without explanation, she embraced him, clinging to him as if her life depended on it. His lanky arms wrapped around her, holding her in that clumsy way of his. The camera bag slung over his shoulder fell forward, knocking into her hip, but she ignored it. When he started to let go, she held on tighter.

"Hey, now. Are you okay?"

She shook her head against his chest. "I got a letter from my birth mom."

"You did? What'd she say?"

Her little brothers came to the door then. "Don't forget to leave room for Jesus," Clay said, quoting the well-known words of their mother.

"And the Holy Spirit," Clark added.

Leland released her to say hi to the boys. The three of them exchanged high fives and *what's ups*. It was no secret that her brothers idolized Leland. If forced to choose, Claudia had no doubt both boys would go with Leland.

"Do you want to film us playing roof ball?" Clay

asked, referring to one of the many games they'd invented.

"Not right now." Leland shifted his camera bag and squatted so he was eye level with both boys. "Will you guys do me a favor?"

"What is it?" they asked.

"Will you go back in the house and let me talk to your sister for a minute?"

While her brothers clearly didn't like the idea, they agreed. Once they'd retreated inside the house and closed the door, Leland turned back to Claudia. "So, what'd your birth mother say?"

Claudia retrieved the letter from her back pocket and handed it to him. "She wants to meet me. Her name's Bianca Morgan, and she lives on Rose Island, Texas."

Leland skimmed the letter. "Rose Island is about an hour away from my grandmother's house in Houston. If you want, we could drive down to Mimi's and meet your birth mom next weekend."

"No." Claudia's one-word answer came out sharper than intended. "I'm not ready to meet her. At least, not right now."

"Why not?"

She shrugged. "I don't know. I guess I feel that I already have a family with more aunts, uncles, and cousins than anyone needs. Plus, I don't want to hurt my parents. They've been through enough this year."

"Do you think meeting your birth mom would upset your mom and dad? Have they said something?"

"No. I just don't want to meet her right now."

"Fair enough." Leland glanced back down at the letter before returning it to Claudia. "Your birth mom seems nice."

"She does, and I don't want to hurt her either. I just don't want to meet her right now."

Leland worked his thumb underneath the strap of his camera bag. "Didn't you tell me that your parents said they'd help you find your birth mom when you turned eighteen?"

"They did." Claudia had been nine when her parents had said that. Clark was a newborn, and everyone kept saying how he looked just like Dad. That'd sparked Claudia's interest in her own biological parents, but now, things were different.

"So what changed your mind?" Leland asked. "Why don't you want to meet her?"

"I just don't."

"It might be kind of interesting."

"Why? So you could film it?"

He shrugged. "Only if you wanted me to."

"No. This is my private life. I don't want you recording it."

He nodded. "I understand."

She knew he didn't. Not really. Leland was a filmmaker, and recording everything around him was just what he did. Still, she didn't want this part of her life on display for all the world to see.

She took a deep breath. "I really don't want to talk about this anymore. I just want to finish getting ready for the party, okay?"

"Okay." He blinked. "Do you still want me to film the party?"

"I do."

"Good."

A car pulled up to the house and started honking. "It's my Aunt Dede and Uncle Geoff," Claudia said, waving. "Come on. I want you to meet them."

She led him across the yard to meet the first of her many relatives expected to come today. Before she knew it, more guests would arrive, filling the small house with friends and family. They'd all wish her happy birthday, tell funny stories, eat amazing food, and rejoice in the fact that her father had survived cancer.

When her grandmother arrived, Claudia would ask to hear her adoption story. Nona loved telling how Claudia's parents had wanted a baby more than anything. How they'd prayed for months until God finally answered their prayer. Claudia loved the part about Nona going to the airport with all the other relatives to meet this most wanted baby for the first time.

Without a doubt, it'd be a perfect day, which Leland would capture on film and edit to make even more meaningful. Maybe tonight, after everyone left, she'd reread Bianca Morgan's letter and stalk her birth mother online. She might even write Bianca a letter. But honestly, what was the point in meeting her?

Claudia had her own family after all. Why did she need someone else's?

Chapter 5

Bianca

As I CLEANED my living room before the high school Bible study I hosted at my apartment every Monday night, I prayed that God would ease my anxiety regarding my daughter. It'd been over twenty-four hours, and I still hadn't heard from her.

The law office informed me that they'd delivered my letter Sunday morning. Maybe, after reading it, my daughter had looked me up online, discovered I was fat, and didn't want to meet me.

Come on, girl. Let's be positive, I told myself. *It's not always about the weight.*

The doorbell rang, so I scooped up the laundry basket full of clutter and raced down the hall to stash it in my bedroom. On the way back, I smashed my toe against one of the slabs of granite leaning against the wall. Falling to the floor, I grabbed my toe and howled in pain.

"Bianca?" called a voice from the other side of the door. "Are you okay?"

"Yes. Come in."

Joy Serrano, my favorite high school senior, pushed open the door. I knew Bible study leaders weren't supposed to have favorites, but Joy was my absolute favorite.

And just to set the record straight, this had nothing to do with the fact that she was Daniel's daughter. No, Joy was my favorite because she was easygoing and had an infectious smile that lit up her entire face. She participated in our discussions, always did her homework, and just made everything better.

She also had type one diabetes, something I'd known nothing about until meeting her. After learning about her disease, I'd come to believe she was the strongest person I knew.

"Did you stub your toe again?" Joy asked.

I shifted on the floor. "I don't think it's broken, but it hurts like crazy." Pushing past the pain, I stood and hobbled to the couch where I collapsed against the cushions.

Joy sat beside me. "Did you talk to your dad about installing your countertops? Is he going to do it?"

Last week, I'd told the girls what happened with my contractor and how I was going to see if my dad could finish the project. Usually, he enjoyed projects like that, but how could I ask him now that he was so upset with me?

I rubbed my toe, grateful the pain was subsiding. "My dad's been a little busy, so I'm probably going to have to find someone else."

"You could hire my dad," Joy said.

I felt a little thrill before coming to my senses. "Doesn't your dad work as an IT manager for the island?"

"He does, but he loves working on home improvement projects. He's run out of things to do around our house, so he's been doing some work for our neighbors. He'd probably install your countertops for free since that's his idea of a good time."

An image of Daniel standing in my kitchen, a tool belt slung low around his hips, flashed through my mind. I mostly saw him at church, looking professional in slacks and a button-down, but I was certain he could pull off the hot construction worker look.

"Bianca?"

"Yes, honey, sorry." I picked up my prayer journal and fanned myself. "I'll have to think about that."

A knock on the door interrupted us. "Come in," I called.

Three other girls for the Bible study entered, and we

exchanged greetings. I told them about my injury and said there were snacks and drinks in the kitchen, compliments of Vicki.

"I love your sister and her bakery," said Kayla, Joy's best friend.

I smiled. "Vicki definitely has a talent for fattening people up."

Joy smiled at my self-deprecating joke. "Do you want me to bring you something to eat?"

"No. Thanks, though."

"Okay." She joined the other girls in the kitchen, and I listened as they laughed and talked about their day. I loved these girls and thought of them as my surrogate daughters. Thank goodness I had them in my life while I waited to hear from my own daughter.

Kate Tate's daughter, Phoebe, arrived, jingling the keys to her new Mustang convertible, a gift from her father. I'd watched the video she'd posted on social media showing Dr. Tate surprising her with the gift on her sixteenth birthday. The car seemed a little excessive to me; then again, Dr. Tate was loaded. So, I supposed it was none of my business what he did with his money.

Once everyone arrived and was settled around the coffee table in my living room, we began by going over last week's homework. For the most part, I kept Bible study homework to a minimum, believing the habit of daily scripture reading for these girls was more important than length.

Next, we talked about this week's lesson, then we discussed prayer requests. Matt's girlfriend, Hannah, asked us to pray for her grandmother who was going parachuting this weekend.

"It's her eighty-fifth birthday," Hanna explained. "Even though Nana said jumping out of an airplane is perfectly safe, that seems really dangerous to me."

"It is dangerous," Phoebe stated. "Horrible things go wrong with those parachutes all the time. I heard about this guy who—"

"*Phoebe*," I gently said, giving her a pointed look. "Let's just remember to pray for Hannah's Nana, okay?"

Phoebe started to speak but changed her mind and simply nodded. I'd talked to her before about being more of an encourager. While I agreed that jumping out of an airplane on your eighty-fifth or any other birthday didn't sound safe, adding to Hannah's fears wasn't helpful.

"Okay," I said, redirecting the conversation, "who else has a prayer request?"

The girls chimed in with various concerns. Joy went last, telling us that she'd renewed her permit and was learning how to drive.

"You're eighteen and you don't have your license

yet?" Phoebe asked in a voice that was the opposite of encouraging.

Joy stiffened but didn't respond. Before I could speak, Kayla gently patted Joy's arm. "It's okay. Tell them what happened."

Joy nodded. "Okay. My mother died in a car accident when I was nine. I was in the back seat, so driving scares me. That's why I haven't gotten my license yet."

All the girls, even Phoebe, murmured words of sympathy. I'd known that Joy's mother had died in a car wreck, but I hadn't known that Joy was in the car at the time.

"I'm so sorry," I told her. "That must've been horrible."

Joy offered a brave smile. "It happened a long time ago, but yeah, it was pretty bad. Until now, I haven't been motivated to get my license."

"Tell them why you want to get it now," Kayla said.

"Okay." Joy gathered her light brown hair at the nape of her neck and laid it across her shoulder. "My boss, Mrs. Maisel, wants to hire me full time this summer, but I have to have my license so I can help with deliveries."

"Joy, that's wonderful." I imagined this opportunity meant a lot to her given how much she loved working with the interior designer.

"I'm excited," Joy said. "The only problem is *my dad*."

"What's wrong with your dad?" I asked, trying to hide my belief that her father was perfect. Absolutely perfect.

"Well, he's the worst driving instructor in the world. Every time I drive with him, he gets so nervous that he makes me nervous too."

The girls all smiled and shared their own stories of learning how to drive with an anxious parent. Kayla talked about backing her family's suburban into the sheriff's car the first time she drove. Everyone laughed at that, grateful it hadn't been them.

"Okay, girls," I said, pulling the conversation back to our prayer needs. "Does anyone else want to share a request?"

A few of the girls talked about upcoming tests and issues with their boyfriends, then it was my turn. "I have something I'd like to share. Something kind of big."

"You found a boyfriend," Hannah said, her eyes dancing.

"No. I wish. I'm still waiting for God to answer *that* prayer."

The girls laughed, then they listened as I told them about having a baby my senior year of high school. I think my news shocked them. When I told them about reaching out to my daughter, they were very encouraging, saying I'd probably hear from her soon.

"I hope so," I said. "I'm trying not to be anxious, but waiting is hard."

Phoebe nodded in agreement. "Waiting is so hard. When I found out my dad was buying me a new car for my birthday, I had to wait three weeks before getting it. Do you know how hard that was?"

Why yes, Phoebe, I do. Waiting for a new car is exactly like waiting to meet your long-lost daughter. Forcing a smile, I reminded myself that Phoebe was young and didn't know better. Of course, she'd equate her misery with mine.

"Well, hopefully, I won't have to wait three weeks," I said cheerfully. "Hopefully, the next time I check my messages, there will be something from her."

AFTER THE GIRLS left, I stood in the kitchen staring at the uneaten food. Vicki was always bringing me sweets from the bakery. In the past, I'd asked her not to tempt me like that, but she never listened.

While I appreciated my little sister's generosity, I found the sugary leftovers impossible to resist. Once I started eating, I could never stop. On more than one occasion, I'd stood in this very spot shoveling brownie after brownie into my mouth until I felt so sick I could barely move.

Tonight, however, I found the strength to take everything downstairs to the salon's break room. Now, the other stylists would have to deal with the temptation.

Before heading back to my apartment, I glanced out the window, surprised to see Joy standing in front of the salon. Opening the door, I called her name. "What are you still doing here?"

"My dad's truck broke down," she explained. "He's trying to borrow a car from one of our neighbors, so he should be here soon."

"I can give you a ride home," I said.

"Oh, that's okay. I don't mind waiting."

"And I don't mind taking you. Call your dad and tell him I'm bringing you home."

"Are you sure?"

"Positive. I have to go to the store anyway to get cream for my coffee, so it's no problem. Come on in, and we'll go out the back door where I'm parked."

She came into the salon and waited while I ran upstairs to collect my purse and keys. A few minutes later, we were headed out to my car."

"Here you go," I said, handing her the keys.

"What?"

"You said you wanted to learn how to drive, so you

should drive."

She stared down at the keys as if they were a foreign object. "Are you sure? I'm a really bad driver."

I laughed. "Of course, you're a bad driver. You've had your permit for what? Five minutes?"

She grinned. "A little longer than that."

"Okay, but my point is I don't care that you're a bad driver. I'm a really good teacher."

"All right."

We climbed into my car with Joy in the driver's seat. Placing her hands on the steering wheel, she sighed. "I'm nervous all of a sudden."

"To drive with me? Don't be. You're going to do great."

"Okay." With a deep breath, she started the engine. So far so good.

"You know what?" I said. "I just thought of a fabulous idea. Why don't you let me teach you how to drive?"

"Really?"

"Yes. I'd love to help you get your license."

"That'd be great. I have to have it by the end of the month. Otherwise, Mrs. Maisel said she'd have to start looking for someone else."

"Then we better get started."

Smiling, she put the car in gear, and that's when

everything went wrong. Instead of putting the car in drive, she'd put it in reverse, causing it to bolt backward and nearly take out the row of mailboxes behind us.

"I'm sorry," she said, after slamming on the brakes just in the nick of time.

"It's okay." I laughed, relieved she hadn't actually hit anything. "You're okay, and so am I. Just put the car in drive and head toward the road."

She did as I said, slowly making her way across the parking lot. Every few feet, she'd hit the brakes, causing me and the car to lurch forward.

Wow, she wasn't kidding about being a horrible driver. No wonder her father was nervous about driving with her. If she was this bad in the parking lot, how would she be once we reached the road?

"I'm sorry, Bianca."

"It's okay, honey." I tugged at my seatbelt, which had locked up, pinning me in place. "Maybe just try to be a little more gentle with the brake."

"Okay."

By some miracle, we managed to make our way through town to the road that led to the other side of the island where Joy and her father lived.

"I'm really bad. I know," she said.

I shrugged. "Well, I wouldn't say you're ready to take your test today, but you'll get better."

"I hope so." She looked at me and smiled as the car slowly veered off the road onto the shoulder.

"Joy! Eyes on the road."

She jerked the steering wheel hard. "Sorry. Maybe you should drive now."

Are you kidding me? Of course, I should drive now.

"No, honey. You're doing fine. You've got this. Just concentrate, okay?"

"Okay." Driving at least ten miles under the speed limit, she managed to stay on the road. Every so often a car would zoom past us, causing her to suck in a sharp breath and tightly grip the steering wheel.

Near the cemetery where my brother was buried, Joy took a left into an older neighborhood. The big palm trees lining the street were impressive, and we passed the cutest neighborhood park. While the homes here had been built years ago, most of them had been renovated with fresh paint and new landscaping.

"This is me," she said, stopping in front of a darling bungalow with dark blue paint, white trim, and a yellow door.

"This is your house? It's so cute."

"Thanks. You should've seen it when we first bought it. It was a complete dump."

"Well, it's adorable now."

Joy put the car in park. "We just refinished the

hardwood floors. It looks really nice now."

"You said *we*. Did you help your dad with the work?"

"A little bit. I'm mostly the idea person, but my dad makes me help with some of the work. He wants me to understand what I'll be asking once I become an interior designer."

"That's a good idea."

She nodded. "I've learned a lot working for Mrs. Maisel, but my dad has taught me a lot, too."

Speaking of her hunky father, the front door opened, and my heart lifted as Daniel stepped onto the porch. Feeling self-conscious, I smoothed back my hair before climbing out of the car.

"Hi," I said, my voice making a strange squeaking noise.

Daniel offered an amused grin as he came toward me. "Hi, Bianca. Thanks for bringing her home."

"I drove," Joy said, joining us on the walkway.

"I saw that. How'd you do?"

"Horrible."

"That's not true," I said. "You did great, and you'll get better each time you practice. I'm just so proud of you for working toward getting your license."

"Thanks, Bianca." She gave me a hug, then quickly said good-bye when her phone rang. "Sorry, it's Kayla.

We have a math test tomorrow. Thanks for bringing me home."

"You're welcome, honey."

Answering the phone, Joy ran into the house, leaving me alone with her father. Turning to me, he smiled in a way that nearly made my insides come undone. "So, how'd she really do driving?"

I shrugged. "She could use a little more practice."

He chuckled, the sound rumbling in his chest. "Yeah, I bet."

I smiled as a warm, tingly feeling danced through me. "I told her I'd love to help her learn how to drive. I'm free most nights."

"Oh, that's generous of you, but it's too much."

"I don't mind." I shifted my weight off my bad toe.

Daniel frowned. "Are you injured? I noticed you were limping when you got out of the car."

"I just stubbed my toe on my countertops again."

He rubbed his beard and studied me carefully. "How'd you manage to stub your toe on your countertops? Karate practice or something?"

"No." I laughed and told him the saga about my contractor disappearing.

"You paid him before he finished your job?"

"I know. Everyone tells me I shouldn't have done that, but I was trying to be charitable. You know, feed the hungry, give shelter to the homeless, help your contractor pay off his hardware bill before he starts your project."

Daniel smirked. "I've done something like that before."

"You have?"

He nodded. "You want to believe people are good and they'll do the right thing. For the most part they do, but sometimes you get burned."

I nodded, thinking this man was my soul mate. One day, we'd tell our children, *Yes, darlings, Mommy and Daddy fell in love because of a silly financial mistake Mommy made.*

"So, do you think he'll come back?" Daniel asked.

"I don't think so. It's been a month, and I've kind of given up hope. He seemed honest, and I want to believe he'll eventually come back, but there's only so much pain my toe can take."

He smiled and started to say something, but the sight of a Lexus pulling into the driveway interrupted him. Just my luck, it was my archenemy, Kate Tate.

Kate parked and stepped out of the car. "*Daniel,*" she said in a sultry voice. "I brought you and Joy dessert. It's a flourless chocolate cake that everyone raves about."

"It looks amazing," Daniel said. "Thanks, Kate."

"You're welcome. If you're free, I thought we could

share a piece and talk about the ideas I have for the church playground."

"Sure, that'd be great."

As if noticing me for the first time, Kate threw a cursory glance my way. "Bianca, I heard about your *birth* daughter. Goodness, you're full of surprises."

The disdainful way she spoke took me right back to the first day of middle school when I'd apparently made a huge fashion mistake by wearing shorts in August. Kate, who'd worn stylish jeans and a sweater in the middle of a heat wave, had looked at my bare legs, horrified. *Well, aren't you courageous, Bianca, choosing shorts for the first day of school.*

"I need to go," I announced, remembering my New Year's resolution to be more kind, especially to people I didn't particularly like.

"Why don't you stay for dessert," Daniel suggested. "I'm sure we could use your input on the playground."

Although he sounded sincere, I knew he was just being polite. Obviously, he was far more interested in Kate than he was in me.

I mean, why wouldn't he be? Kate looked like a supermodel, while I resembled . . . well, I didn't know what I resembled, but it definitely wasn't a supermodel or any other kind of model for that matter.

"Thank you, Daniel, but I actually have an early

morning, so I should go. Thanks for letting Joy come to Bible study."

"Thanks for having her," he said.

I forced a smile at Kate and said good-bye. Then, I climbed into my car and drove away.

Ugh. I was such a fool. Of course, a guy like Daniel Serrano wasn't interested in me. Had I honestly thought he could see through my layers of fat to realize I'd make a great girlfriend?

Facing facts, I drove home, trying not to feel sorry for myself. It was only as I climbed the stairs to my apartment that I remembered I'd forgotten the cream for my coffee.

Chapter 6

Daniel

WEDNESDAY AFTERNOON, DANIEL sat at the kitchen table, staring at his computer screen. Once again, he reread the letter he'd been trying to write to his daughter for the past two months. With a frustrated sigh, he deleted the page and tried again.

> *Dear Joy,*
>
> *There's something I've been wanting to tell you. Something that's hard for me to say, so I thought I'd write you this letter.*
>
> *I want you to know that I never could've asked for a better daughter. You've been the light of my life, and I'm so proud of you.*
>
> *When your mother died—*

"Dad," Joy called, opening the front door, "I'm home."

Daniel jumped in his seat and closed his computer. Standing, he slipped his laptop into the backpack he used for work.

"Dad?"

"In the kitchen, honey." Despite trying to sound like everything was fine, his voice was tight with guilt and fear. Keeping this secret was beginning to take its toll.

"Something smells good." Joy entered the kitchen and opened the oven. "Chile rellenos, my favorite. Are they ready?"

Peering past her into the oven, Daniel nodded. "I think so." He grabbed the potholder from the hook and removed the casserole dish. "I just need to make the salad, then we can eat as soon as you're ready."

"Great." Joy washed her hands at the sink.

"How'd school and work go today?" Daniel asked, opening the refrigerator to collect the ingredients for the salad.

"Okay."

"Just okay?"

With a deep sigh, she sat at the table to test her blood sugar. As a type one diabetic, testing her blood sugar and taking insulin before every meal was a normal part of her life. Without careful regulation, her blood sugar could become too high, causing serious damage to her health.

"School was fine, but after work today, Mrs. Maisel

suggested I drive her home."

"That was nice of her."

Joy inserted a testing strip into her glucometer. "Yes, but she made me pull over after one block and let her drive. Apparently, she values her life too much to put it in danger with my driving."

"Is that what she said?"

"Pretty much."

Daniel winced. "Ouch."

"Yeah." Joy lanced her finger and put a drop of blood on the testing strip. "She was nice about it, but she doesn't see how I'm going to be able to get my license in time."

"Oh, honey, I'm sorry." Daniel's heart ached for his daughter. The fact that she was even trying to get her license was a huge step. She'd gotten her permit when she'd turned fifteen like the rest of her classmates, but full-blown panic attacks had prevented her from learning how to drive.

"You'll get there," he said, wanting it to be true. He'd taken her driving the other night, but it hadn't ended well. Although he considered himself a calm person, he'd snapped when she'd driven through a red light, nearly killing them both. She'd started crying, then said she didn't want to drive with him anymore.

While he understood, he couldn't figure out why

teaching her how to drive was so difficult. He'd taught her how to do math problems in her head, manage her diabetes, and do a number of other tasks. Why couldn't he teach her how to drive?

He'd been surprised, shocked actually, that Joy had driven with Bianca from one end of the island to the other. Bianca was obviously far more patient than him or Mrs. Maisel.

Then again, Bianca was one of a kind. Not only was she beautiful, but Daniel found her smart, funny, and easy to talk to.

He also loved the sound of her laughter, and when she smiled at him . . . well, Bianca Morgan had one of those smiles that just made you happy, just made you feel that everything was going to be okay.

He'd wanted to ask her out when he first moved to the island with Joy four years ago. He hadn't known anyone, and Bianca had made it her mission to introduce Joy and him to everyone at church. She'd even been sweet enough to invite them out to her family's ranch for a barbecue.

Then, Joy had started attending Bianca's Monday evening Bible study, something that quickly became a highlight for Joy. Before he knew it, his daughter had found something in Bianca that Daniel couldn't give her—a mother.

After that, he feared starting a relationship with Bianca would complicate things for Joy, something he definitely didn't want to do. So, he'd put Bianca in the category of *just friends* where she would probably remain forever.

"How are your numbers?" he asked, slicing a red pepper for the salad.

Joy looked up from the device which held the results of her blood sugar test. "They're good."

"Good." He didn't ask for specifics, knowing she couldn't stand it when he hovered. If he wanted, he could use the app on his phone to follow up, but Joy was a responsible kid, plenty capable of figuring out how much insulin to tell her pump to release. She'd been dealing with her diabetes for ten years after all.

That didn't mean he didn't worry about her. No, he worried about her all the time. She was the most important person in his life, and everything he did was for her health and happiness.

"Listen, honey. How about I take you driving tonight after dinner?"

She groaned. "I think I'll just have Bianca teach me. She said she didn't mind."

Daniel tossed the salad. "She told me the same thing, but I think it's too much."

"What if I paid her? I've got money in savings from

my job."

Wincing, Daniel pulled down two plates from the cupboard. He didn't want Joy spending her hard-earned money on driving lessons. Besides, he didn't think Bianca would accept payment for something like that.

As he opened the drawer for the silverware, he was struck by an idea. What if he made a deal with Bianca that would give them both something they wanted? Would she be interested? If she was, that would certainly make things easier.

Maybe then, after solving his daughter's driving issues, he could figure out a way to tell her the secret that weighed so heavily on his heart . . . the secret that Joy deserved to know regardless of its implications.

Chapter 7

Bianca

*A*FTER WORKING IN the salon all day, I was worn out. It'd been one of those crazy busy days where I barely had time to eat lunch or use the bathroom. I often binged on days like these, mindlessly shoving food down my throat between clients. Then, I'd eat my dinner in front of the TV, wondering why I felt so full.

Tonight, however, I had a counseling session with Yadira. I'd started seeing the eating disorder therapist last year. So far, I'd only lost one pound, but I supposed that was better than gaining a pound.

As I sat in Yadira's office, I told her about waiting to hear from my daughter. I'd actually told Yadira about the baby several months ago. I hadn't meant to, but the story came tumbling out one rainy evening when I was feeling particularly vulnerable.

"It sounds like Anna and your sisters took the news well," Yadira said. "I know you were worried they might be upset you'd kept your daughter a secret for so long."

I took a sip of my water. "Both Jillian and Vicki have been great. When I talked to Anna on the phone, she was really excited for me."

"I'm excited for you as well," Yadira said.

"Thank you." We talked about how my anxiety over waiting to hear from my daughter affected my eating. Then, I told Yadira about my conversation with Daniel the other night. "I thought things were going well, but once Kate arrived . . . well, she just makes me feel so bad about myself, you know?"

Yadira gave a nonjudgmental nod. She'd heard me talk about Kate and other people that made me feel bad about myself. "So, sometimes when you have a conflict with others, it leads to a binge. How'd it go this time?"

"I didn't binge," I said, smiling. "I thought about it, but I didn't. I just crawled into bed, read my book, and went to sleep."

"Why do you think you were able to maintain control? What made a difference this time?"

"I don't know. Maybe I was too tired or maybe it was the fact that the sweets were all the way downstairs. I did write in my journal, but it wasn't like I reached any profound conclusions."

"No?"

I shook my head. "Honestly, isn't that the million-dollar question? I mean, why can I refrain from binging sometimes and other times there doesn't seem to be any end in sight?"

"Well, that's what we're trying to figure out. That's why you're here. All I can say is it's different for each person. Let's talk about Kate."

"I'd rather not."

Yadira smiled. "What is it about Kate that makes you want to eat?"

I shrugged. "I guess she just makes me feel bad about myself. I've known her since the sixth grade, and she's never liked me. I get it. Kate's one of those people that just doesn't like fat people."

Yadira pressed her lips together. She'd heard all about my theory of certain people automatically judging me because of my weight.

I knew it was true because for a brief period I'd been thin and had experienced special treatment. My skinny days had happened after the baby. Without even trying, I'd lost a ton of weight. At first, I thought the birthing process had shut down my appetite. Looking back, I realized I was probably clinically depressed.

Whatever the reason, I started college in the fall at the perfect size. I'd always had lots of friends because I made the effort to be outgoing, but at college, I didn't even have to try. Good-looking people went out of their way to talk to me and invite me to all sorts of events. Guys actually paid attention to me.

During our dorm's water balloon fight, I'd met Zach, an engineering major who loved comic books. Zach was a good guy who played the keyboards at church. We hit it off right away, spending every hour together.

As a result, my depression vanished and my appetite returned. Although I tried to limit my portions, my jeans became tighter and tighter. I tried reducing my calories, but that just made me cranky, resulting in late-night binges. Then, I'd wake the next morning, vowing to stick to an impossible diet of carrot sticks and skinless chicken breasts.

I found myself in a vicious cycle of dieting and binging. While I couldn't blame our breakup entirely on my issues with food, it definitely played a role.

Yadira slipped her right skinny leg over her left. "People judge others all the time. It's our human nature regardless of how much we try not to. But I believe after spending time with people that initial judgment becomes less important."

"I agree."

"And in some ways, you've judged Daniel Serrano based on his outward appearance."

"What do you mean?"

"You think he's cute, therefore, you think he's a good person."

"Well, he is cute, and he is a good person."

Yadira smiled. "I guess my point is you can't change other people. All you can do is change yourself, which is why you come see me each week."

"But you think I should change how I feel about Kate. You think I shouldn't worry about how she treats me."

Yadira bit her bottom lip. "I think you should change how much power you give her. And you did that last night by not binging after she upset you."

"I did, didn't I?" I said, feeling proud of myself.

AFTER THERAPY, I walked down Main Street back to my apartment. Yadira was right about Kate. She was also right about Daniel, too. I had judged him based on the fact that I was attracted to him. For all I knew, he might be a horrible person.

Except, deep in my gut, I knew he wasn't. Part of that was due to the fact that he'd fathered such an incredible daughter.

I thought about my own daughter. Would she get along with Joy? They were almost the same age after all. What if Daniel and I started dating and ended up getting married? Joy and my daughter would become sisters and—

I jumped as a truck startled me by pulling up to the curb. "Need a ride?" the driver asked, speaking through the opened passenger's side window.

Unable to help myself, I grinned, thrilled to see Daniel grinning right back at me.

Chapter 8

Claudia

Dear Bianca,

I received your letter and

A *ND WHAT?* THOUGHT Claudia. What exactly was she supposed to say to this woman? Her birth mother?

Claudia repositioned the pillows on her bed, trying to get comfortable. Bianca's letter had arrived several days ago, and she still didn't know how to respond.

She wanted to thank Bianca for giving her life and placing her with a family that'd been perfect. But meeting Bianca in person? That wasn't something Claudia could do right now.

At the same time, she didn't want to hurt her birth mother's feelings. Leland had said Bianca seemed nice. Claudia agreed, but that didn't mean she had to meet her. Did it?

A loud crashing sound came from her brothers' bedroom down the hall. Clark and Clay yelled at each other. Then, Claudia heard Mom's firm voice rise above the fray. "Just clean it up, boys, okay? Both of you."

Claudia reached for her headphones only to remember she'd left them downstairs. It was times like these that made her question her decision to live at home this year.

She'd chosen not to live in the dorm because she'd wanted to be close to her family as her father went through treatment. Plus, the idea of moving out at seventeen was a little unsettling for both her parents and her.

Overall, she had no regrets about staying home, but sometimes, like tonight when she was trying to concentrate and the boys were all wound up, she fantasized about living on campus next year.

There was a soft knock on her bedroom door, and she quickly stashed the notebook with the letter under her bed. "Come in."

Her mother opened the door and smiled. "Am I interrupting?"

"No, come in. Is everything okay?"

"The boys broke a shelf in their closet, but they're fine." Mom entered the room, closed the door, and sat on the edge of Claudia's bed. "We haven't really had time to talk since your birthday. How are you doing?"

"Good."

"Were you studying?"

Claudia shrugged. "Not really." She hadn't told her parents yet about hearing from Bianca, nor did she intend to right now. Honestly, she was just trying to figure out her own feelings before sharing them.

"It's been such a whirlwind week with the party, recovering from the party, and dealing with the boys' project for Cub Scouts. You and I haven't really had any time to connect. I was thinking we could grab lunch tomorrow if you're free."

"I'm free, and lunch would be perfect."

"Good." Mom smiled. "Did you have a nice birthday? I feel like there was so much focus on your father's good news that the celebration wasn't really about you."

Claudia shook her head. "Celebrating Dad's recovery was the best birthday gift in the world."

"I have to agree." Mom picked up the stuffed elephant Claudia had received as a baby from her grandmother. "I heard Nona retelling the story of your adoption."

Claudia nodded. "I asked her to tell it. I like hearing it. I like the part where she's speeding to the airport, gets pulled over, and talks her way out of the ticket."

Mom laughed. "I like that part too, but my favorite

part is when Nona talks about holding you for the first time. How the earth stood still as she looked into your eyes. How you looked back at her, and she just knew God had created you to be in our family."

Goosebumps prickled Claudia's skin. "You said that's how you felt the first time you held me."

"It was. We were in the hospital in South Carolina, and you were so tiny that I worried I might drop you. I think the nurse was worried, too, but I instantly felt like you were mine."

Mom's eyes filled with tears as the boys came down the hall, shouting, "Mom, Mom."

"Pretend we're asleep." Mom dove into the bed, her back to the door. Claudia lay down as well, facing her mother.

"Try not to laugh," Mom said, closing her eyes.

"You try not to laugh."

As the sound of Clay's and Clark's footsteps came closer, Claudia shut her eyes and breathed deeply.

The door creaked open. "Mom?" Clark whispered.

Mom didn't answer.

"I guess they're asleep," Clay said, keeping his voice low.

A beat of silence followed, then her brothers whispered something to each other that Claudia couldn't hear. A moment later, the door closed.

Both Claudia and her mother opened their eyes at the same time, huge smiles on their faces. Then, Claudia screamed because the boys were standing at the edge of her bed staring down at them.

"Ha," Clay said. "I knew they were faking it."

"Yeah, me, too," Clark said.

Claudia and Mom burst into laughter, howling so hard their bellies hurt.

"You guys are big fakers," Clay said, jumping on the bed.

Clark followed, and Claudia and her mother grabbed the boys and began tickling them as they laughed with abandon. Clay laughed so hard he farted, which caused all of them to laugh even harder.

"Hey, what's going on up here?" Dad said with mock sternness as he came into the room.

"It's Dad." Clay stood and launched himself off the bed into his father's arms. Dad caught him and swung him around. Clark came next, and Claudia's heart lifted at the sight of her strong father holding her brothers.

This time last year, Dad had been too weak to roughhouse with the boys. Now, everything was better. Everything was perfect.

No way was she jeopardizing this by doing anything as foolish as meeting her birth mom. No way.

Chapter 9

Bianca

TRYING TO PLAY it cool, I rested my arms on the open window ledge of Daniel's truck. "What are you doing downtown tonight? Not enough excitement for you in the suburbs?"

"Something like that," he said with an easy smile.

I laughed, partly because being around him made me nervous, and partly because downtown Rose Island during the off-season in the middle of the week wasn't exactly exciting. There were a few people eating at the new restaurant that'd just opened, but other than that, the street was quiet.

Daniel tapped his thumb on the steering wheel. "Joy and I were talking, and I was wondering if you'd be interested in striking a little deal."

"What kind of deal?" I asked, thinking *Yes, let's get married and have lots of babies before it's too late for me.*

"Well, I was thinking maybe I could install your

countertops in exchange for you teaching Joy how to drive."

I stared at him with what I imagined was an expression of disbelief. "You want to install my countertops, and all I have to do is teach your daughter how to drive?"

"Well, I wouldn't exactly phrase it that way, but yes. What do you think?"

"I think you might change your mind once you see my countertops. They're really heavy."

He shrugged. "I have a friend that can help if I need him, but I don't think it will be too hard. Do you think I can stop by and see them sometime?"

"You can come see them now."

"Okay."

Because we were so close to the salon, he drove forward half a block and parked. I unlocked the salon door and led him upstairs to my apartment.

Once inside, I said, "Come on in. Welcome to Casa Bianca."

Casa Bianca? Really, Bianca?

Daniel stepped into my apartment and gestured across the living room. "Are those your countertops?"

Feeling the need to be ornery, I waved a dismissive hand. "Nah, they're just slabs of granite I like to keep around for decoration."

"Good to know." His mouth tugged upward in a smile as he walked across the room.

In the mirror above my entry table, I caught a glimpse of my double chin and cringed. Suddenly, I felt foolish for flirting with Daniel. What was I thinking?

If I hadn't felt a connection with him, hadn't felt this mutual attraction between us, it would've been no big deal. I was used to being the pal after all. Used to having good-looking guy friends who confided in me about everything from problems with their girlfriends to fears about losing their jobs.

When it came to romantic relationships, however, I always fell for the guy who either had no interest in me or was no good for me.

"This shouldn't be too hard," Daniel said, when he finished examining each slab of granite.

"No?"

He shook his head. "Where's the kitchen?"

"This way." I led him around the wall to my kitchen.

He looked at everything, opening and closing my messiest cupboard. "Just out of curiosity, was your runaway contractor going to do anything else besides the countertops?"

"Is that your way of telling me my kitchen is outdated?"

"No, I didn't mean anything by that. I was just curious."

"It's okay. This kitchen was already here when we bought the building. I know it's old. To answer your question, yes, my runaway contractor was going to replace the flooring and appliances, which I already bought. They're in the back room at the hardware store."

"What about the wall?"

I glanced at the wall that separated my kitchen from the living room. "Everyone says I should knock it down to open the floor plan, but I'm nervous about doing that."

"Are you afraid of seeing the kitchen mess every time you're in the living room?"

"Exactly."

He nodded. "I helped my neighbor knock down his wall. His wife had the same worry as you, so we raised the countertop to hide the kitchen mess."

"That's a good idea."

He nodded and gestured at the food-splattered wall behind the stove. "What about the backsplash?"

"I thought maybe I'd try to do the backsplash myself once the countertops were installed. I've seen it done on one of those design shows, and it didn't look too hard."

Daniel smiled. "Famous last words."

"Yeah?"

He nodded. "Actually, the backsplash isn't that hard to do."

"No?"

He shook his head and gave the kitchen one last look. "Well, if you're interested, and you don't mind covering the cost of any additional supplies, I'd be willing to install the countertops, the flooring, the appliances, and help you with the backsplash. I can even knock down the wall if you want."

I cocked my head to the side. "What's the catch?"

"The catch?"

"Yes, that's an awful lot of work on your part."

He rocked back on his heels. "Well, the catch would be you teaching Joy how to drive."

"I can do that, but teaching her to drive doesn't seem like much in exchange for getting my entire kitchen renovated."

"Have you seen my daughter drive?"

I laughed. "Yes, and I still think you're not getting a fair deal. What if I throw in a year's worth of free haircuts for both you and Joy?"

He smiled and absently ran a hand through his short cropped hair. "I think negotiations are supposed to go the other way, Bianca. You're supposed to offer less, not more."

I smiled, loving the way he said my name. "You're probably right, but I wouldn't feel good taking advantage of you like that."

"Again . . . have you seen my daughter drive?"

"She's not that bad." I laughed at this little exchange between us. "Joy definitely needs practice, but I'm confident I can help her."

"So, it's a deal?"

"It's a deal."

He held out his hand and I shook it, thinking this was the best deal I'd ever made in my entire life.

AFTER DANIEL LEFT, Vicki came over to ask my opinion about the sleek, black cocktail dress she was wearing. Holding out her hands, she spun around. "Well, what do you think?"

"I think you look amazing."

"Really? You don't think it's too tight?"

"No, you look great. What's the occasion?"

"I'm going to see a concert in Galveston at The Grand."

"With whom?"

She hesitated before admitting she was going with Seth Watson, her long-time admirer.

"Wow. What's that about? Did he somehow age an

extra five years?"

"Ha ha. No, he just came into the bakery today—"

"In his turnout gear?"

She rolled her eyes. "No, he wasn't wearing his turnout gear. He just mentioned that he had an extra ticket to the concert, so I figured why not. We're just going as friends."

I raised a brow. "Maybe that's what you think, but I guarantee that's not what Seth will be thinking when he sees you in that dress."

Self-conscious, she ran a hand over the bodice. "Should I wear something else? I don't want him getting the wrong idea. I love this gown, but maybe I should wear that dress I wore to church last week."

"Don't you dare. This is perfect for a night out at The Grand."

"Okay." She started to leave, then she asked if I'd heard anything from my daughter.

"Not yet."

"I'm sorry. I know you're anxious, but it really hasn't been that long."

"It feels like an eternity."

"I'm sure it does. What about Daniel? I just saw him driving out of the parking lot. Is everything okay with Joy?"

I nodded and told her about the deal I'd just struck

with Daniel.

"Good for you," she said.

"I know, right?"

"Why do you think he's being so nice? Do you think he has ulterior motives? Do you think maybe he likes you?"

"I wish, but no. I think he really doesn't want to be the one teaching Joy to drive. She's pretty much the worst driver in the world."

"Really?"

"Yes, but there's a reason for it." I explained about the accident that killed Joy's mother and how it left Joy feeling extremely anxious about driving. "I'm sure that affected Daniel, too. I think he just wants to make learning how to drive a pleasant experience for Joy."

"Maybe, but it seems like he's going out of his way to make things pleasant for you, too."

The idea of that being even remotely true caused a thrill to skitter through me. I knew if I thought about it too much, I'd come to the conclusion that it was too good to be true. Still, I couldn't help but hope it was slightly true.

Chapter 10

Daniel

*T*HURSDAY NIGHT, JOY and Daniel drove up the mountain to talk to Bianca's dad about buying the truck Walter was selling. Daniel's truck had over 250,000 miles and was starting to shake whenever he drove faster than twenty-five miles per hour.

All day, the sky had been overcast. When they reached the Morgans', the rain began, accompanied by lightning and thunder.

Walter invited them into the barn to wait out the storm with him and his beautiful golden labs, Duke and Lady. Daniel was impressed by the barn, which boasted a fully stocked workshop.

In addition to every tool and gadget a person could ever want or need, Walter had no less than fifty projects going at one time from refurbishing old furniture to renovating cars. While Daniel tended to be the kind of guy who finished one project before beginning another one, he admired Bianca's father for his ingenuity.

When the storm lifted, Daniel and Joy took the truck for a spin. Upon their return, Daniel and Walter spent a few minutes negotiating a fair price. Once the check was written, the men shook hands, and Walter invited Daniel and Joy to dinner.

"The family usually gets together on Sundays," Walter explained, "but Luella and I have other plans this weekend, so we're having family dinner tonight."

"We don't want to intrude on your family time," Daniel said.

Walter waved a dismissive hand. "Nonsense. You're here and there's plenty of food, so come join us. I insist."

Daniel and Joy agreed, and they strode across the lawn with Walter to the house. As they entered through the kitchen door, Luella, a large woman with bushy brown hair, turned from the oven and smiled. "Daniel, Joy. I'm so happy to see you." She crossed the room and gave them each a hug.

"They're staying for dinner," Walter told his wife.

"Wonderful."

"I hope we're not interfering," Daniel said, repeating what he'd told Walter.

"Not at all. Walter loves feeding people, and so do I. You two are welcome anytime."

"Thank you," Daniel said.

Joy nodded. "Yes, thank you. What are we having? It smells delicious."

Walter unwrapped a foil-covered pan that'd been sitting on the kitchen counter. "Brisket, and of course, it smells delicious. It's the second-best barbecue in Texas."

"*Second* best?" Joy asked.

"Yep." Walter winked. "Luella is originally from Lockhart, the barbecue capital of the world. Most people agree that my barbecue is outstanding, but changing my stubborn wife's mind is impossible, so we let her have her way in declaring mine the second best."

Luella batted a hand through the air. "I said that one time, and he's never forgiven me."

Joy and Daniel laughed as Bianca came into the kitchen. "Well, hello, Serrano family. What are you doing here?"

"Bianca!" Joy stepped toward Bianca and gave her a hug. "We just bought your dad's truck, and he invited us to stay for dinner."

Bianca grinned. "That's great."

"Yes, we're happy to have them," Luella said, patting Joy's arm. She suddenly frowned and patted Joy's arm again. "What's this?"

"It's my insulin pump." Joy lifted her sleeve to reveal the hard, square-shaped plastic container that

Daniel had always thought resembled an oversized package of dental floss.

"Your insulin pump?" Luella said.

"She has type one diabetes," Bianca explained, opening the silverware drawer.

The furrow between Luella's brows deepened. "Diabetes? That can't be right. You're not fat."

"*Mom,*" Bianca warned, mortified.

"It's okay." Joy smiled like it was no big deal. Daniel supposed his daughter was used to the ignorance surrounding her disease. "I have type one. You're probably thinking about type two, which can be caused by poor eating and lack of exercise. Type one is different. I've had it since I was eight."

"Oh," the older woman said, clearly not understanding.

Bianca counted out several forks and set them on the counter. "Type one is an autoimmune disease, Mom. Joy's pancreas doesn't produce insulin. Weight has nothing to do with it."

Daniel glanced at Bianca, impressed. Most people were clueless when it came to T1D—type one diabetes.

Luella pointed to Joy's pump. "So that thing gives you insulin whenever you need it?"

"Not exactly. I have to test my blood sugar before I eat, then I enter that number into my device so my pump can send me the right amount of insulin, which is based on my numbers and what I'm going to eat."

"I see." Luella stared at Joy as if expecting her to combust at any moment.

"Come help me set the table," Bianca said, breaking the tension by giving Joy a handful of knives. Bianca grabbed the forks, and the two of them went into the dining room.

Once they were out of earshot, Luella turned to Daniel. "She takes that insulin before every meal?"

He nodded.

"And before every snack, too?"

"Yes."

Luella was quiet for a moment. "Daniel, what are the side effects of doing that?"

"The side effects?"

"Yes. Every medication has side effects. What are the side effects of taking insulin on a regular basis?"

For the first time since Joy's diabetes was mentioned, Walter spoke. "Honey, I think the biggest side effect is not dying."

"*Walter!*" Luella scolded.

The older man shot Daniel a look of apology. "I'm sorry. That was rude of me."

"It's okay. It's true."

Luella, who seemed flustered, shook her head. "It

just seems so excessive to take insulin for every meal and every snack."

Daniel offered what he hoped was a comforting smile. "I know it's overwhelming, but Joy needs insulin to live. Without it, her body can't process the nutrients it needs. Like she said, she was diagnosed when she was eight, so we've dealt with this for a long time. I'm not saying it's easy, but it's our normal."

Walter snuck a bite of meat from the platter on the counter. "She seems pretty healthy."

"She is," Daniel agreed. "She does a good job managing everything."

Luella glanced over her shoulder toward the dining room, then back at Daniel. "Will she always have diabetes?"

He sighed as Joy came back into the kitchen with Bianca. "Luella just asked if you'll always have diabetes."

His strong, beautiful, amazing daughter lifted her chin. "I hope not."

The older woman's face flooded with relief. "Oh, that's wonderful. So, you might outgrow it?"

Joy shook her head. "No. Right now there's no cure. We're praying that one day there will be."

"Oh." Luella's expression faltered. She stared at Joy. "You're very brave, aren't you?"

Joy shrugged. "I don't know about that. It's just

how things are, you know?"

The kitchen door opened, and Keith entered, carrying the diaper bag and an empty car seat. His boys followed, each of them holding a covered dish.

"Don't tell me your mother made sweet potato pie *and* mashed potatoes?" Luella said, peering down at the dishes in her grandsons' hands. "I told her she didn't have to do that."

"I guess she wanted to," the youngest boy said.

Keith greeted his in-laws and set down the diaper bag and empty car seat before shaking Daniel's hand. "Hey, Daniel. Did you buy the truck?"

"I did. Thanks for telling me about it." Daniel knew Keith from church as well as the men's Bible study they attended on Tuesday mornings. Joy said hi to the boys whom she knew from school as well as youth group.

Minutes later, Jillian entered, holding a sleeping baby. "Sorry we're late. The baby was fussy, and we couldn't find the car keys."

"And Mom couldn't figure out what to wear," the youngest boy said.

"*Drew,*" Jillian scolded.

"Well, it's true."

"Sometimes the truth is best left unsaid," Keith said, tousling his son's hair.

Was it? Daniel wished he could believe that, then he

wouldn't feel so guilty about keeping his secret from Joy. He'd given up on the idea of writing a letter. Now, he was determined to just tell her once things settled down.

Vicki arrived next, and Luella wasted no time in enlisting everyone's help in carrying the food to the table. Joy quietly stepped into the living room to test her blood sugar before joining everyone in the dining room. Once they were all seated, Walter said a blessing, and they dug into the meal.

Daniel had to admit it was a little overwhelming passing food, answering questions, and hearing everyone talk at once. Usually, his meals with Joy were sedate. Dinner with the Morgan family couldn't have been more different.

Luella asked if Daniel had any siblings. "My sister and her husband live in Spain. He works in shipping, and she stays home with their three kids."

"Our cousins went to Spain for spring break," Drew said. "They live in Germany."

Drew's words sparked a lively conversation about the Petersons and when they were planning on coming back to Rose Island. Daniel had heard all about the whirlwind love story between Nick and Anna.

Jillian and Keith's baby, who'd been sleeping in her car seat during the meal, woke up howling. For such a little thing, she had an incredibly strong pair of lungs.

Sighing, Jillian pushed away from the table and scooped up the baby. "I'm going to see if I can nurse her back to sleep."

"Anything I can do to help?" Luella asked.

"No." Jillian sounded stressed out as she left the dining room.

Keith waited a beat before announcing he was going to check on his wife and baby.

AFTER DINNER, VICKI, Luella, and Walter bundled up the baby and went for a walk while everyone else did the dishes. Jillian said that Joy and Daniel were guests and didn't need to help, but they insisted.

"You don't need to help, either," Keith told his wife as she stood at the sink, rinsing dishes. "You didn't sleep well last night, so why don't you go upstairs and lie down."

"I'm fine." Jillian reached for another plate.

"You're not fine." Keith turned off the faucet. "Go upstairs and take a break. Your parents have the baby, and we've got the dishes, right, boys?"

"Yeah," Matt said, taking his mother's place at the sink.

Jillian, who obviously didn't like being told what to

do, snapped. "I don't want to take a break, Keith."

Daniel took that as his cue to leave the kitchen. In the dining room, he found Joy and Bianca looking at the large family portrait hanging above the buffet.

"Are you the little girl with the French braids?" Joy asked.

Bianca nodded. "That photo was taken on the day we began construction on this house."

"You all look so happy," Joy said.

"We were happy. It was a great day."

Daniel began stacking plates to clear the table. "You haven't always lived here?"

"No." Bianca picked up a few serving bowls. "We used to live on the beach in a little turquoise cottage called The Blue Crab. My parents wanted more land, so we moved up here and kept the beach house as a rental property."

Daniel nodded and followed Bianca and Joy into the kitchen with his stack of plates. Right away, he noticed the absence of both Keith and Jillian. They must've moved their argument elsewhere.

"Want to help dry the pots and pans?" Drew asked, tossing a towel to Joy.

Because her hands were full, Joy caught the towel with her mouth and nodded. Everyone laughed, then Bianca and Daniel returned to the dining room to clear the rest of the table.

Daniel gestured back at the family portrait. "I never could figure out how to braid Joy's hair like that when she was little. I was an expert with pigtails, but French braids were beyond me."

"At least you tried. If my dad was put in charge of our hair, I'm pretty sure he would've taken us to the barbershop for crew cuts."

Daniel smiled. "I don't know, your father seems pretty talented. I'm amazed by how many projects he has going on in the barn."

A disheartened expression crossed Bianca's face. "He likes his projects, that's for sure. But seriously, Daniel, you're a good dad."

Guilt crushed down on him. Was he a good dad? Wouldn't a good dad stop stalling and talk to his daughter about everything?

"You don't think you're a good dad?" Bianca said.

"No, I mean, thank you." *Was it possible to make this exchange any more awkward?* "Joy's an easy kid, so raising her has been . . ."

"Joyful?"

Daniel looked at Bianca and smiled. "Yes. Raising her has been joyful."

"I'm sorry about my mom's comments regarding Joy's diabetes."

Daniel shrugged. "She's just concerned. I get that. Most people don't know the difference between type one and type two. I'm impressed by your understanding of it."

"Well, diabetes is a huge part of Joy's life, so I educated myself. I want to be supportive."

"You are."

Looking up from underneath long eyelashes, Bianca smiled. "Thank you, Daniel."

The way she looked at him and said his name tugged at his chest. Despite Bianca's love of sarcasm, she exuded a sense of warmth and comfort he craved.

"What?" she asked, staring at him.

Shaking his head, he turned away. "I guess we better get these dishes cleared."

Daniel thought he heard a hint of disappointment as Bianca said, "I guess so."

Chapter 11

Bianca

THE NEXT MORNING, Daniel came to the salon. "Can I speak to you in private?" he asked.

The seriousness in his voice concerned me. "Sure. Is everything okay?"

He nodded but didn't give any indication what this was about. Upstairs in my living room, he shifted from one foot to the other. "Your dad called me this morning."

"He did?"

"Yes. He wanted to know if I was interested in helping him install your countertops."

"Oh. What did you say?"

He shrugged. "I told him the truth. I told him I was planning on renovating your entire kitchen in exchange for you teaching Joy how to drive. I hope that was okay I told him. He seemed surprised by our deal. I didn't mean to cause problems if—"

"No, it's fine."

What in the world had inspired my dad to think about installing my countertops? While we'd been cordial to each other last night, it wasn't as if we'd had one of those love and forgiveness conversations.

"Okay." Daniel nodded. "I just wanted to double-check before I got started."

"Thank you." I pushed out a deep breath. "My dad and I are having a difference of opinion right now. I didn't mean to drag you into it. At the end of the day it's going to be fine, so please don't worry about it. I made a deal with you, and I want to keep my end of the bargain."

"Good." He smiled. "That's really good. I tried driving with Joy again last night, and let's just say it didn't go well. So, I'm relieved you're still interested in our deal."

"Of course. I'm looking forward to helping her."

"Good."

With that settled, we turned to leave the apartment. At the fireplace, Daniel paused and stared at the framed picture of my daughter and me. When he didn't say anything, I felt the need to tell him my whole life story.

"This is my daughter," I said, picking up the picture and handing it to him. "I don't know if Joy told you, but I had her my senior year of high school and gave her up for adoption. I'm hoping to meet her again some-time soon."

He nodded and returned the picture to the mantle. "Joy told me."

"Well, that's why things have been tense between my father and me. He disapproves of my decision to contact her."

Daniel stared at me blankly, clearly uncomfortable that I was divulging such personal information. Yet, I couldn't stop myself from explaining. "He thinks I'm making a huge mistake, but I'm not changing my mind. This child is my own flesh and blood, and I need to meet her."

Something flashed across Daniel's face as though he wanted to say something.

"What?" I asked.

He shook his head. "Nothing."

"Tell me. You obviously have something on your mind, so tell me what you're thinking."

"It's really not my place."

"Do you agree with my father? Is that it?"

"Well . . . I . . ."

"Do you think it's a mistake for me to meet my daughter?"

Daniel's eyes darted around the room, probably looking for the escape hatch. "It's really not my place to say, Bianca. I don't know your situation or—"

"I'd like to know your opinion. You have a daughter about the same age as mine. If Joy was adopted, would you want her to meet her birth mom?"

Daniel shifted uncomfortably. "I don't know."

"That means no." I had no idea why I was being so combative. I guess I just wanted him to take my side.

Daniel stroked his beard. "It's just that people have this idea that once a kid turns eighteen, that's it. They're legally an adult, so they can go out into the world and make their own decisions. Maybe some kids are like that, but it seems to me that most of them still have a lot of growing up to do. They still need their parents' guidance. I guess . . . I don't know what I'm saying."

"You're saying you think I'm making a big mistake by contacting my daughter."

"I'm saying I don't know."

SATURDAY MORNING, JOY and Daniel arrived to begin my kitchen project. Given the uncomfortable conversation I'd had with Daniel yesterday, I was nervous about seeing him again. Fortunately, he seemed fine and completely focused on the logistics of renovating my kitchen.

"So, you're helping your dad today?" I asked Joy.

She nodded. "I usually work for Mrs. Maisel on Saturdays, but she closed the shop today because her son is getting married. Plus, my dad said I had to help, since I'm the one benefiting from the driving lessons."

I smiled at Daniel, relieved when he smiled back. Part of me wanted to apologize for being so disagreeable yesterday. I supposed I was just being overly sensitive.

"Well, I better get to work," I said. "I'll be downstairs in the salon. If you need anything, shoot me a text or come down and get me."

Daniel nodded, but Joy asked about the wall separating the kitchen from the living room. "My dad said you don't want us to knock it down. Are you sure? I think opening the view would be really nice."

"*Joy*," Daniel warned.

"What? I'm just asking."

"I know, but Bianca already said no."

I reached for my water bottle. "It's okay. It never hurts to ask, but yes, I'm sure I don't want the wall knocked down."

"Okay," she conceded. "If you change your mind, we can knock it down later."

"That's what your dad said, and I appreciate that. But I'm not going to change my mind."

Grabbing my phone, I said good-bye and headed out into the hallway. To my surprise, Daniel followed me.

"Do you have a second?" he asked, pulling the door closed.

"Sure."

"I just wanted to apologize for yesterday. I shouldn't have said anything about your daughter. I think if you want to meet her, you should."

I shook my head. "No, I'm the one who should apologize to you. I know I can be a little hard."

He shook his head. "I'd never describe you like that."

"No?"

"No."

A moment of awkward silence fell between us. Then, Daniel excused himself and went back inside the apartment, leaving me to wonder what that was all about.

⁂

As I worked in the salon that morning, I listened to Daniel and Joy moving around upstairs. At lunch, I ran up to check on their progress and was pleased to see they'd already ripped out the old countertops and had installed the largest slab of granite.

"This is amazing," I said, running a hand over my new counter. "I love it. Can I bring you something to eat for lunch?"

Daniel gestured to their ice chest. "Thank you, but we brought our own food."

"Then I'll bring you an early dinner. I insist. How does pizza sound?"

"It sounds great," Joy said. "My dad and I love pizza."

"Perfect. What kind should I get?"

"My favorite is pepperoni, sausage, and pineapple," Joy said, not the least bit shy about voicing what she wanted.

I grinned. "That's my favorite, too. Daniel, what about you? Do you want a meat-lover's pie?"

He shook his head. "No, I like pepperoni, sausage, and pineapple."

Back downstairs, I chatted with everyone about my kitchen remodel. Those who'd been in my apartment asked if I was going to take down the wall.

"What is it with everyone and the wall?" I asked. "I like the wall, so I'm not taking it down."

After seeing my last client, I ran across the street and picked up pizza, salad, and drinks. Climbing the stairs to my apartment, I imagined myself living an alternative life where Daniel was my husband and Joy our daughter. We'd be one of those single-kid families that traveled to Morocco or Fiji for summer vacation.

Every night we'd eat dinner together, discussing literature, history, and other interesting topics. Even though we could afford a bigger and more expensive home, we'd choose to live in the little apartment above the salon because it was cozy and allowed us to save money for travel and other adventures. Of course, we'd have to move once the other babies came along.

The thought of having children with Daniel made me sigh. Then, I thought of my own daughter. How would she fit into this scenario?

Reaching the top of the stairs, I shook away the fantasy. Best to stay in the land of reality.

Inside my apartment, I found Joy and Daniel cleaning up the day's mess. The countertops were installed and absolutely beautiful. Already, my kitchen looked one hundred percent better.

"Well, what do you think?" Joy asked, making a sweeping gesture with her arm across the kitchen.

"I love it. The countertops look even better installed than they did in the living room."

"Good," Daniel said.

We exchanged a smile, and I asked if he was hungry.

"I wasn't until you brought the pizza. Now, I'm starving."

"Bianca," Joy began, "my dad showed me the tile for your floor. I think it's going to look really nice with the countertops, but what about painting the cabinets?"

"Painting the cabinets?"

She scrolled through her phone and showed me a picture of what she had in mind.

"That's beautiful," I said, "but—"

"I'd do it for another year of free haircuts," Daniel said.

"You would?"

He smiled at me and nodded. "I think it'd look really nice, and Joy's usually right about things like this."

I glanced around my kitchen, trying to imagine what it would look like when everything was complete. "Why don't I just do a lifetime worth of free haircuts for both of you," I said.

"Yes," Joy said. "That's perfect. We accept."

Daniel chuckled. "Once again, I don't think that's how negotiations are supposed to work."

"Well, that's my final offer. You guys have done so much work, and I know painting the cabinets will be a big chore. Plus, you still have the appliances, the flooring, and the backsplash."

Daniel shrugged. "It sounds like a lot, but it shouldn't be too hard."

"And, don't forget, you still have to teach me how to drive," Joy added.

"True, but I feel like I'm getting the better end of

the deal."

"I don't feel that way," Daniel said.

"Me neither," Joy said.

I nodded. "Okay."

With everything settled, we took the pizza and drinks onto the balcony. It wasn't too cold tonight, but I turned on the heat lamp to take off the evening chill.

Joy lifted her hands toward the heat. "That feels great."

"I love these heat lamps. I'm sure people in Minnesota or Canada think I'm crazy, but I don't like to be cold."

"Me neither." Joy opened her backpack to test her blood sugar. She had a stylish, leather backpack from Myabetic that carried all her supplies. "Go ahead and eat if you're hungry. It will take a few minutes for my insulin to kick in."

I glanced at Daniel, not sure what to do. He shrugged. "I usually wait for her, but you don't have to."

"No, I don't mind," I said.

The three of us chatted until Joy's insulin took effect, then we dug into the pizza. Just as we finished eating, Vicki came into my apartment and waved at us through the window. I beckoned for her to join us. After giving my kitchen a quick look, she came outside.

"I love the countertops," she said.

I nodded. "Didn't they turn out great?"

"They really did. Here's your mail." Vicki plopped about a month's worth of mail on the side table next to me.

"Thanks."

"You might want to think about checking your mailbox once in a while," she suggested.

"Isn't that what I have you for?" I teased. "Plus, what's the point? Nothing good comes in the mail anymore."

Daniel nodded. "That's true."

I smiled and turned to my sister. "You're all dressed up. Do you have another date tonight?"

She nodded and mentioned the name of a guy I'd never heard of. "He's a lawyer I met at The Grand the other night."

Not bothering to keep the judgment out of my voice, I said, "You're going out with a guy you met while on a date with a different guy?"

"I told you, Seth and I are just friends, so it wasn't a real date. But yes, I met Ambrose when Seth took me to The Grand."

"Poor Seth," I said, shaking my head.

"Seth is that cute firefighter with the dimples, right?" Joy asked.

Daniel cleared his throat. "I think he's a little old for

you, honey."

Joy laughed. "Of course, he's too old for me, Dad. He's like twenty-eight."

"Thirty-one," Vicki said, lifting her chin.

"Wow, I didn't know he was that old," Joy said.

Daniel caught my eye and winked. "Thirty-one is not *that* old."

"Exactly," I said, thrilled by Daniel's wink.

"Anyway, I need to go." Vicki glanced at Joy and Daniel. "It was nice seeing you two again."

"You, too," they both said.

With that, my little sister left, off to break another man's heart.

Glancing at the mail, I sighed. "I remember as a little kid thinking my mom was crazy for throwing out half the mail. Now, I do the same. I just wish for once I'd receive something good."

"Maybe this is your lucky day." Joy smiled at her father. "Remember when I threw a fit because you refused to answer that letter from a lawyer claiming to represent a distant relative who'd left us an undisclosed fortune? You said it was a hoax, but I didn't believe you."

Daniel chuckled. "He just needed three hundred dollars for his fees, then he could release the money."

I absently glanced at the pile of mail, noticing a

hand-addressed envelope from Kansas. I didn't know anyone from Kansas, did I?

As though drawn by an invisible force, I picked up the letter and opened it. Inside, I found a folded piece of paper I somehow knew was the letter I'd been waiting for.

Oh, why hadn't I checked my mail earlier? Why had I just assumed my daughter would contact me via email?

Joy said something, but I didn't hear her. Instead, I stared down at the most incredible words I'd ever seen.

Dear Bianca,

My name is Claudia Cavenaugh, and I'm the child you gave up for adoption.

Chapter 12

Bianca

M Y HEART JOLTED, and my vision blurred as I tried to read more. I must've made a gasping noise because Joy asked if I was okay.

Nodding, I pressed the letter to my chest. "My daughter's name is Claudia."

"What?" Joy said.

I lowered the letter and did my best to speak over the lump in my throat. "This is from Claudia Cavenaugh. My daughter."

Daniel's eyes widened as Joy gave a little squeal. "Oh, my gosh. What does it say?"

"I don't know. I'm too excited to read it."

"I'll read it," Joy offered, coming over to sit next to me.

"Joy, honey. Let's give Ms. Bianca a little space. Come back inside with me and—"

"No, it's okay. I'm shocked and scared and thrilled

and—" I handed the letter to Joy. "Will you read it for me? Please?"

"Of course."

"Is that okay?" I asked Daniel, remembering what he'd said about kids turning eighteen. Maybe he thought Joy was too young to be part of this conversation. Then again, she was a month older than my own daughter.

"She can read the letter if that's what you really want," he said.

"It is."

Joy smoothed out the letter on her jeans. With a deep breath, she began to read.

Dear Bianca,

My name is Claudia Cavenaugh, and I'm the child you gave up for adoption. Thank you for your letter, which I received on my birthday.

I also want to thank you for giving me life. I can't imagine having a baby at my age and giving her up for adoption. I'm sure that was really hard.

I want you to know that you couldn't have picked a more perfect family for me. My parents tried for a long time to have kids. They always say getting me was an answer to their prayers. They've been happily married for twenty-five years and have been the best parents ever.

I have two little brothers my parents call miracle babies. Doctors don't know why my mom got pregnant after so many years of infertility. She just did.

My brothers' names are Clark and Clay. Clark is seven, and Clay is six. They were born exactly one year apart to the hour. Although they're very rowdy, I love them and would do anything for them.

I'm a freshman in college, studying music and French. I play the violin and hope to study abroad in France my junior year. And no, I don't know what I want to do with my life. My parents ask me this all the time.

I usually say teach, but my passion is composing music. I love writing songs. It's hard to earn a living as a songwriter, so I'll probably have to teach to support myself.

My boyfriend, Leland, is studying to become a filmmaker. He's actually helping me with this letter.

Leland and I found some pictures of you online. He says I have your smile, and I think he's right.

Last year, my dad was diagnosed with prostate cancer. He'd had it before, but this time, he had to have surgery and chemotherapy. It was terrifying, and we thought we might lose him.

Even though I had a scholarship to study on the East Coast, I decided to stay in Kansas and live at home. I'm really glad I did because I was able to help my family during my dad's treatment.

I'm happy to tell you that my dad is completely better. He still gets tired, but every day he gets stronger.

Anyway, the reason I'm telling you all this about my dad is because I'm not ready to meet you at this time. I don't want to hurt your feelings, but right now, I need to do what's best for my family.

I'm sure this is hard to hear, and I'm sorry. You seem like a very nice person, and I don't want you to take my decision personally.

From the pictures on your social media sites, I can tell that family is important to you. I hope you can understand how much my family means to me, too.

I've enclosed a picture of me, and you can look at my social media sites, but please don't friend or follow me right now. I haven't told my parents about your letter because I don't want to upset them.

If you'd like to contact me, you can email me at ClaudiaCavenaughlovesFrance@yahoo.com.

I'm sure that someday I'll want to meet you.

I've always been curious about my medical history.
    Thanks for understanding,

Sincerely,
Claudia Cavenaugh.

Tears streamed down my face as Joy finished reading the letter. I was both happy and devastated. Happy because Claudia, my daughter, seemed happy. Happy because she had everything I'd ever wanted for her.

And yet, I was devastated that she didn't want to meet me.

"Oh, Bianca." Joy's eyes filled with tears as she placed a hand on my arm. "I'm so sorry she doesn't want to meet you."

"Thank you. Intellectually, I understand, but it hurts." I reached for another napkin and blew my nose. "She said she sent a picture?"

Joy reached into the envelope and handed me a small photograph. The sight of my daughter all grown up knocked the wind out of me.

"She's beautiful," Joy said.

I nodded. Claudia was gorgeous with thick blond hair, bright blue eyes, and high cheekbones. Wearing a shimmery silver formal gown, she stood in front of a lake, holding her violin. Her hair was pulled into a double-knot updo, and she wore dangly earrings, similar to a pair I owned.

"She does have your smile," Joy said, leaning over to look at the photo.

"She has my smile, but not my body, thank goodness. Look at her. She's as tiny as Vicki. And her hair is so blond."

"But it's thick like yours," Joy said.

Daniel surprised me by coming over to sit beside me on the couch. I showed him the photo, and he smiled. "She has your little nose."

"My little nose?" I pressed a hand to my nose, feeling self-conscious. Nobody had ever commented on my nose before. Was something wrong with it?

Smiling, he pulled down my hand. "I'm sorry. I didn't mean to embarrass you. It's a nice nose."

"A nice nose?"

"It's cute, okay? You have a cute, little nose."

"I do?"

"*Dad*," Joy said, embarrassed. "Don't be weird."

"Sorry."

Joy pulled her phone out of her back pocket and shook her head.

I started to tell Daniel it was okay, but Joy's next words stopped me. "She has a video on YouTube."

"What?" I said.

Joy handed me her phone, and holding my breath, I

watched in amazement as my daughter came to life, playing the most beautiful violin solo I'd ever heard.

"She's incredible," Daniel said.

I swiped at the tears streaming down my cheeks and nodded. My daughter truly was incredible.

AFTER JOY AND Daniel left that night, I drove up to the ranch to show my parents Claudia's letter and video. My mother reacted with just as much excitement as I had, especially when she saw the video.

"Oh, Bianca, look at her. She's gorgeous. And the way she plays that thing . . . that violin . . ." My mother blinked back tears, then she turned up the volume and watched the video again.

My dad, on the other hand, showed little emotion. In fact, his only concern was my daughter's name. "Why do you think they named her Claudia?" he asked.

"What?" I said, annoyed.

"Claudia . . . I just . . ." He shook his head like Claudia was the worst name you could give a child.

Biting the inside of my cheek to control my temper, I said nothing. Then, I turned back to the video and joined my mother in watching it again.

Claudia's parents could've named her Mud, and I wouldn't care. She was incredible, and even though she didn't want to meet me right now, I felt nothing but love and admiration for her.

To: ClaudiaCavenaughlovesFrance@yahoo.com
From: BiancaMorgan@TheLastTangle.com
Subject: Hi!

Dear Claudia,

Thank you so much for writing to me! I received your letter tonight, and I was so excited, I don't know if I'll ever be able to sleep.

I want you to know that I understand why you don't want to meet me right now. I'm sorry about your dad, but I'm so glad to hear he's doing better. That must've been such a scary time for you and your family.

I also want you to know that you have an open invitation to visit me whenever you want. I have a guest room in my apartment where you can stay anytime. My family also has a little hobby ranch with lots of room for guests.

Not to pressure you, but I think you'd love Rose Island. It's so pretty here with the beach, the wild roses, and the ocean. You and your brothers would love the new zip line. It starts at the top of the mountain near the Rose Museum and goes all the way down to the beach with only a few stops in between.

You said you've always been curious about your medical history. I'm happy to say there's not much to report. For the most part, the Morgans are a healthy bunch. My nephew has dyslexia, my dad is stubborn, my mother often speaks without a filter, and I'm overweight. Other than that, I can't think of any medical issues to tell you about.

Joy, a girl from the Bible study I lead, found a video of you playing the violin. I'm not a huge crier, but the way you played was so beautiful, I bawled my eyes out. Did Leland film that?

Well, I don't want to overwhelm you with this letter, so I'll say good-bye for now. If you have any questions for me, I'd be more than happy to answer them.

Take care and write soon, if you want.

Love,
Bianca

Chapter 13

Daniel

AT BREAKFAST THE next morning, Joy chatted endlessly about Bianca's daughter. "Do you think Claudia will change her mind about meeting Bianca? Do you think she'll come to the island? Maybe Bianca will visit her in Kansas first."

Daniel stirred cream into his coffee. *You need to tell her,* a voice inside him whispered. *Just stop being so weak and get it over with.*

"I was thinking I might email Claudia," Joy said.

Daniel stopped stirring his coffee. "Why?"

"Well, I was thinking maybe it would help. Maybe I could get her to change her mind about meeting Bianca."

"Honey, I know your heart is in the right place, but I think you need to stay out of this."

Joy waved a dismissive hand. "I knew you were going to say that."

"Say what?"

"Say that I should stay out of it. Seriously, Dad, if I would've listened to you last night, we would've missed out on learning about Claudia."

Daniel raised his brow. "You don't think we were imposing by staying?"

"No, Bianca's our friend, and she wanted us there."

Daniel took a sip of his coffee and set it back down on the table. He didn't know what to think about sitting with Bianca during what was a private moment.

And why in the world had he told her she had a cute nose? What had that been about?

This is why you're so awkward with women, he told himself. *Especially women you really like.*

AT CHURCH, DANIEL sat in the back row by himself while Joy joined the choir. Although his daughter didn't have the greatest singing voice—something he would *never* tell her—he was proud of her effort. It took a lot of courage to do something you weren't good at.

Behind him, he heard Kate Tate's voice. Hopefully, she wouldn't want to sit with him again.

While Daniel was sure most men found the divorcée attractive, Kate wasn't his type. For one thing, she was way too high maintenance for his tastes. And second, he didn't like the smell of her perfume or the color of her nail polish. Did that make him shallow? He hoped not. She just didn't do it for him.

"Hey, stranger," called a friendly voice behind him that thankfully didn't belong to Kate.

Relieved, Daniel turned to see Bianca standing with her mother. Coming to his feet, he said hello.

"Daniel." Luella gave him a huge hug. "It's so good to see you. How's Joy doing?"

"She's doing great." He gestured toward the front of the church where Joy was studying her music.

Luella followed his gaze and pressed a hand to her heart. "What a sweet, sweet child. You must be so proud of her."

"She is sweet, and I am proud of her."

A beat of silence followed in which Daniel found himself staring at Bianca. She looked so pretty this morning in her blue and white dress. He wanted to ask how she was feeling about everything. Had she found out any more about Claudia? Had they spoken on the phone or talked via text?

Interrupting his thoughts, Luella tugged on Daniel's arm. "Come on, Daniel."

"What?" he said, confused.

"You can't hear your daughter sing when you're in the back pew. You need to sit up front with us."

"*Mom*," Bianca warned, looking embarrassed.

"Don't tell me not to meddle."

"That's exactly what I was going to tell you." Bianca gave him a quick glance. "I'm sure Daniel is perfectly happy sitting back here by himself."

Bianca's reaction surprised him. He studied her carefully, trying to figure out what she was thinking. Did she feel uncomfortable that he'd been there last night? Had he embarrassed her with the cute, little nose comment?

Daniel smiled at Luella. "Thank you for the offer, but this church has great acoustics. I can actually hear just fine in the back."

Bianca nodded. "Plus, you don't have to worry about getting caught nodding off when the sermon goes into overtime."

Daniel laughed as Luella responded with mock outrage. "Bianca Grace Morgan, hush. What a horrible thing to say."

Bianca's eyes danced with amusement. Then, she smiled at Daniel in a way that caused a strange feeling to settle in his gut. A strange warm feeling he actually liked.

"Won't you please join us?" Luella pleaded. "I really don't like the idea of you sitting back here alone."

Hearing Kate's voice approaching, Daniel nodded.

"Okay, Ms. Luella. If you insist."

"I absolutely insist," the older woman said, beaming.

He glanced at Bianca, hoping she didn't mind. Avoiding Kate was only one of the reasons he'd agreed to Luella's offer.

JOY'S EYES WIDENED as Daniel joined the Morgan family in the front row. Walter and the others quietly greeted him, and he took a seat between Bianca and her mother.

Although there wasn't a lot of room, Daniel didn't mind. It was actually nice being able to see Joy. And sitting next to Bianca, who smelled amazing, was nice too.

After church, Luella and Walter scooted out quickly because they were meeting some old friends. Keith and Jillian also left right away because the baby was throwing a fit and the boys had a lot of homework to do.

Before Joy and Daniel could say their good-byes, Vicki introduced them to Ambrose, her date from last night. Joy said hello before hoisting her backpack on her shoulder and joining her friends in exiting the church.

Ambrose turned to Daniel and asked what he did for a living. That sparked a conversation about a new software program Ambrose's law firm had recently implemented. As the men talked, they slowly moved down the aisle, following Vicki and Bianca.

Every few minutes, they had to stop walking because someone wanted to say hello to Bianca or give her a hug. Bianca was a people magnet, something Daniel deeply admired given how awkward he could be around people. Everyone loved Bianca, and Daniel didn't blame them. Being around her just made you happy.

She was fun and exciting without the drama. Well, maybe she had a little drama, but it was fun drama. Not exhausting drama if that made any sense.

Maybe he should encourage Joy to reach out to Claudia. Bianca deserved to be happy. If anyone could change Claudia's mind about meeting Bianca, it would be Joy.

On the steps outside the church, Vicki asked if Daniel had plans for lunch. "Ambrose, Bianca, and I are going to walk over to Juanita's. You and Joy should join us. Have you ever been there?"

"I have, and it's delicious."

"So you'll come?" Vicki asked.

Daniel shook his head. "Unfortunately, Joy and I have a lot of work to do today. Maybe another time, though."

Bianca frowned. "I thought you didn't work on Sundays. Are you cheating on me, Daniel?"

"Busted," Vicki said in a low voice.

Daniel's face grew warm. "Oh, I don't work on major projects on Sundays, but that's the day Joy and I catch up on our laundry, clean the house, make a menu, and go to the grocery store. You know, all that life stuff you never have time for during the week."

"Wow," Bianca said, teasing him. "And I thought my life was exciting. Laundry, cleaning, and going to the grocery store. You really know how to live on the edge, Daniel."

"Don't forget menu planning," Vicki said.

Bianca laughed, and Daniel did too. Then, he stopped being stubborn and agreed to join them. "When you put it that way, I kind of have to accept."

"We don't want to force you," Bianca said.

"No, it's fine."

"Of course, it's fine. It's lunch at a Mexican food restaurant. What's better than chips and salsa on a Sunday afternoon? Besides, you haven't lived until you've tried Juanita's carne asada."

"Well, I definitely can't turn down carne asada." Daniel called to Joy and told her about the plan for lunch.

"Actually . . ." Joy offered an apologetic smile. "I was hoping to go down to the beach with my friends. Is that okay? We'll grab lunch at one of the food trucks, and Kayla said she could give me a ride home."

Daniel glanced at the group of girls Joy had been talking to, recognizing most of them. "Yes, that's fine."

"Why don't you have Kayla drop you off at my place?" Bianca suggested. "As long as your dad doesn't mind, I can take you driving."

"I don't mind at all," Daniel said.

"Okay, see you later." Joy waved good-bye and headed back to her friends.

"She seems like a good kid," Ambrose said.

"She's an awesome kid," Bianca said.

Daniel grinned at Bianca, thinking he couldn't agree more.

Chapter 14

Bianca

"*Y*OU'RE WELCOME," VICKI said as she and I climbed the stairs to our apartments after lunch.

I frowned. "You're welcome for what?"

"For arranging that lunch so you could have a little *Daniel time*."

"*Daniel time?*"

She cracked up. "What? Now that he's renovating your kitchen you're not into him anymore?"

I shrugged. "I wouldn't go that far, but I definitely don't want to jeopardize my sweet deal with the kitchen renovation."

"Right," she said, her tone skeptical.

"What about you and Ambrose?"

"Oh, he's nice, but—"

"Not the one?" I asked.

She stopped walking and gave me an icy cold glare. "Why do you think so little of me?"

"I don't."

"Well, you act like I'm too picky. I wish I liked Ambrose like that. I wish I liked Seth and all the other guys I've dated over the years. I want to get married and all that. I just don't want to make the wrong choice."

"I know, and I respect that."

"Do you?"

I nodded. "I'm sorry, Vicki."

"Thank you." She opened the door to her apartment and said good-bye.

"Vicki—"

"It's fine," she said. "I'm just tired of the dating scene. I'm tired of trying, you know? It's exhausting."

"I know. Just don't give up."

With a sad smile, she told me we could talk later. Then she went inside her apartment and closed the door.

As I headed to my own place, I couldn't help but wonder if Daniel felt the same way about me as Vicki felt about all those guys. Maybe in Daniel's eyes I was sweet and nice, but I just wasn't *the one*.

BECAUSE DANIEL WAS working on my kitchen Monday evening, I held Bible study in Vicki's apartment. In celebration of St. Patrick's Day, she'd decorated her place with green shamrocks and leprechauns.

She'd also provided the girls with an abundance of shamrock-shaped cookies topped with my favorite buttercream frosting, tinted green for the holiday. I limited myself to one cookie, grateful I could leave the rest with Vicki instead of being tempted by having to deal with them in my apartment.

During sharing time, I told the girls about receiving the letter from Claudia and stalking her on the internet. Everyone was excited I'd heard from her, but they also understood my disappointment.

When Bible study ended, I encouraged the girls to take the leftover sweets home to their families. Even so, there was still an entire plate of cookies left over.

Vicki covered the plate with Saran wrap and handed it to me to take home. "Thanks," I said, not sure if I had the self-control tonight to actually put them in the break room.

"I'll take them downstairs if you want," Joy offered, knowing that's what I did with the leftovers.

"Thank you. I appreciate that."

She took the plate while I returned to my apartment to admire Daniel . . . I mean, to admire the progress Daniel was making on my kitchen. I was so impressed that after working his IT job all day he was willing to come over and spend time on my project.

After Joy and Daniel left, I brushed my teeth, all the time fantasizing about sneaking downstairs for a soft, buttercream-topped cookie. *What was wrong with me? Why did I have such strong cravings for food that ultimately made me sick?*

As I crawled into bed, I told myself to just go to sleep. *You'll feel stronger in the morning, and the cookies won't be such a temptation.* With those words on my lips, I threw back the covers, rationalizing that I might as well have just one and get it over with.

Of course, I hadn't stopped at just one. No, if I could stop at one cookie, then I wouldn't have a problem with cookies. Instead, I ate until my stomach felt like it was hanging down to my knees.

Defeated, I crawled back in bed and awoke in the morning with a horrible headache. Glancing at the clock, I realized I needed to hurry if I wanted to have time for my morning bike ride. Part of me thought about skipping it. What was the point in exercising if I was going to negate the benefits by binging?

Clinging to Yadira's encouragement to view my morning bike ride as a gift and not a punishment or a way to lose weight, I forced myself outside. Once on the trail, I felt better.

Despite the roll of flab hanging over my yoga pants, today was a new day, full of opportunities. I could start over. I could be strong and make choices that led to a better life.

I didn't have to be defined by what I did and didn't eat. I was a child of Almighty God after all. If He could part the Red Sea, surely He could heal me.

The rest of the day went well, and by the time Daniel and Joy arrived, I was feeling better. Joy and I went driving, using the truck instead of my car because Daniel wanted her to feel comfortable driving the truck.

Sitting in the passenger's seat of my dad's old vehicle brought back all sorts of memories, making me sad for how things were between us right now. The Bible said not to let the sun set on your anger, but our family hadn't quite mastered that concept yet.

Not that my dad would admit to being angry. If pressed, he'd probably say he was disappointed in the decisions I'd made. He'd also probably insist that Claudia's refusal to meet me was proof I'd made a mistake in contacting her. Plus, he'd acted so strange about her name.

"Which way should I go?" Joy asked, interrupting my thoughts.

I smiled at her, grateful for the distraction. "Take a left out of the parking lot, and we'll go up First Street until we hit Blackberry."

"Okay." She followed my directions and drove fairly

well. At least, she drove better than she had the first few times, which was progress.

"You're being so quiet. Are you thinking about what a horrible driver I am?" Joy asked.

Shaking my head, I smiled. "No, I was thinking about how much you've improved."

"Really?"

"Really. I was also thinking about my dad. He had a truck just like this when I was in high school. He bought it so he could pull the horse trailer for my shows."

"Your shows?"

"I used to do horse shows."

"Really? I didn't know you had a horse. I always wanted one."

"You'd love it. People complain about it being a lot of work, but I absolutely loved the time I spent with Mr. Whiskers."

"Mr. Whiskers? That was your horse's name?"

"Whiskers for short, but yes. He was such a great horse. Very kind and smart. In the summers, I worked as a trail guide at Camp Windham, and Whiskers was so patient with all those kids."

"Sounds like fun." Joy pulled the truck to a stop at the sign. "Camp Windham? I've heard of that before. Where is that?"

"It's the summer camp behind my family's property. Have you never been there?"

She shook her head.

"I have amazing memories of playing there as a kid. Do you want to see it?"

"I'd love to."

"Okay, good. We can drive up there now."

Taking Joy up to Camp Windham was so much fun. Of course, it wasn't fun when she almost hit the deer, but that wasn't Joy's fault. That crazy animal literally jumped right in front of us.

Despite the *No Trespassing* signs, my sisters, Marcus, and I had spent hours of our childhood exploring the camp. The owners never minded because we were good kids and never damaged the property. In fact, sometimes we improved things by raking leaves or weeding the flower beds.

Because I knew where the secret key was hidden, I was able to show Joy the dining hall, the cabins, and the adorable little chapel. It broke my heart to see that the camp had fallen into disrepair since closing a few years ago.

Most of the buildings needed new roofs as well as new paint. The road leading to the camp could definitely use several loads of gravel to fill the potholes. In fact, had Joy not driven the truck, I don't know if we would've been able to make the trip in my car.

I'd heard the property was unofficially for sale. Maybe someone would buy it and give it the new life it deserved, although from the looks of it, that would take a lot of work, not to mention a fortune.

When the sun fell and it was too dark to see without the use of the flashlight app on our phones, Joy and I headed back to town. Her driving was definitely improving, but she still had a long way to go before she'd be able to take her test. Hopefully, she'd make the deadline Mrs. Maisel had set. Part of me was considering talking to the older woman and seeing if she'd be willing to give Joy a little extra time.

Back at my apartment, Joy pushed open the door. "Dad, we're back."

"In here," Daniel hollered, his voice strained.

Joy headed toward him. When she rounded the corner to the kitchen, she gasped. "*Dad.*"

"I'm okay. I was cutting the tile for tomorrow, and the saw slipped, but I'm fine."

"You're bleeding."

"I know, but I'm okay, honey. It was an accident."

Scared of what I'd find, I strode toward Joy. "We need to take my dad to the hospital," she said, her face white and her eyes wide with fear.

"No, it's just a scratch," Daniel said, standing at the sink. "I'll be fine."

"It's not just a scratch. Show Bianca the cut."

"Joy, I'm fine."

My stomach pitched as I glanced at Daniel who was pressing a bloody dishtowel to his hand. Gripping the counter, I tried to steady myself. There was a reason why Jillian, instead of me, was the nurse in our family.

"I'm sorry about the dishtowels," Daniel said, reaching for another one. "I'll replace them."

"It's okay. Don't worry about that."

He nodded and removed the bloody towel to examine the wound. I should've looked away because the sight of his open gash caused my head to spin. My legs wobbled, and the room tilted. I tried to hold on, but next thing I knew, I found myself on the floor, my knee throbbing.

"Bianca." Kneeling above me, Daniel called my name in the smoothest, most calming manner. "Bianca, can you hear me?"

I looked into his eyes, which were marred with concern. Beside him knelt Joy, her face even whiter than before. "*Bianca.*"

"Hey." Glancing around the room, I tried to remember what happened. "Why am I on the floor?"

"You passed out," Daniel said. "Are you okay?"

I blinked. "I think so. I feel a little sick to my stomach, and my knee hurts."

He nodded. "You hit your knee when you fell. Can you move it?"

I tried to do so, but the pain made me wince. "Ouch."

Daniel placed his good hand on my shoulder, something that helped ease my suffering more than a thousand Advil could ever do.

"Is her knee broken?" Joy asked.

Daniel shook his head. "I don't think so. Why don't you get Bianca a bottle of water from the ice chest?"

"Okay." She stood and did as he suggested.

Daniel turned his attention back to me. "Have you ever passed out before?"

"Once, when Drew crashed his bike into the garage door. And when Jillian had the baby, but don't tell anyone about that."

"I won't."

"I don't like the sight of blood."

He grinned. "I kind of figured that."

Joy brought me the water, and Daniel helped me sit up to drink it. I purposely kept my gaze away from his injured hand and the bloody dishtowel covering it.

"How do you feel?" he asked, watching me intently.

"I'm okay."

He nodded. "I don't think you broke anything, but you should probably see a doctor."

"You *both* need to see a doctor," Joy said, sounding way more worried than she needed to be. I hadn't thought she'd be the kind of person to overreact in a situation like this.

Then again, I'd just fainted in my kitchen at the sight of a little blood. You couldn't exactly achieve a bigger reaction than that.

"Joy's probably right," Daniel conceded. "Do you think you can stand if I help you?"

I shook my head, not because I wasn't ready to get off the floor, but because I was afraid helping me stand would make Daniel realize how much I weighed. "It's okay. I can get up on my own."

"Let me help you." Before I could protest, Daniel placed his strong arm underneath mine and lifted me to my feet as if I weighed nothing at all. Still holding on to me, he asked, "How do you feel?"

With your arm against mine? Amazing.

"My knee hurts," I said.

"What about your head? Do you feel dizzy, like you might pass out again?"

"No."

"Good. Do you think you can walk downstairs? If

not, I can carry you."

I suddenly had a horrible vision of Daniel lifting me into his arms, then swaying because of my girth, before finally smashing to the ground. The headline would read, "Innocent Father Crushed To Death By Overweight Hairdresser."

Determined to avoid such a scenario, I managed to push through the pain and limp down to the parking lot. Because of her father's injury, Joy insisted on driving.

"The clinic's not that far," Daniel said. "I can drive."

Joy narrowed her eyes and stashed her backpack behind the seat. "You're not driving. I am. Now, scoot over."

"Yes, ma'am." Daniel slid across the seat to sit between Joy and me. "Are you okay going to the Urgent Care instead of the hospital?"

I nodded, and Joy headed out of the parking lot. While the trip was a little rough with Joy almost hitting a delivery truck, we made it in one piece. At the clinic, we went our separate ways with me seeing a doctor who determined that my knee had been badly bruised but wasn't broken.

Because my blood pressure and other vitals were normal, the doctor gave me a pair of crutches and sent me on my way with instructions to take it easy and continue icing it to reduce the swelling. In the waiting room, I found Joy reading a paperback by Karen Kingsbury.

"Great author, great book," I said.

She closed the book and set it on the coffee table. "I just found it here in the waiting room, but I'm going to buy the digital copy so I can read it on my phone. It's really good."

I nodded. "All her books are good. Have you heard from your dad?"

"They're stitching up his hand now. He should be done soon."

"You didn't want to stay and watch?"

"No. I've never passed out at the sight of blood, but being around doctors isn't exactly my favorite thing."

"I imagine not. I'm sure you've seen your share of doctors and hospitals."

"I have."

I studied her carefully, suddenly worried about her. "Do you need to eat something? It feels like we've been here forever."

"I'm okay. I tested my blood sugar and had a snack from my backpack."

I resisted the urge to ask if that was enough. I didn't want to smother her, but still, I couldn't help but worry.

As if sensing my concern, she smiled at me. "I'm fine, Bianca. Seriously."

"Okay," I said, sarcastically. "Sorry for being such a kind and caring person. Sorry for worrying about your health and wellness."

She rolled her eyes, then gently nudged me with her elbow. I laughed, hoping things would be this easy with my own daughter if I ever got to meet her.

"You probably already know this," Joy said, "but this building used to be a grocery store."

"That's right." I looked at her, surprised. "How'd you know that?"

"My parents brought me here. There was this brown horse out front—you know, one of those plastic mechanical kinds for little kids. My dad had a ziplock bag full of coins, and he let me ride until I got bored."

I studied Joy carefully, surprised she'd been on the island with her parents back when the Urgent Care was a grocery store. "I had no idea you visited the island when you were little. How old were you?"

"Seven. I have really good memories of that vacation. We were here for the Fourth of July, so there was this huge parade and fireworks at night."

"I wonder if I saw you? I've never missed a Fourth of July on the island."

"Wouldn't that be crazy?"

"It would." I smiled at Joy, imagining she'd been such a cute kid. "You know, they actually moved that horse you're talking about to the Rose Museum."

"Really? My dad and I will have to go see it."

"You haven't been up to the museum yet?"

"No. My dad said I almost fell off the cliffs when I was little, so he's kind of freaked out about going up there again."

"Well, you can tell him there's a stone wall around the viewing area now, so he won't have to worry about you."

"He'd still worry about me. That's what he does."

At that moment, Daniel came into the waiting room, his hand bandaged. He gestured at my crutches. "What'd they say about your knee?"

"Bruised but not broken. It should be better in a few days. What about your hand?"

"A couple stitches, so basically the same."

"That's not the same," I said, smiling.

"Well, what I mean is, the stitches will dissolve in a few days, so completing your project won't be a problem."

I waved a dismissive hand. "Don't worry about that. I've waited this long for my new kitchen. A few more days isn't going to be the end of the world."

He gave a curt nod. "All the same, I intend to uphold my end of the bargain."

"I do, too," I said, appreciating the fact that Daniel was a man of his word.

To: ClaudiaCavenaughlovesFrance@yahoo.com
From: JoySerrano@gmail.com
Subject: Bianca Morgan

Hi, Claudia!

You don't know me, but my name is Joy Serrano. Bianca is my Bible study leader, my driving instructor, and my friend. I was with her the night she received your letter, so that's how I got your email address.

I just wanted to reach out and tell you how happy Bianca was to hear from you. She's always wanted to meet you and find out how you turned out. It sounds like things are going well for you. I'm glad your dad is better.

Your brothers sound really cute. I'm an only child, but I always wanted brothers and sisters.

Anyway, Bianca and I watched a video of you playing the violin. Wow! You're so talented. I wish I was musical like that. I sing in the choir at church, but I'm not very good. Sometimes, Mr. Brown, the choir director, tells me not to sing so loudly. Seriously, I'm that bad. My dad's offered to pay for singing lessons, but being in the choir is something I want to do for fun.

Okay, enough about me. I just wanted to say "hi"

and tell you I understand why you don't want to meet Bianca right now. I'm sure it's scary for you to think about meeting your birth mom given what your family has been through. I admire you for wanting to protect them.

I also want to tell you that Bianca is the best. My own mother died when I was nine, and Bianca has been like a mother to me. I honestly don't know anyone more kind, sweet, patient, and fun as Bianca. She's hilarious, too. She's always making sarcastic comments and cracking jokes.

Anyway, I just thought you might like to hear from someone your own age that Bianca is a great person. I'm not trying to change your mind . . . okay, maybe I am, just because I know how much Bianca would love to meet you. But seriously, she really is wonderful.

I hope you don't mind me emailing you. Bianca doesn't know I'm sending this, so please don't think she put me up to it. She totally respects your decision not to meet her, even if she wishes you didn't feel that way.

Like I said, she's a great person. Hopefully, one day, you can see for yourself.

Well, have a great day!

Sincerely,
Joy Serrano

Chapter 15

Bianca

*I*N THE MORNING, my knee hurt worse than it had the night before. Following the doctor's instructions, I iced it and took ibuprofen. Needless to say, I didn't go for my bike ride, something I deeply missed. Instead, I took my Bible and coffee onto my covered balcony.

Having quiet time for prayer and scripture reading was important to me, but I often neglected it for the simple fact that I could be lazy. Sometimes, it was just easier to fill my time with social media or email. These days especially, I checked my email every chance I got, hoping to hear back from Claudia.

Recently, I'd read a book called *Bored and Brilliant* by Manoush Zomorodi. Manoush believed the increase of technology and the convenience of smartphones hindered us. Instead of being creators, we'd become consumers, something that wasn't good for us long-term.

As if to prove her point, my phone dinged with a text from the pizza restaurant, asking me to fill out a survey regarding my recent purchase. Was that really necessary right now?

Determined to spend this time with God, I turned off my phone, opened my Bible, and resisted the urge to post a photo with the caption, "Just spending a little time with the Lord this beautiful morning. #Blessed."

Enough, I told myself. *Enough. Let's focus on what's most important, okay?*

IN THE SALON that day, I tried not to complain about my knee. As the bruise turned purple, looking more painful than it actually felt, everyone commiserated with me.

Of course, that didn't stop them from laughing when I explained how I'd been injured. For some reason, everyone found it hysterical that I'd passed out at the mere sight of blood.

My own mother laughed the hardest. To embarrass me further, she told the other hairdressers and our clients how I'd thrown up *and* fainted during the birth of my niece Linda Faith.

"Have you ever seen a baby being born?" I asked in my defense.

"Yes, it's miraculous," Jenny said, sweeping the area around her station. "I was in the room when my sister gave birth. What a powerful, spiritual experience."

"Well, that may be true," I conceded, "but the birthing process is also disgusting."

That just made everyone laugh harder. My mother laughed so hard she almost fell out of the salon chair. It was then that I said, "Maybe it's time for you to find a new hairdresser, Mom."

"Oh, Bianca, don't be so melodramatic."

While the mood had been light, and I'd been joking around just as much as everyone else, my mother's comment struck a nerve. How many times when I was a child had she told me not to be so melodramatic? Wasn't I allowed to say something when people hurt my feelings? Wasn't I allowed to express my opinion?

I thought about the donuts in the break room Vicki had brought over this morning. *Yes, that's exactly what you need*, the childish part of my brain said, lighting up at the thought of a sugar fix.

No, you need to tell your sister to stop sabotaging your efforts to be healthy, the responsible part of my brain insisted. *Sugar makes you crazy, so just stop, okay?*

Forcing a smile, I pushed both thoughts away and did what I always did. I cracked a joke, putting everyone at ease by pretending I wasn't bothered by anything.

Good job, my inner child said, *now, go reward your-self with a cookie.*

⁕

BECAUSE OF HIS injury, Daniel didn't work on my kitchen that night or the next. One of my clients told me Kate had brought him dinner and stayed to watch a movie.

"Isn't that nice," I said, tamping down my jealousy. If only I'd thought about taking him dinner and staying for a movie.

After lunch the following day, Daniel came into the salon while I was cutting Sonya Tuskaloski's hair. He asked about my knee, and I told him it was sore but much better.

"You don't need the crutches anymore?"

I shook my head. "No, I stopped using them after the first day. How's your hand?"

He held up his bandaged hand. "Not bleeding, fully covered, and in no danger of causing anyone to black out."

"Ha, ha." I rotated the salon chair so I could reach the back of Sonya's hair.

Daniel folded his arms across his chest. "So, hey. I wanted to install the backsplash today, but because of my hand, I need some help. Joy's working for Mrs.

Maisel, and my neighbor isn't feeling well... You mentioned that you were interested in learning how to install the backsplash? Do you still want to do that?"

"Yes, I'd love to help," I said.

"Yeah?" He smiled as though pleased by my answer. "Are you sure?"

"Definitely. Let me finish up here, then I'll be done for the day, and I'll be all yours." As soon as the words left my lips, I realized the mistake in what I'd said.

Embarrassed, I didn't dare look at Daniel for fear he'd see the heat burning my face. Instead, I focused all my attention on Sonya's hair.

"Great." Daniel's voice held a hint of amusement. "I'll take everything upstairs, then when you're ready, we can get started."

"Sounds good." I tried to act casual, and as Daniel headed toward the back of the salon, I told myself not to look. Then, I snuck a peek just as he turned to look at me. Quickly, I turned away, mortified.

Breathe, girl, breathe. You don't want to pass out on him again.

As though reading my mind, Daniel chuckled. Then, he pushed open the back door and headed upstairs.

"Who is that?" Sonya asked, her thick Slavic accent punctuating every word.

"Daniel Serrano. I'm teaching his daughter to drive in exchange for having him renovate my kitchen."

Her brow lifted. "So that's what they're calling it these days."

I laughed.

"You're going to help him today?"

I nodded. "I've been watching a lot of home improvement shows, and I thought it might be fun to install my own backsplash."

Sonya scoffed. "Those projects always take more time than they're worth. Although"—she offered a sly grin—"I'm thinking from the looks of it, you won't mind spending a little extra time on this project."

I rolled my eyes, despite thinking I couldn't agree more.

Chapter 16

Daniel

NOT SEEING BIANCA for two days gave Daniel a lot of time to think. Although they'd exchanged a few texts, it wasn't the same as talking to her in person. Despite not wanting to, he'd missed her smile and the way she made him feel when he was around her.

Bianca didn't exhaust him like all the other women who'd brought over dinner to help him recover from his injury. How they found out he'd been hurt, he had no idea. Part of him wondered if Kate Tate had a tracking device on him because she was actually waiting in the driveway when Joy drove him home from the Urgent Care.

He really hadn't wanted her to stay, but Kate insisted on heating up dinner and making sure he was comfortable. Then, she'd invited herself to watch a movie with him since her kids were gone with her ex-husband.

He really needed to grow a spine and learn how to say no. Kate just seemed kind of lonely, and Daniel didn't want to hurt her feelings.

Well, none of that mattered now. Just seeing Bianca and being in her apartment took away all the tension he'd been feeling since almost slicing off his hand.

Now, Bianca was going to help him with the backsplash, and that would be fun. He chuckled to himself, thinking how much he liked Bianca's sense of humor and how she just made things more enjoyable.

Relying mostly on his good hand, he laid out the tile and marked the wall. By the time Bianca came upstairs, he had everything ready to go.

Her face beamed as she hobbled into the kitchen. "I'm so excited to learn how to install the backsplash. What do we need to do first?"

He smiled at her standing there in her fancy dress and designer shoes. "Well, first, you should probably change into something you don't mind getting messy."

"Oh, sure." She laughed her good-natured laugh. "I'll be right back."

"I'll be right here."

As she left the kitchen, he rolled his eyes at his pathetic attempts to flirt with her. Hadn't he told himself earlier that starting a relationship with her was a bad idea? He'd never forgive himself if he ruined Joy's friendship with Bianca.

Think of her like a sister, Daniel told himself. *And whatever you do, don't look at her eyes. Those soft brown eyes of hers are a trap. And her lips—*

"How's this?" Bianca asked, returning to the kitchen. She'd changed into a T-shirt and a pair of jeans that showed off her curves. She'd also done something to her eyes to make them even bigger and prettier than normal.

You're looking at her eyes. Daniel gave a curt nod and turned away. "That's fine. Now, what do you think about this pattern for the backsplash?"

She walked over and began rearranging the tile. He tried not to inhale her scent or think about pulling back her hair and kissing her neck as she moved the tile one way, then the other. Finally, she settled on a pattern, and they got to work.

Picking up a piece of tile, Daniel demonstrated how to spread the thinset with the trowel.

"Like this?" she asked, smiling up at him.

"Exactly." He placed his tile on the wall and had her do the same. Because she pressed hers a little too hard into the adhesive, he had to straighten it out before moving on. They continued like that until they reached the end of the row and started over.

"Joy told me you came to the island when she was seven," Bianca said, breaking their companionable silence.

"That's right." Daniel pulled Bianca's last tile off the wall, removed the excess thinset, and handed it to her to try again.

She sighed and reinstalled it, using a little less pressure this time. "Sorry. I'm trying to keep it straight, but it's harder than it looks."

"Five seconds to learn, a lifetime to master, and all that."

She smiled. "It's more difficult than it looked on TV, but it's fun."

"Good," he said. "I'm glad you're having a good time."

"Speaking of good, Joy did a pretty good job driving us to the Urgent Care the other night, didn't she?"

"She did. You're a good teacher."

"Well, I wasn't looking for a compliment, but thank you."

"You're welcome." They lapsed back into silence, until Daniel asked how she was feeling. "The work isn't too hard on your knee, is it?"

"No. My back will probably be a little sore in the morning from leaning over, but every time I come into the kitchen, I can be proud of how I helped."

He nodded. "That's how I feel about so many projects around the house. I love my day job, but there's something satisfying about creating something you get to see every day. It's not always like that with work."

"I guess I get that feeling of accomplishment in my job," she said. "Although, my clients go home and sometimes I don't see them until next time."

"But they come back, so you obviously know you're doing something right. I often only hear back from my clients when things have gone horribly wrong."

"I'm sure that can be a little frustrating."

"A little. But it feels good when things get fixed and everyone is happy."

She nodded before returning to their earlier topic. "So, when you came to the island, did you come because of work or vacation?"

"Vacation."

"Really? Why Rose Island? Why not South Padre or Galveston or some other more popular place?"

"Well, my wife, Libby, always wanted to come to Rose Island. She'd once met someone from here and thought they were wonderful. Anyway, I decided to surprise her by bringing her here for the Fourth of July."

"Oh, Daniel. That's so sweet. I bet she was incredibly happy."

Incredibly happy? Daniel held back a sardonic grunt. Libby had been incredibly *not* happy as they'd crossed the bridge and she realized where they were.

"What?" Bianca looked at him with so much compassion that he almost told her. Then, he came to his senses.

Keeping his mouth shut, he removed the last tile Bianca had installed. He held it up for her to see. "You probably don't want to use this one. It's defective. See the flaw?"

She stared at the tile in his hand and shrugged. "I kind of like it. The flaw gives it personality."

He shook his head, amused by her ability to see the good in a piece of imperfect tile. Then, he tossed it in the trash and reached for a new one.

Chapter 17

Bianca

AT WORK THE next afternoon, I made my way through several clients before heading over to volunteer at our church's Dinner and a Movie Night. In the parish kitchen, I cut tomatoes and onions with Caroline Kempner. Caroline, her husband, and their eight boys had recently moved to the island in search of a simpler life.

"I can't imagine anything being simple with eight boys," I told her.

She laughed and admitted I was probably right. "Still, it's relaxing living in a place where the boys can ride their bikes and we can go to the beach every day. Plus, Doug's new job is an answer to prayer. After surviving a year without a steady income, having a salary makes everything simpler."

I nodded and asked how she'd found the time and energy to work tonight. "I would think volunteering would be the last thing you'd want to do at the end of a long day."

"Are you kidding?" Her eyes sparkled as she spoke. "Chopping these tomatoes with you is a huge break for me."

"It is?"

"Yes. You and I are having an adult conversation. Nobody is tattling on their brother, making a mess, or complaining about what's for dinner. What could be more wonderful? It's like an all-expenses-paid vacation for me, and I get the added benefit of feeling like I'm contributing to our church family."

I laughed. "I hadn't thought about it like that."

Smiling, she slid the sliced tomatoes on her cutting board into the large, metal serving bowl. "In all honesty, Dinner and a Movie Night was a huge blessing for our family when we first moved here. Doug had been out of work for so long that all our money needed to go toward getting caught up with our bills. For the longest time, we didn't really have any money for entertainment. This ministry provided us with a free outing we looked forward to each month. Giving back by volunteering is satisfying, you know?"

I nodded. I'd never really struggled with money. My parents had paid for college, and I'd gotten a good job after graduating. I was easily paying my bills and putting money into savings, so it'd never occurred to me that Dinner and a Movie Night might mean so much to people like the Kempners.

Around five o'clock, Caroline and I switched from meal prep to working on the serving line. We had a great time saying hello to everyone, including some of my school teachers and several clients.

When Caroline's adorable family arrived, all the boys except one of the twins were thrilled to see her. The boys talked over one another, telling her about the dog throwing up in the living room and Daddy knocking over the gallon of milk that Gavin had left on the counter.

Caroline laughed until the unhappy twin started crying, saying he missed her and it felt like she'd been gone a million years. Doug pushed out a slow breath, patted the boy's head, and sent his wife a pleading look.

Caroline turned to me. "Do you mind if I leave and go back to my family?"

"No, go ahead." I glanced at the other volunteers. "We've got this, right?"

They all nodded and encouraged Caroline to call it a night.

"Thanks." Caroline took off her apron and left the kitchen to join her family. The boys greeted her with hugs, and the sad one wrapped his arms around her leg, refusing to let go until his father lifted him upside down in the air.

While I could see having such a big family was a lot of work, part of me longed for Caroline's chaotic life. Those little boys were such a blessing, and it was obvious her husband adored her.

Would I ever find a man like that? A man who was willing to marry me and give me children? Or would Claudia end up being my only biological child?

The question bounced in my head as Daniel and Joy arrived. *Is that some kind of sign, Lord? Yes? No? Maybe?* I waited for a response but didn't hear anything.

"My dad just showed me pictures of the back-splash," Joy said. "I love how it turned out. It really complements the countertops, and I think it will look even better once we paint the cabinets."

"I agree," I said.

"Once *we* paint the cabinets?" Daniel asked his daughter. "Does that mean you'll be helping?"

She grinned. "Hey, I'm the lead designer on this job. I'll help if I can, but it sounds like you've already got a great assistant."

I laughed at the realization she was talking about me. "I don't know how much I helped. Your dad did most of the work."

"Nah," Daniel said. "We made a good team."

I willed myself not to look at him for fear he'd see how much I wanted that to be true.

WHEN THE VOLUNTEER cleanup crew arrived, I made myself a plate of food and joined my sisters in the dining hall. Jillian had left Linda Faith at home with Keith tonight, and she seemed extremely relaxed as she chatted with Vicki.

Sitting beside Vicki, I glanced across the hall and spotted Daniel and Joy, sitting at a table with Phoebe and Kate. In church last week, my mother had saved me from being forced to watch Kate flirt with Daniel.

Tonight, however, Kate was making up for lost time. Dressed in skinny jeans and high heels, she threw her head back, laughing uproariously at everything Daniel said.

"You're not going to let her get away with stealing your man, are you?" Vicki asked.

I lathered my roll with butter. "He's not my man."

"Who are you talking about?" Jillian peeked over her shoulder. "Daniel Serrano? Are you still interested in him?"

"She is, and given how he was looking at her to-night, I'd say he's interested in her as well."

"Daniel was looking at me?" I asked, unable to help

myself.

Vicki nodded.

I sighed. Was it possible that Daniel had feelings for me? Given how he was acting with Kate, I had to believe he just felt sorry for me because my crush on him was so obvious. That had to be it.

"If I were you," Vicki said, interrupting my thoughts, "I'd march over there right now and tell Kate to stand down."

I rolled my eyes and glanced across the room. Daniel was now actually nodding as Kate flipped her hair this way, then that. Were those new highlights in her hair? Had she betrayed me by going to a different salon to get her hair done?

Frustrated by the jealousy boiling inside me, I stood and moved to the other side of the table so I wouldn't have to keep watching Kate and Daniel. "If Kate is the kind of woman he's interested in, what do I care?" I declared. "I made a deal with Daniel to teach his daughter how to drive in exchange for having my kitchen renovated. As long as he follows through with his end of the bargain, he can keep company with whomever he wants."

"Is that so?" Vicki asked.

Knowing I was being ridiculous, I laughed. Then, I heaved a huge sigh. "Always the bridesmaid and never the bride."

"Hey," Vicki said, "as a proud member of the Morgan Sister Spinsters' Club, I resemble that statement."

Jillian waved a dismissive hand. "Don't give up hope. When you least expect it, love will find you."

"You keep saying that," I said, taking a bite of my spaghetti, "but I'm beginning to doubt you. Besides, if I ever found a man interested in me, by the time I convinced him to propose, get married, and try for a baby, my eggs will have all shriveled up and died."

Across from me, Vicki groaned. "Shriveled eggs. Such a lovely image, Bianca. Thank you for sharing."

"What? It's true. You think you have all the time in the world, and then bam! Your biological clock shatters, and it's too late. When Mom was your age, she already had three kids. She had her fourth baby at my age, and then that was it for her. No more babies."

Vicki shook her head. "You're just full of good news, aren't you?"

"I'm just telling the truth."

Vicki waved at something or someone behind me. "Come join us."

Even before looking, I knew it was Daniel. Coming around the table, he sat next to Vicki. "So, what are you ladies talking about?" he asked.

My face turned red, but Jillian came to the rescue by

mentioning one of her classmates who'd just sold a start-up company for millions of dollars.

"Wasn't he the one who used to eat glue in Sunday school class?" I asked.

Jillian nodded. "That's the one."

I smiled at Daniel. "You're a smart guy. How much money do you think it takes to eradicate one's reputation as a glue eater?"

"I don't know, but I imagine a lot." Daniel grinned at me in such a way that I felt it from the tips of my toes to the top of my head. He honestly had the best smile in the world. Joy had that same smile, and I just loved it.

I allowed myself the fantasy of thinking about two or three little kids with my cute nose and Daniel's warm smile. Strangers would stop us on the street to admire our growing brood and—

"Excuse me," a small voice said, interrupting my daydream. "May I clear your plate, please?"

I turned to see a sweet girl wearing a name tag on her apron that read, "Avery." The child had Down syndrome, and I recognized her immediately as Avery Gray, the daughter of our former governor and his mistress, Lyla Gray.

My family's history ran deep with Lyla, as she'd written a book about military heroes that included my brother. She'd also been present at the time of Marcus's tragic death, but that was something I tried not to think about.

Avery motioned to my plate and asked again if she could take it. "Yes, thank you." I stacked my silverware and napkin on top of my plate and pushed it toward her.

A woman carrying a toddler in a backpack walked over and placed a hand on Avery's shoulder. "Did you ask if we could clear any plates?"

"I did, Justine," Avery said excitedly. "She said *yes!*"

Justine smiled. "Great. Do you want any help?"

"No, I got it."

"You're such a great helper, I might not let you go home when your mom and Hank return from their honeymoon."

Avery froze and looked up at Justine with wide eyes. "You're not going to let me go home?"

Realizing the child misunderstood her, Justine quickly corrected the situation. "Oh, Avery, I was just teasing. Of course, I'm going to let you go home. I just meant that I'm grateful for your help."

Avery gave a huge smile before hugging Justine. Then, she turned back to our table and told us that she and her mom were moving to her new daddy's house. "And you know what?"

"What?" I asked.

"He painted my room pink because I love, love, love pink."

"I can tell," I said, noting her pink sweatshirt and pink nail polish. I scooted my chair away from the table to give myself a little more room. "You sure are one lucky girl to have a new daddy and a new pink room."

Right away, Avery's gaze dropped to my belly. Leaning forward, she placed her hands on my stomach and spoke in a tone of reverence. "Do you have a baby in your tummy?"

"Avery, no." Justine pulled Avery away from me.

Humiliated, I gave an embarrassed laugh as if this were all a big joke.

"I'm so sorry," Justine said.

"It's okay." Placing a hand on my stomach, I smiled at Avery. "I don't have a baby in there. I've just eaten too much spaghetti." I tried to sound light and playful as though everything was fine.

"Not a baby?"

"No." My face burned with shame, and I didn't dare look at Daniel. "What about you?" I asked, tickling Avery's tummy. "Do you have a baby in there?"

She giggled and patted her round stomach. Then, she lifted her shirt to reveal a bright white belly. "Yes, I have a baby in my tummy. A spaghetti baby!"

WHEN AVERY ASKED if I had a baby in my belly, I knew I couldn't take it personally. Avery was just a little girl who'd innocently pointed out the fact that I was so fat that I looked pregnant. Still, hearing those words hurt.

After our plates were cleared, I excused myself to check on something in the kitchen. Nobody said anything as I left the table and snuck out the back door.

All I wanted to do was crawl into bed with a carton of ice cream. I knew binging at a time like this didn't make sense. Any normal person would use this event to turn their life around and lose weight.

But how?

Eat less and exercise more? How many times had I heard that advice? And how many times had I tried so hard to lose half a pound only to gain back three?

Following the stone wall that surrounded the prayer garden, I headed home, planning to stop at the convenience store for something sweet. When I reached the garden's entrance, however, I paused.

Seeing nobody was there, I took the path that led to a bench by the fountain. Sitting down, I took one deep breath after another. Then, I closed my eyes and prayed.

I didn't ask God to help me lose weight. No, I'd long since given up that impossible fantasy. Instead, I simply prayed that He would help me make peace with my body.

Help me continue to exercise and make healthy choices out of respect for all you've given me. And help me to get over the hurt and humiliation I'm feeling right now. I want to honor you with my life and my body, Lord, but I don't know how to do that.

And regarding Kate, take away my jealousy. I want to be a better person. I know the only way to do that is to forgive her for all the mean things she's said to me over the years.

Help me forgive her. Help me to just let everything go and remember that you love me.

Footsteps on the gravel path startled me. Opening my eyes, I cringed at the sight of Daniel coming toward me.

What was he doing here? Hadn't he seen enough of my humiliation tonight?

"Hey," he said, kindly.

"Hey."

He came over to the bench and just stood there without speaking.

"Did you need something?" I asked, an edge in my voice.

He shoved his hands in his pockets. "Well, I was just wondering, Bianca, if you knew where the bathroom was."

"The bathroom?" I glared at him. How could he be

so insensitive to follow me out here and ask about the bathroom? Couldn't he have just asked Jillian or Vicki?

"Sorry," he said, a glint in his eye. "I was trying to be funny, but . . . Are you okay?"

"You mean other than being completely mortified and humiliated?"

"Yeah, other than that."

Willing myself not to cry, I nodded. "I'm fine."

He shoved a hand through his hair. "Do you mind if I sit down?"

I shrugged. "It's a free country."

He sat beside me on the small bench. I blinked hard, determined to keep my tears at bay. When he placed a hand on my back, however, I broke.

"Hey, now," he said as a giant sob racked my body. He slipped his arm across my shoulders. "It's going to be okay, Bianca."

"Is it?"

"Yeah. Of course, it is. I've read the book. I know how it turns out. The good guy wins."

His words and touch just made me cry harder. I tried to control myself, but the tears kept coming.

To his credit, Daniel didn't run away. He just sat there, holding me as if he didn't mind my breakdown.

When my tears finally ended, I wiped my eyes and moved away from him. "I'm sorry I'm such a blubbering fatso."

He shook his head. "I don't think you're a blubbering fatso."

"No?"

"No."

Pushing out a deep breath, I spoke with a wobbly voice. "The thing is, I thought I'd come to peace with my body. After months of therapy, I thought I'd finally accepted the fact that I was a larger woman. But hearing Avery ask if I was pregnant . . ."

I shook my head, determined not to cry again.

"It made you feel bad," Daniel said matter-of-factly.

"Yeah, it made me feel really bad. I know she wasn't trying to be mean, but her words really, really hurt."

"I know. I'm sorry that happened to you."

"Thanks."

Silence fell between us, then Daniel spoke. "Can I tell you something?"

I nodded.

"Okay. The thing is . . . I didn't really come out here looking for the bathroom."

I smiled and nudged him with my shoulder. "I know."

He grinned and nudged me back. "In all seriousness . . ." He wiped his hands on his jeans. "I'm sure you know that Joy thinks the world of you."

I nodded. "I feel the same way about her. She's such a special kid."

"I agree, but her mom—" He stopped abruptly and stared at the fountain. "I don't want to talk bad about Joy's mom, but I don't know how to tell you what I need to tell you without mentioning Libby."

"Okay," I said, apprehensive.

He hesitated for a long time before speaking. "Libby had a lot of mental health issues. She could be sweet and kind, but most of the time, she made things tough."

"I didn't know that."

He nodded. "That's why Joy was so concerned about all that blood on my hand. Her mother tried to kill herself by slashing her wrists, and Joy found her."

"Oh, Daniel." I placed a hand on his arm.

He patted my hand and offered a sad smile. "Because mental illness can be inherited, I've always worried about Joy."

"I can understand that, but Joy seems really well-adjusted."

"She is well-adjusted. Type one diabetics have a higher rate of depression and anxiety than the general population, but I think Joy is truly happy." Daniel looked at me and smiled for real this time. "Anyway, that's my point. She's happy, and I think a lot of Joy's happiness is because of you."

"Because of me?"

He nodded. "You've been a good role model and friend to her. You've taught her that true happiness can only come from believing in God. In many ways, you've given Joy what her mother took from her. You've given her stability, love, and deep friendship. At the risk of sounding presumptuous, you've been the mother she never had but so desperately needed."

My heart swelled with love. "That doesn't sound presumptuous. That sounds beautiful."

Tears stung my eyes as I smiled at Daniel. "Joy has been like a daughter to me. In fact, without her friendship, my own daughter's decision not to meet me would've been so much harder."

"I'm glad to hear that." Daniel looked down at his hands, then back at me. "The whole point of telling you this is to say that even if you were the largest, most ugliest person in the world, I'd only be able to look at you and see beauty."

"What?"

He shook his head. "That came out wrong. What I'm trying to say is you're beautiful, Bianca. I'm sure you know that, but—"

I stared at him incredulously. "A little girl just asked if I was pregnant."

He shrugged. "Little kids say all sorts of things. My

point is . . . after that first Bible study at your apartment Joy's freshman year, she came home and told me about you.

"I'd met you, and I knew you were wonderful and beautiful on the outside, but I didn't know how wonderful and beautiful you were on the inside. Over the years, you've shown that in the way you've treated Joy and the other girls in the Bible study."

I stared at him, my heart pounding. "You think I'm wonderful and beautiful?"

"I do. Is that okay I told you that?"

I nodded, afraid if I spoke I might explode with pure happiness. Daniel Serrano thought I was wonderful and beautiful on both the outside and the inside.

Chapter 18

Claudia

CLAUDIA WATCHED AS Leland sat across from her at the Student Union Building reading the emails from Bianca and Joy. When he finished, he asked, "Does this make you change your mind about meeting your birth mom?"

"Not really."

"No? You're not even the least bit curious?"

She shrugged. "Maybe I'm a little bit curious, but it's not like I can just drive down to Rose Island and meet her."

Leland closed the laptop. "I told you my grandmother lives in Houston. I've really been wanting you to meet her. We could drive down next weekend—"

"You never said anything about wanting me to meet your grandmother."

"Well, I'm saying it now." He wrapped his fingers over his camera case, which was sitting on the table between them.

"I haven't even told my parents about Bianca yet," she protested.

"When are you going to do that?"

"I don't know."

"You could always tell them after you meet her. It might be easier that way."

"Maybe."

His eyes widened just a bit. "Does that mean you want to go? Should I see if we can stay with Mimi?"

"I don't know. I need some time to think about it. If I do decide to go, I don't want you filming our trip. This is private."

"I know." He kept his eyes down, avoiding her gaze. "Although, I could always film it and not use it. Just so you'd have a record of the experience."

Something inside her snapped. "Is that why you're so eager for me to meet her? So you can record my experience? I already told you I don't want you filming it."

"I know."

"Then why do you keep pushing me?"

"I'm not."

The lump in her throat tightened. When they'd first met, she was so fascinated by his passion for filmmaking. Leland's ability to talk to everyone and draw them out of their shell was something she admired about him.

Lately, however, his camera felt like the third person in their relationship. Maybe he'd be happier with someone else. Someone who didn't mind being filmed all the time.

Recently, they'd watched a documentary called *Expedition Happiness*. The film was about a couple from Germany who converted an old school bus into a loft on wheels. The couple crossed Canada before driving up to Alaska and then all the way down to Mexico, documenting each step of their journey.

While Claudia enjoyed watching the film, she didn't think she could be so open about her life like that. Leland, on the other hand, was inspired by the movie to brainstorm ideas for documentaries he could make about his own life or the lives of people around him.

Not that he wasn't always brainstorming ideas. As an artist, his brain never shut down. He couldn't watch a simple movie without pointing out continuity errors or how the filmmaker had missed an opportunity by shooting it one way and not the other.

Claudia did the same thing when it came to music. She couldn't help pointing out songs that were rewrites of other songs or places where the melody fell flat. And if she ever got a new idea for a piece she was creating, she'd drop everything to work on it. That was just the artist's way, she supposed.

Out of all her friends, Leland was the only one who understood this. He also never complained about the hours she spent practicing or how she could lose track of time when learning a new piece. She needed to remember that whenever they disagreed like this.

"I gotta go," Leland said, glancing down at his phone. "I'm supposed to be helping them edit that commercial for the drama department. I'll call you later, okay?"

"Okay." She tried not to sound disappointed that he was leaving. He'd been on his way to the drama department when she'd stopped him and made him read Bianca's and Joy's letters.

Still, she couldn't help but wish he'd stay to help her figure out what to do. At this point, not telling her parents about Bianca felt just as bad as telling them.

Chapter 19

Bianca

ORMALLY, A COMMENT like Avery's would've sent me off on an endless sugar binge. Instead, my thoughts kept circling back to the fact that Daniel thought I was wonderful and beautiful, not just on the outside but on the inside, too.

When I got home that night, instead of sneaking down to binge on leftover sweets from the bakery, I found the journal Yadira had given me during our first therapy session. Just holding it relaxed me, and I spent the next hour writing down my thoughts and feelings regarding what'd happened with the do-you-have-a-baby-in-your-tummy incident.

In the end, I came to three major conclusions.

1. I had a big belly. That was just a fact of life. Was I willing to do something about it like starve myself, exercise more, or give up my favorite treats? Not really. At least, not right now.

Well, was I willing to spend ten extra minutes on my abs workout every day? Yes, I could do that. I could even commit to holding a plank twice a day since that was supposed to be the best core exercise, according to this month's issue of *Fitness Magazine*. Next month, the experts would probably conclude that the plank actually made you fat.

Regardless, starving myself to slim down just wasn't going to happen right now, so I needed to accept the body I had at this moment. My body could still be a temple for God. It was simply a mega-sized one.

2. Because I knew I'd be working in the kitchen at church, I'd worn a blouse that I didn't mind getting ruined by spaghetti sauce. The style of that particular shirt wasn't very flattering on me. In fact, Jillian had worn a similar top when she was nine months pregnant even though it wasn't officially a maternity blouse.

   Maybe if I didn't want to look pregnant, I should stop wearing clothes that could be mistaken for maternity clothes.

3. Not only had Daniel come out to the prayer garden to talk to me, but he'd told me I was beautiful. He told me I'd been like a mother to

Joy. He'd opened up about his wife, trusting me with something extremely personal.

He didn't profess his undying love for me or ask if I'd be the mother of his future children, but he'd been supportive and kind. He'd been a good friend when I'd needed one, and I really appreciated that.

So there you had it. Yes, I was fat. That hadn't changed.

But maybe I was learning to be more gentle with myself. Maybe treating myself kindly was something I could be proud of and count as a success.

I placed the journal back in my nightstand drawer, turned off the light, and snuggled under the covers. Then, I said my prayers, thanking God for everything that'd happened today, including my time with Daniel in the prayer garden.

You know I really like him, Lord. He's so cute and has a good heart. And he's such an amazing father. Spending time with him makes me happy.

But I also adore Joy and would never want to do anything to jeopardize my friendship with her. So, if you've placed Daniel in my life to only be a friend, that's okay, but I want to get married and have more children. I want to be a wife and a mother. Have I ever told you that?

I laughed because when had I not told God the desires of my heart? When had I ever been shy about asking for what I most wanted?

I continued praying, lifting up all the girls in the Bible study, my parents, my sisters, the stylists in my salon, and everyone striving for world peace. Then, I prayed for my daughter.

I know Claudia has a family that loves and supports her, but if it be your will, Lord, please encourage her to reach out to me. Help her to know that I don't want to interfere with her family, I just want a chance to get to know her. Amen.

Picking up my phone from the nightstand to make sure I'd put it on "Do not disturb" for the night, I saw that Daniel had texted. "Can I join you on your bike ride tomorrow morning?"

My heart lifted with excitement, and I actually laughed. Daniel wanted to go bike riding with me? Tomorrow?

Smiling, I texted, "Do you think you can keep up?"

He returned my text immediately. "Probably not, but I'd like to try."

"Okay. Meet me behind my building at six."

"Six in the morning?" he asked.

"Yes. Is that too early for you?"

"It is, but I'll be there."

Smiling so hard my cheeks hurt, I set down the

phone. Then, I tried not to let my excitement for tomorrow keep me from sleeping.

THE NEXT DAY, I awoke feeling like a kid on Christmas morning. As I brushed my teeth and put on my makeup, I wondered if Daniel would think I was beautiful if I met him without any makeup. Better not risk it.

Downstairs, I found Daniel waiting for me with his bike. "Good morning," I said, feeling giddy.

"Good morning. It looks like it's going to be another beautiful day."

"Definitely."

We hopped on our bikes and rode along the trail that followed Harbor Street past the marina where Keith kept his boat. Staying on the trail, we cycled past the Pelican Pub and The Blue Crab. I waved at the tenants staying in our beach house for the winter, and they waved back.

"That's Nick and Anna's house," I said, pointing to the luxurious home next door.

"It's impressive."

I nodded, and we continued our ride. At the golf course, we climbed off our bikes and took a rest on a bench overlooking the water. Daniel pulled a mandarin orange from his jacket pocket and peeled it before handing me a slice.

"Thanks." I popped the orange into my mouth, savoring its sweet taste. "And thanks for talking last night. What you said really helped."

"Did it?"

I nodded. A beat of silence fell, and I worried I'd only imagined him calling me wonderful and beautiful. Maybe he'd used that word to describe the prayer garden or maybe he'd called me wonderful and beautiful last night but now regretted it.

Daniel glanced across the bay at the pink and blue sky. "Does living here ever get old? The mornings are so breathtaking with that sunrise."

I paused, taking in the mist coming off the water and the colors of the sky. It was definitely one of those perfect mornings. "Living here doesn't get old, but when I was a kid, I didn't always appreciate it. I thought island life was too slow, and I yearned to move to the city. After several years in Austin, I was happy to come back home."

"Isn't that the story of life?" Daniel mused. "I was raised in El Paso and always thought the desert dull. I didn't appreciate its subtle beauty until I came home after college."

"Is the desert beautiful?" I asked. "I'm not saying

that to be rude, but I never think about the desert as being beautiful. I just think of it being brown and arid and full of rattlesnakes and cacti."

He offered a knowing smile. "You've never been?"

"Not really. My family drove through El Paso on the way home from California one summer. I think we stopped at the gas station, but we didn't do anything there."

"I'm sure a lot of people have a similar experience with west Texas. The desert has a beauty that's easy to overlook, especially from the highway. When you hike around the Franklin Mountains, though, you can see thousands of birds, plants, and animals. During the rainy season in June, everything comes alive, and it's incredible."

I smiled. "It sounds like you miss it."

He gazed out across the water before turning back to me. "There are definitely aspects I miss, but Rose Island is home now. We've been here four years, and I can't imagine living anywhere else."

"Good," I said.

"Good?"

I nodded. "I like having you and Joy here. I like . . ."

The air grew thick between us, and I looked away, embarrassed by how much I wanted him to kiss me. I fumbled for the words that would make my feelings less obvious. "I like having you here just in case I have another breakdown in the prayer garden."

He smiled before reaching into his wallet and retrieving a piece of paper. "After we talked last night, I got to thinking you might find this helpful. It's a prayer that has given me a lot of strength."

He handed me the paper, and I unfolded it. "Abandonment Prayer," I said, reading the title.

He nodded, and I read the prayer aloud.

Father, I abandon myself into your hands. Do with me what you will. Whatever you may do, I thank you. I am ready for all. I accept all. Let only your will be done in me and in all your creatures.

"Oh, Daniel." I smiled at him, incredibly emotional that he'd shared this prayer with me. "This is exactly what I was praying about last night."

"Yeah?"

I nodded. "Thank you for sharing it with me. It's beautiful."

"You're beautiful." His gaze dropped to my lips.

My heart thudded as I stared at him. He didn't just say that, did he?

In answer to my question, he reached out and brushed a strand of hair off my face, tucking it behind my ear. As though embarrassed by the gesture, he pulled away, dropping his hand to his lap.

I swallowed hard, not wanting the moment to pass. "I think you're beautiful too, Daniel. *Handsome*, I mean." Heat burned my face. "*Ugh.* I sound like such a dork."

He grinned. "Well, I just so happen to have a thing for dorks."

"You do?"

"I do."

His hand returned to my face, resting briefly on my cheek. Then, he cupped the back of my head, pulled me close, and kissed me.

With my heart pounding, I kissed him back, swept away by all I felt for him.

AFTER RETURNING HOME from my bike ride, I couldn't stop smiling. Singing aloud, I showered, dressed, and took a little extra time with my hair. Any minute, Daniel would arrive to work on my kitchen.

When the doorbell buzzed, I skipped across the room like a schoolgirl, excited to see him again. "Hi," I said, flinging open the door.

"Hey." Instead of Daniel, Keith stood there, a panicked expression on his face.

"What's wrong?"

My brother-in-law glanced over his shoulder toward

Vicki's place, then looked back at me. "I need to come in."

"Of course." I stepped aside, and he entered the apartment, immediately closing the door behind him.

"What's going on?" I asked. "You haven't been drinking again, have you?"

"No."

Raising my brow, I gave him my you-better-not-be-lying look.

"I haven't, Bianca. Honest." Cracking his knuckles, he began pacing the room. "It's Jillian. Well, it's this big surprise party I'm planning for her birthday."

"You're planning a big surprise party for my sister's birthday?"

He nodded. "I'm inviting over a hundred guests."

"You're kidding? When is it?"

"Two weeks from today," he said, sounding defeated.

"Two weeks from today?"

"Yeah."

I stared at him in disbelief. "It's two weeks from Saturday, and you didn't bother to tell me?"

"I'm sorry. I just wanted it to be a surprise, and you're not exactly the best at keeping secrets."

"What are you talking about? I'm great at keeping secrets. I didn't tell anyone about Claudia for *eighteen years.*"

"I know, but this is different. This is something I think you wouldn't be able to keep from Jillian."

Knowing he was probably right, I sighed and took a seat on the couch. "I'll try not to let that comment hurt my feelings, but seriously, Keith. Do you hear yourself? I thought we were friends."

Keith sat beside me. "We are friends. That's why I came to you. Vicki is going to lose it when she finds out what happened to the invitations."

"Vicki knows?"

He nodded.

"I can't believe you told Vicki about the party but not me. How long has she known?"

"Does it matter?"

"How long has Vicki known, Keith?"

He offered a remorseful grimace. "Since Christmas."

"Since Christmas? You've been planning a surprise party for my sister since Christmas, and you're just now telling me? Am I even invited to this event?"

"Of course, you're invited, but that's one of the problems."

"What's one of the problems? Inviting me?"

"No. Vicki thought it would be more elegant if we sent paper invitations. She spent all this time addressing the envelopes in calligraphy and sealing them with this special gold sticker she ordered online. Then, Drew lost them."

"Oh no."

Keith nodded. "Yeah. He lost all one hundred seven invitations. Vicki said they had to be mailed on the third, but I was out of town. Drew insisted he could drop them in the mailbox by his school. Apparently, he put them in his backpack for safekeeping, but then he lost the backpack."

"Where did he lose his backpack?"

Keith gave me a look of exasperation. "I don't know. Probably the same place he lost his glasses and retainer and everything else he's lost since the beginning of time."

"Okay." I realized my question was pointless. The entire island was well acquainted with Keith and Jillian's frustration over their youngest son's tendency to misplace his belongings. "I'm sure his backpack will show up, but because you're running out of time, you should probably send a digital invitation."

"Okay. Can you help me with that?"

"Let me get my computer." I pushed myself off the couch and strode across the room to the entry table. As I reached for my laptop, my phone dinged with a text from Daniel, telling me he was on his way.

Smiling, I texted back, "See you when you get here."

"That's not Jillian, is it?" Keith asked, sounding half crazy.

"No, it's Daniel." Using all my self-control, I tried to hide my smile. "He's headed over to work on the remodel."

"Oh, that's right." Keith turned to look at my kitchen, but because of the wall, he couldn't see anything. "How's that going?"

"Good." Unable to help myself from thinking about kissing Daniel this morning, I laughed.

"What?" Keith asked.

I shook my head. "Nothing. I was just remembering something that happened earlier today."

Keith looked at me with suspicion. When I didn't elaborate, he asked if I was going to have Daniel knock down the wall to open up the room.

"No." I sat beside Keith on the couch and logged into my computer. Glancing at the time, I realized I had only twenty minutes before my first appointment. Usually, I liked opening the salon before everyone arrived, but helping my brother-in-law right now was more important.

Plus, Jenny and the other stylists were plenty capable of taking charge until I arrived. And the longer I stayed in my apartment, the greater the possibility I had of seeing Daniel before work.

"What's going on with you?" Keith asked, studying me carefully.

"Nothing. Why?"

"You're a million miles away."

"No, I'm not." I pulled my attention back to the computer. *Stop daydreaming, girl.* "I'm just trying to figure out how to forgive you for telling everyone but me about the party."

Keith sighed. "I didn't tell everyone, and I'm really sorry, Bianca. Will you please, please forgive me?"

"Since you asked so nicely, yes, I'll forgive you. Now, look at these invitations and tell me what you think."

I turned the screen toward him, and he pointed to the first one on the page. "That's good."

"Are you sure? Does it go with the theme of your party?"

He frowned. "The theme of my party?"

I nodded. "What do you have planned so far?"

"Oh, okay." He relaxed and filled me in on the details.

I had to hand it to him. Without any help from me, he'd managed to rent the ballroom at the Rose Museum, hire a caterer, order the cake from Vicki, find a DJ, and come up with a scheme to get Jillian to the party.

I stared at him, impressed. "It sounds like you have

everything under control. Let me ask you this."

"What?" He scooted forward on the couch as if worried he'd forgotten something important.

"Are you sure you want to go through with this party?"

"Of course. Why wouldn't I?"

"Well, I don't know how well you know my sister, but she's not big on surprises. She's more of the plan-a-year-in-advance-and-execute-that-plan-to-the-exact-detail kind of girl."

"I know, but she needs this. Things have been stressful with the baby, and I want to do something to boost her spirits before I leave on my next overseas trip."

Keith worked as an independent contractor for the Army, which meant he spent several months of the year abroad. Although Jillian hadn't said anything, I imagined she was anxious about him leaving.

"Why don't you take her out for a nice dinner while I watch the baby?" I suggested. "Or maybe you could give her a spa day with her sisters? Maybe—"

Keith placed a hand on my arm. "Bianca, I know you're only trying to help, but I want to throw my wife a surprise party for her birthday. She's never had one, and I'm afraid if I plan a different event, she's going to feel a need to take charge."

"Jillian take charge?" I asked sarcastically.

"Be nice."

"Okay, but—"

"Just help me with the invitation. If you want to come decorate on the day of the party, that would be great, too. But don't try to talk me out of this. I'm going through with it. All I need from you is your support."

"Okay," I said, a little worried. Emotions had been tense between Jillian and Keith at dinner the other night. When I'd run into Jillian at the grocery store this week, it looked like she'd been crying even though she insisted it was just allergies.

"Everything is okay with you guys, right?" I asked, my stomach knotting.

"Yeah." Keith looked away. "I'm sure it's fine. I'm just worried about her."

"Why?"

He looked at me, his eyes filling with incredible pain. "Do you think she's happy, Bianca?"

My heart broke for him. "Of course, she's happy. She seems really tired, but I think she's happy. She seemed happy at movie night. Are you worried she's depressed?"

"I don't know."

I studied him carefully. "Did something happen?"

"No. Not really." He leaned against the couch and placed an ankle on top of his knee. "The baby is keeping her up at night, so she's not getting enough sleep. But around three this morning, I woke to find her gone."

"Gone?"

Keith nodded. "Linda Faith was sound asleep in the bassinet beside our bed, but Jillian wasn't there. At first, I thought she might be in the bathroom, but she wasn't. So, I walked down the hall and . . ."

Keith took a deep breath as wild images raced through my head. Did my sister have some kind of postpartum psychosis where she engaged in strange behavior like dancing on the roof in her nightgown or watering the fake plants?

Was she suffering from some kind of mental illness like Daniel's wife had? Goosebumps prickled my forearms. "Where did you find her, Keith?"

He sighed. "In the laundry room."

"What was she doing?"

Slowly, he exhaled. "She was folding towels."

I pressed a hand to my heart, realizing it was racing. "And . . ."

"And that's it. She was just folding towels. I told her she shouldn't be doing laundry in the middle of the night, but she just got mad. We ended up having a huge fight over the stupid towels."

Feeling both relieved and confused, I offered Keith an encouraging smile. "If it makes you feel any better, my parents have had lots of stupid fights, and they've been happily married for years."

"I know, but I hate fighting with Jills. I love her so much, and we were apart all those years. I don't want to spend a single second fighting with her."

"Well, if you don't want to fight, you could start by remembering she can't stand having people tell her what to do."

"I know, but do you think she should be doing housework in the middle of the night when the baby is sleeping? Does that seem normal to you?"

It didn't, and I was a little worried about my sister, too. "Have you talked to her about it?"

"I've tried. I keep offering to help when I'm home, but she's so adamant about doing everything on her own. I have no idea how she's going to return to work, especially when I leave for my next trip."

"Does she need to go back to work? I mean, aren't you guys rich?"

Keith smiled. "Hardly. But you're right. We could probably manage without her income. I just don't know if staying home with the baby is something she wants to do. I don't care either way. I just want her to be happy, you know?"

"I know." Something inside my chest ached with jealousy. What I wouldn't give for a man like Keith who just wanted me to be happy.

An image of Daniel popped into my mind. Could he ever feel that way about me? It was too soon to tell, but I hoped so. I really hoped so.

Chapter 20

Bianca

B ECAUSE WE WERE so busy at the salon, I didn't get a chance to talk to Daniel until three that afternoon when he asked if I could come upstairs and take a look at something. Optimistic, I hoped that was code for *I need to see you and maybe even kiss you again.*

As it turned out, he actually wanted to show me that he'd finished painting my cabinets. Just like Joy said, they looked gorgeous with the countertops and new flooring. "It's perfect," I said, admiring his work.

He beamed proudly. "You really like it?"

"I love it. I can't believe how different the room looks. You did such an amazing job."

He grinned. "I'll install the appliances next week, then you'll finally be rid of me."

I frowned. "I don't like the sound of that."

"No?" His gaze met mine. "Does that mean you want to keep me around by having me knock down the wall?"

I laughed. "It's always about knocking down walls with you guys."

"With us guys?"

I nodded. "Keith was here earlier and asked if I was going to have you knock down the wall."

"What'd you tell him?"

"I said no . . ."

"You don't sound very convincing."

I glanced at the freshly painted cabinets, the backsplash, the countertops, and the flooring. "Wouldn't knocking down the wall mess up my beautiful kitchen?"

His eyes lit with excitement. "No, I can easily cover everything with tarps."

"Really?"

"Really."

"If I said yes, how long would it take?"

His face broke into a huge grin. "I can do the cutout this afternoon and reframe it next week. Things are light at work, so I could probably have the whole job done by next Saturday."

"That soon?"

"Yep."

I hesitated. "What if I don't like it?"

"If you don't like it, I'll rebuild it for you."

"Wouldn't it be hard to match the paint? Wouldn't

people be able to tell there was once a hole in the wall?"

"Maybe a little, but I could get pretty close. Of course, all this is assuming you're not going to like how it looks, but I don't think that will be the case."

I smiled. "It's just such a big decision."

"It is," he agreed. "After all, if you choose wrongly, thousands of people could lose their lives."

It took me a second to realize he was joking. When I made the connection, I laughed and shook my head. "I know it's crazy to be worried about this."

He shrugged. "It's your kitchen. If you want to wait, then you should wait. You're the one who has to live with the change, so you should do what you think is best."

I looked at the wall, then back at him. "Okay, let's go for it. Let's knock down the wall."

His grin was a mile wide. "Great. Let me just run out to the truck and get my sledgehammer."

"Your sledgehammer?" I laughed because he looked like a little kid, barely able to hide his excitement in receiving permission to knock something down with his sledgehammer.

Smiling, he closed the gap between us and wrapped his arms around me. "You have the best laugh."

"I do?"

"You do." He kissed the top of my nose.

"Gross." I wiped off his kiss with my hand and broke free of his grip.

"You don't like that?"

"No. Lips and noses don't go together. Don't ever kiss me on the nose again." Although my voice was happy, I was completely serious. Being kissed on the nose or seeing someone kissed on the nose had always grossed me out.

"But your little nose is so cute. It was one of the first things I noticed about you."

I glared at him with mock anger, and he just laughed. "Okay, lips and noses don't go together. Got it."

"Good."

He pulled me back into his embrace, and I went willingly. "You know what does go together?" he asked.

"What?"

"You and me."

Despite the corny line, my stomach did a free fall. "You think?"

"Yeah, I do." Brushing back my hair, he kissed me, making me believe that we really did go together.

THREE HOURS LATER, my apartment resembled a disaster zone. Dust covered the plastic tarps Daniel had thrown over the furniture, and debris littered the floor and surfaces.

Nevertheless, the wall was down. Standing at the kitchen sink, I could see all the way to the front door.

"What do you think?" Daniel asked.

"I think I love it."

"Really?"

I nodded. "It's going to be so nice when I have guests over and I'm working in the kitchen. Now, I won't feel separated from everyone. Thank you, Daniel. Thank you so much."

He winked at me. "You're welcome."

A bolt of electricity passed between us. Had it only been this morning since our first kiss? I felt so close to him. Then again, I'd had a crush on him forever.

"Well," he said, breaking eye contact with me, "I should probably clean up this mess before the boss fires me."

I smiled. "While you're doing that, why don't I run out and grab some take-out Chinese food for dinner?"

"That sounds great."

"Should I get enough for Joy? Is she coming over after work?"

"She's actually going to Kayla's for dinner. I'm picking her up later."

"Okay. I'll get our food and be back in a minute."

Daniel reached for his wallet, but I waved him off. "It's my treat tonight, okay?"

He hesitated a second before returning the wallet to his pocket. "Okay, but next time you'll have to let me treat you."

"It's a deal." Grabbing my purse, I headed out the door, thrilled he wanted there to be a next time, too.

WHEN I RETURNED with dinner, Daniel had cleaned up the mess, uncovered the couch, and set the coffee table with plates, napkins, silverware, and drinks.

"*Daniel.*" My heart turned to mush at the sight. "What a sweet thing to do."

"I was going to light a candle, but I was afraid that might make my intentions too obvious."

"Your intentions?"

He nodded. "I'm trying to woo you, woman. Can't you tell?"

I laughed, feeling so happy. He took the bags of food from me, and we sat on my couch.

As we ate, we talked about Claudia. "I don't know what I'll do if she doesn't change her mind about meeting me. I sent her an email, but other than a quick reply thanking me for being understanding, I haven't heard from her. Do you think I should write to her again? I don't want to be pushy, but it's hard waiting around, wondering what she's thinking."

"I'm sure it is."

I sighed. "There's this website that has tons of stories about women meeting the kids they gave up for adoption. I've read every account, and it seems like a lot of kids weren't ready to meet their birth parents until they had kids of their own. Maybe I just have to be satisfied knowing she turned out okay."

"With your family's genetics, how could you ever worry about her not turning out okay?"

I took a sip of my drink. "The thing is only half of Claudia's genetics came from me. The other half came from her father, and he wasn't exactly the nicest person in the world."

Daniel stopped eating. "What do you mean?"

I shrugged, not wanting to talk about Chad tonight. Not now when Daniel and I were having such a nice dinner.

Daniel's face grew serious. "Did he force himself on you?"

"No. Maybe he was the one who pushed, but we were both drinking. I was flattered by his attention. I thought he really liked me, so I exercised poor judgment. Actually, I didn't exercise any judgment at all. I was just stupid."

My stomach roiled at the memory of that night. I'd willingly walked away from the bonfire and the other kids at the beach. Willingly lain down with Chad. Willingly ignored the consequences of my actions.

"I felt so grown up and in charge of my sexuality that night," I said. "But it was all an illusion. Having sex like that didn't make me in charge of anything. The next day, he barely acknowledged me. And later, when I told him about the baby, he looked at me with annoyance and said, 'Why are you telling me this? It's probably not even mine.'"

"Oh, sweetheart."

I swallowed the lump in my throat. "It was his all right. I even told him that I'd never been with anyone else, but he didn't believe me. Anyway, that was the last time I ever saw him. I guess he's living in New York or Boston or someplace like that."

Daniel took my hand. "That guy was a jerk. You know that, right?"

I nodded and bit down hard, refusing to waste any more time thinking about him.

Still holding my hand, Daniel said the exact words I needed to hear. "Judging from Claudia's letter and the video of her playing the violin, it seems like she turned out pretty good."

"She turned out amazing. I just wish I could meet

her in person. I know I need to embrace the words of the Abandonment Prayer and surrender my desire to meet her to God, but it's hard."

He smiled. "Yeah. Placing your life in God's hands is one thing. Actually, following through can be a little more tricky."

EVERY FEW MONTHS, my sisters and I gathered for a wild night of scrapbooking. When Anna lived on the island, we always met at her place while the cousins spent the night at the ranch with my parents. Now that Anna lived in Germany, we gathered at my apartment where we could video chat with her on my big screen TV above the fireplace.

When I mentioned all this to Daniel during one of our morning bike rides, he asked if I found it ironic that my sisters and I used technology to communicate with Anna while engaging in an old-fashioned, labor-intensive activity like scrapbooking.

"I hadn't thought about it like that, but you're right. It is a little ironic." We were sitting on our bench by the golf course, watching the sunrise. "I just have this theory."

"I'm sure you do," he said, flashing a grin.

"What's that supposed to mean?"

He laughed. "You just have lots of theories and ideas about life."

"Is there something wrong with that?"

"Not at all. It's actually something I like about you."

I refrained from asking what else he liked about me. No sense in appearing desperate for his attention.

"So, tell me your theory about scrapbooking," he said.

"Well, I think no matter how much technology advances, women will always crave a creative outlet like scrapbooking, sewing, or knitting. There's a woman in California who teaches classes on making beautiful handcrafted felt flowers. Even though you could probably buy something like that at a big box store for less, there's something appealing about working with your hands or purchasing something handmade. It just seems wholesome, you know?"

Daniel pulled an orange from his jacket pocket and peeled it. "It's the hundred-dollar tomato hypothesis."

"The what?"

"Well, you can buy an organic tomato from the farmer's market for a few dollars, or you can grow one yourself. You just have to buy the soil, the tools, the seeds, pay for the visit to the chiropractor, and build a higher fence to keep the deer out. In the end, the cost averages to about $100 for an incredibly delicious tomato you grew yourself."

I laughed, thinking this was a perfect example of why I liked spending time with Daniel. Not only was he a great listener, but he always had something interesting to say.

Plus, he had the best smile in the world. And when he pulled me close to kiss me or just hold me . . . well, that was the greatest feeling of all.

ON SCRAPBOOKING NIGHT, I relayed Daniel's $100 tomato theory to Anna and my sisters.

"That makes sense," Anna said, stifling a yawn as she nursed her baby.

Even though technology had bridged the distance between Germany and Rose Island, it couldn't do anything about the time zone. Early evening in Texas was middle of the night for Anna.

"Hey, can you see my new kitchen?" I asked, jumping up to tilt the TV so she could look through the space where the wall once stood.

"You took down the wall!" she exclaimed. "I love it, and I love the painted cabinets and new countertops."

I smiled. "I do, too. I was nervous about the project, especially taking down the wall, but Daniel promised to rebuild it if I didn't like it. I told him he was crazy, but he said he didn't mind."

Vicki spoke with a teasing lilt in her voice. "What else did Daniel say?"

"What do you mean?"

Anna's baby, Zoey, who'd been nursing this whole time, popped her head up and grinned at the computer screen. Laughing, Anna quickly covered herself. "Vicki's right. Your voice is all *Daniel this* and *Daniel that*."

"No, it's not." I suddenly felt protective of my brand-new relationship with Daniel. I adored him, but what if things didn't work out between us? What if he changed his mind about seeing me? I didn't want to embarrass him or myself. Or Joy, for that matter.

"Daniel's renovating my kitchen in exchange for my help with his daughter," I said, returning to the scrapbook table. "We've spent a lot of time together because of the remodel, but as soon as he finishes, I probably won't see him much."

"Too bad," Vicki said. "He's really cute."

I thought of Daniel's milk chocolate eyes, beautiful smile, and broad shoulders. "He's okay."

My sisters and Anna laughed. "Are you kidding?" Jillian said. "Daniel is super cute, and that's coming from a very happily married woman."

I smiled, relieved to hear her say she was happily married. After my conversation with Keith, I'd been worried. Maybe Jillian just needed a little sister time to laugh and take a break from her family and newborn baby.

"Daniel is one of those guys who can pull off the scruffy beard look," Vicki said. "He has the perfect amount of facial hair—just past five o'clock shadow and miles away from *Duck Dynasty*."

I nodded, thinking Vicki was exactly right. Daniel could easily be a model for some facial hair product.

"I should ask him to give Keith some pointers," Jillian said, cropping a picture. "The few times Keith has tried to grow a beard, it's come in lopsided. He starts trimming one side only to find it uneven with the other side. Then, he trims that side. In the end, he just shaves the whole thing off."

We all laughed, and Anna said it was probably difficult for a former military guy like Keith to handle facial hair. "I don't think Nick could do it."

"Couldn't do what?" Nick asked, appearing on screen in plaid pajama bottoms and a "Beat Navy" T-shirt.

My sisters and I said hi and chatted with our brother-in-law for a few minutes. When he let out a huge yawn, I told him he should go back to bed.

"Why?" He ran a hand over his short cropped hair. "So you can talk about your *love* life, Bianca?"

"Oh, *Nick*." My voice oozed with sarcasm and humor.

"Oh, *Bianca*." He laughed, then he kissed both his wife and the baby before saying good-bye and leaving.

Anna lifted the baby and propped her on her shoulder. "I love this life Nick and I have built in Germany with our children, but I really miss being on the island with y'all."

"We miss you, too," my sisters and I said in unison.

"Do you think Nick will ever receive orders to come home?" Vicki asked.

Anna nodded. "I hope so."

My sisters and I couldn't agree more. After Anna signed off, Keith called to say he couldn't get the baby to stop crying. Even from across the room, I could hear Linda Faith screaming through the phone. Jillian's entire demeanor stiffened as she packed her things and left.

"So, what's really going on with you and Daniel?" Vicki asked as we continued working on our books.

"We're friends," I said.

"And you like him?"

I gave her a huge smile. "Yes, I like him."

"Do you think he might like you like that?"

I nodded. "Well, he kissed me if that's what you mean."

She squealed. "Oh, Bianca. That's wonderful."

"I know, but don't say anything, okay? It's only been a few days since our first kiss, and I'm not ready for everyone to know."

"Why not?"

I covered the back of a picture with adhesive and placed it on my page. "I guess I don't want things to be awkward if it doesn't work out. And I especially don't want things to be awkward with Joy."

"She's really special to you, isn't she?"

I nodded. "She's kind of like my daughter. I feel that way toward all the girls in my Bible study, but Joy definitely holds a special place in my heart."

"I understand that." Vicki placed a hand on my arm. "Just don't sell yourself short when it comes to Daniel, okay? He's a good guy, and you deserve a good guy. Plus, I know he really likes you."

"You do?" I warned myself to stay calm as a feeling of warmth and excitement spread through me.

"I saw you riding bikes with him this morning. I was taking out the trash, and the two of you were walking your bikes toward the building, chatting away. I waved, but y'all were so wrapped up in each other that you didn't see me."

I giggled, thrilled to hear her say that. Still, I pretended it was no big deal. "We weren't wrapped up in each other."

"Whatever." Vicki rolled her eyes. "You do know that guys don't wake at the crack of dawn to go bike riding with someone they're not interested in, right?"

My stomach did that jittering thing it did whenever I thought about the possibility that Daniel might actually like me as much as I liked him. "He's an early morning riser like me."

Vicki laughed, then her voice grew serious. "I just don't want you being afraid that you're not good enough, okay?"

Feeling I wasn't good enough had ruined my chance at happiness more times than I could count. I imagined it'd be easy to let the fear of not being good enough ruin things with Daniel, too.

Instead of admitting that to Vicki, I plastered a smile on my face, sat up straight, and ran my hands down my body. "With a figure like this? Not good enough? Are you kidding?"

She gave a dismissive wave. "Joke all you want, but you and Daniel are perfect together."

Chapter 21

Claudia

O N SUNDAY, TWO weeks after Claudia received Bianca's letter, Aunt Dede and Uncle Geoff came over to the house and announced they were pregnant. Because this would be the first baby born into their family since the arrival of Clay six years ago, everyone was super excited.

While Claudia was happy about her aunt and uncle's news, she had a hard time enjoying the evening or her family. Everyone was getting on her nerves, something she attributed to the fact that she was about to get her period. Plus, she'd barely heard from Leland all week.

She had no idea if he was avoiding her on purpose or just occupied with his current project. When she invited him to come for dinner tonight, he said he couldn't because he had too much work to do.

That was fine. Usually, she didn't have time to sit

around overanalyzing their relationship. This week, however, she had a lull in her schedule because the large family of homeschooled kids she taught music lessons to were out of town.

All her other friends were busy, so she'd spent her extra time catching up on homework and practicing for her upcoming recital. Despite trying to be in a good mood, she just felt annoyed.

"I think it's snowing," Clay said, jumping from the table and running to the window. "Yep, it's snowing all right."

"Can we go outside and play?" Clark asked, joining his brother.

"Clay can, but you've been sick," Mom told Clark. "I want you to stay inside right now, okay?"

"*Mom.*"

"Too bad for you," Clay said, grabbing his jacket and racing outside. Clark stared out the window, looking dejected. Although it'd been a cold and wet winter, there hadn't been a lot of snow, so this was a big deal for the boys who loved playing in the snow.

Dad, who didn't baby the boys as much as Mom did, said, "I bet Clark will be okay outside for a little bit."

"*Randy*, I don't want him getting sick again," Mom protested.

"It'll be okay." Dad pushed away from the table and stood. "Who else wants to come outside and play in the snow? Aunt Dede?"

"Sure." Aunt Dede placed one hand on her flat stomach and reached for her husband with the other hand. "Come on. Let's go outside and take a picture to show the baby his first snow."

Uncle Geoff smiled. "Is this how it's going to be for the next nine months? The baby's first snow, the baby's first trip to the movie theater?"

Aunt Dede laughed and convinced everyone else to come outside as well. Claudia didn't really want to, but she couldn't exactly say no.

Once the pictures were taken, Dad and the boys started throwing snowballs at each other. Mom, Aunt Dede, and Uncle Geoff joined in, but Claudia ducked inside and made herself a cup of hot tea.

Moments later, Uncle Geoff entered the house and joined her in the kitchen. "My Florida blood wasn't made for these harsh Kansas winters," he said. "You know what I mean?"

Claudia smiled. She liked her uncle. Sometimes he could be a little annoying, always talking about how much better Florida was than Kansas, but Aunt Dede loved him, so that was all that mattered.

"Your tea smells good," Uncle Geoff said.

"Here. You can have it. I haven't touched it."

"I don't want to steal it from you."

"I'll make myself another cup. It's no problem." Claudia placed her mug on the counter for him. Returning to the sink, she filled another mug with water and stuck it in the microwave for two minutes.

"Thank you," Uncle Geoff said, sipping the tea. "That hits the spot."

She nodded. "I drink a lot of tea during the winter. It's the only thing that keeps me from freezing to death."

He smiled. "Dede said you don't like the cold either."

"No, I don't."

"Well, given the fact that you were born in South Carolina, that makes sense."

Plus, my birth mother is from Rose Island, Texas. The microwave dinged, and Claudia retrieved her mug. Dunking a tea bag in the hot water, she glanced out the window where her father, her aunt, and the boys were covering themselves with snow as Mom took pictures.

Her uncle followed her gaze. "I guess you and I are the only sane ones of the bunch. Then again, we're the only two not part of that crazy gene pool."

"What?" Although she'd heard him, she didn't quite understand what he meant.

"We're not biologically related to anyone in this family," he explained. "I guess my baby will be, but I'm not. And you're not either. So, it makes sense that we're in here and they're out there."

"Oh, yeah, right." Staring out the window, she watched Mom hand the camera to Aunt Dede before joining Dad and the boys for a picture. Seeing the four of them together without her made Uncle Geoff's comment hit home.

Clark and Clay were the perfect combination of Mom and Dad. Nobody ever questioned where Clark got his chin or where Clay's dark eyebrows came from. Claudia, on the other hand, looked nothing like her parents or her brothers or anyone else in her family for that matter.

"Did I say something wrong?" Uncle Geoff asked. "You look upset."

"No, it's fine." She forced a smile, knowing he hadn't purposely meant to hurt her feelings.

Still, up until this moment, her adoption had never been a big deal. Now, she felt like an outsider . . . like she didn't belong with her family.

The back door opened, and everyone piled into the house, chatting animatedly. Clay ran over to hug Claudia with his cold hands.

"My favorite sister," he cooed. "Give me some love."

"No," Claudia said as Clark snuck around behind her and dumped a snowball down her shirt.

She screamed, knowing she was overreacting but unable to help herself.

Everyone laughed as Dad said, "Our poor Claudia. She's never been a fan of the snow, has she?"

"No," Claudia said, blinking back hot tears. "I'm not like you guys."

"Hey, what's wrong?" Mom asked.

Claudia shook her head, despising how distraught she felt. "Nothing. I'm just not in the mood for all this."

"For my cold hands?" Clark asked, coming closer.

"For my really cold hands," Clay said, joining his brother.

"Guys," Dad said, "back off."

For once, the boys listened.

Claudia could feel her parents studying her with concern. "I'm sorry, but I need to go upstairs and get some studying done." Grabbing her tea, she left the kitchen before she could say anything else she might regret.

"What's her problem?" Clark asked.

Clay responded by saying something Claudia couldn't hear. It must've been hilarious, however, because her entire family cracked up.

Her stomach twisting, she escaped into her bedroom. Maybe meeting Bianca and her biological relatives wasn't such a bad idea after all. Maybe meeting people she was genetically related to would fill the empty space in her heart she'd come to accept as normal. Maybe she'd actually fit in with these people.

Then again, maybe it'd be a complete disaster.

Chapter 22

Bianca

*I*T TOOK A little while to get used to not having the wall in my apartment. Overall, I liked the change and had no regrets.

Still, I felt awfully exposed at the openness whenever I stood in my kitchen. Although, I supposed *openness* was the point of taking the wall down in the first place.

When Joy came over on Monday for Bible study, she asked what I thought about the painted cabinets.

"I love them," I told her. "I never would've had your dad paint the cabinets if you hadn't suggested it, but I'm so pleased with how they turned out. You definitely have an eye for design, my dear."

"Thanks," she said, smiling.

OVER THE NEXT few days, Daniel worked hard to complete my remodel. Just like we'd discussed, he raised the counter to hide the kitchen mess. He also installed my new appliances and worked on reframing the opening. A project at work prevented him from finishing the remodel on Saturday, but I didn't mind.

The following Tuesday, I went over to Daniel and Joy's place for dinner. Daniel met me at the door and kissed me on the cheek. "Welcome to Casa Serrano."

"Gracias."

He winced. "Whoa, we need to work on that accent. It's worse than Joy's."

I laughed. "Do you speak Spanish, Daniel?"

He nodded. "My grandmother was from Honduras. She lived with us growing up and didn't speak English, so Enzo and I had to speak to her in Spanish."

"Enzo?"

"My brother." Daniel suddenly looked uncomfortable. He'd told me about his little sister who lived in Spain, and I knew his mother had passed away before Joy was born, but he'd never mentioned a brother. For that matter, he'd said very little about his father—just that he moved around a lot and that they seldom talked.

"I can't believe you didn't tell me you had a brother. Is he older or younger than you?"

A muscle in Daniel's jaw clenched. "He's my twin."

"You have a twin?" I stared at him, shocked. Wasn't revealing you were a twin one of those things you mentioned when dating someone?

"It's a long story," Daniel said.

"Well, you'll have to tell me about it sometime." Although I pretended everything was fine, I was bothered he hadn't told me about his brother.

I guess I thought we were closer than that. After all, he knew practically everything about me and my family. Why hadn't he told me about his twin?

In the kitchen, I found Joy spreading garlic butter on a loaf of French bread. "Everything smells wonderful. What are we having?"

"Fettuccini Alfredo."

"Yum. That's one of my favorites. What can I do to help?"

"Nothing." Daniel opened the refrigerator. "Make yourself at home, and dinner will be ready in a minute. Would you like a glass of wine?"

"Yes, just a little one."

He poured me a small glass of pinot noir and one for himself. "Cheers," he said, clinking glasses with me.

"Cheers." I took a sip of my wine. "That's wonderful. It's very smooth and tastes like cherries."

He handed me the bottle so I could read the label. "It's from one of the vineyards here on the island."

"I know the family that owns this vineyard. I went to high school with their son. They're really nice people."

Daniel shot Joy a knowing glance, and she laughed.

"What?" Self-conscious, I smoothed down the black dress I was wearing.

Daniel stirred the Alfredo sauce. "Well, my daughter and I were just wondering if there was anyone on the island you didn't go to high school with or isn't a client?"

I laughed and took another sip of my wine. "You have a point. It's a small island, and while many people go away for college and jobs, a lot of them come back."

"That's good to hear." Daniel offered Joy a sad smile. I knew he could barely stand the thought of her going away for college in the fall.

Joy smiled back before turning her attention to me. "Do you want to come see our new garden?"

"I'd love to." I followed her to the backyard, which was small but lush with evergreen bushes, roses, and a large oak tree. A stone path led to a wooden swing hanging from a pergola, surrounded by pots of winter flowers.

Joy gestured to the raised garden bed she'd just built with her father. "It mostly looks like dirt right now, but we've planted carrots, cilantro, parsley, turnips, and lettuce. Your mom said it's important to keep the seeds wet while they're germinating, so we've been watering several times a day."

"My mom?"

Joy nodded. "We ran into her at the garden center. She helped us choose what to plant."

"She loves to garden."

"I can tell. And she knows so much. We were going to put the garden on the other side of the yard, but when she came over, she said it had to go here for the morning sun."

"My mom came over to your house?"

"She did."

"I didn't know that." It was strange to think of my mom coming to Joy and Daniel's house without me. I had no doubt the next time I talked to her she'd tell me every detail of the encounter.

But why hadn't Daniel mentioned it during our bike ride this morning? And why hadn't he told me about his brother? Was his lack of communication something I needed to worry about?

"Dinner's ready," Daniel called from the back door.

"Coming." Joy headed inside.

As I followed, I glanced up to see Daniel waiting for me. Immediately, I was filled with a sense of peace that overpowered me.

Maybe Daniel wasn't as forthcoming as I wanted him to be. One thing was for certain, nobody had ever made me feel so accepted as he did.

AFTER DINNER, JOY offered to do the dishes by herself. I started to protest, insisting it was only fair that I helped clean up, but Daniel took me by the hand and said we were going outside.

I was surprised he'd held my hand in front of Joy. We hadn't talked to anyone about our new relationship or whatever this was between us.

"I'm going to tell her tonight," Daniel said, once we were seated on the swing underneath the pergola in the backyard.

I shifted so I could see his face. "Tell who what?"

He grinned. "Tell Joy that I like you."

"You *like* me?"

He brushed a strand of hair off my face and tucked it behind my ear. "Did you not know that?"

I gave a nonchalant shrug. "I had my suspicions."

He laughed. "You overwhelm me, Bianca."

"I *overwhelm* you? What's that mean?"

"It means . . . I'm falling for you."

My heart slammed into my chest and began pounding so hard I could barely breathe. "*Daniel.*"

"Is that okay?"

I nodded. "Yeah, that's okay."

"Good." A sly grin tugged at one corner of his mouth. He gave the swing a push with his foot, and we sailed through the air.

When we slowed, I asked Daniel why he hadn't told me about my mom coming over for the garden.

He shrugged. "I guess I forgot."

"You forgot?"

"Yeah." He frowned. "I'm sorry. Did I do something wrong?"

I sighed. "You didn't tell me about your brother either. Your *twin* brother."

"No, I didn't."

"Why not?"

Shifting on the swing, he gazed out across the yard. "It's complicated."

"Complicated?"

He nodded. "Do you really want to hear about this?"

"I do."

"Okay." He took a deep breath. "Enzo and I haven't spoken to each other since Christmas. That probably doesn't sound like a long time to most people, but we've always been best friends and have talked or texted nearly every day."

"So, what happened?"

"We had a huge fight."

"What about?"

"Our dad." Daniel fell silent. I could tell this was difficult for him, so I did my best not to push him, even though I was anxious for him to just blurt out the story like I would.

"My dad left our family when Enzo and I were in high school. He basically said he was tired of being a husband and father, and he just left."

"*Oh, Daniel.*"

"It was rough, especially on our mother who was devastated. My sister was so mad she refused to invite him to her wedding, so Enzo and I walked Miriam down the aisle. I honestly didn't think I'd ever see my dad again, and I didn't care.

"After our mom died, he contacted us, but we didn't want to speak to him. He'd been gone almost fifteen years by then, and Miriam was convinced he just wanted money. So Enzo told him to leave us alone. He did, but last December, he showed up at my work. He seemed so old and broken. I couldn't just ignore him."

"Of course not." My heart broke for the whole situation. "What'd you end up doing?"

Daniel ran a hand over his jaw. "I took him to dinner, and he met Joy. I didn't mean for that to happen, but she was out with friends, and we ran into them as we left the restaurant. She'd seen pictures of him, so she knew who he was right away."

For the first time since he began speaking about his father, Daniel smiled. "You know how Joy is. Once she met him, she invited him to stay."

"I can see her doing that."

"Anyway, I didn't tell Enzo because he was spending Christmas with his girlfriend's family, and I didn't want him to be upset over the holidays."

I nodded. "I can understand that. I'd probably do the same thing."

"Well, Enzo can be a little flaky. He prefers the word spontaneous, but it always causes problems. So, without calling or texting or anything, he just showed up out at the house Christmas Eve. He freaked out when he saw our dad. He told me that I was a traitor and that he couldn't believe I'd stabbed him in the back like that."

"Did you try talking to him and explaining what happened?"

"I tried, but at that point there was no reasoning with Enzo. He stormed out and left the island. My dad apologized for putting me in that position, but it didn't change the fact that I'd kept something like that from my brother. And the thing is, I can see Enzo's point. I understand why he felt betrayed."

"Have you tried contacting your brother since then?"

"I've tried, but he won't take my calls."

I slipped my arm through Daniel's and placed my head on his shoulder. Daniel gave the swing a shove, sending us into the air.

"What about going to see him in person?" I asked.

"I've thought about it. Miriam says I should, but she also understands why Enzo was so mad."

"Well, I agree with your sister. I think you should try again with your brother. Maybe enough time has passed that he'd be willing to listen to you."

"Maybe." Daniel didn't sound convinced.

"What about your dad?"

Daniel shrugged. "I don't know. It wasn't as though we had this Hallmark Christmas moment where things ended all magical like. He said some things, but . . ." Daniel shook his head. "I feel like I've unloaded too much on you. I'm sorry."

"Don't be sorry. I'm glad you shared this with me. I'm sorry it happened, but I'm glad you told me."

He squeezed my hand. "All this doesn't make you rethink dating me?"

"No. I wish I could make it better, but it doesn't make me rethink anything about you."

"Good. And you have made it better. Just by listening to me, you've made it way better."

Chapter 23

Daniel

AFTER BIANCA LEFT, Daniel thought about what she'd said regarding Enzo. Maybe enough time had passed that his brother would be open to talking.

He really wanted to tell Enzo about the other thing. The thing he couldn't bring himself to tell Joy. The thing he mostly ignored until it gnawed at his stomach like secrets did.

Wandering into the living room, he found his daughter sitting on the couch, reading one of her favorite books, *The Magnolia Story*. He'd bought the book for her last summer when they'd visited Magnolia Market at the Silos in Waco.

"Look," Daniel began, taking the seat opposite her, "I want to talk to you about something."

"Is it about Bianca?"

"Bianca?"

Joy put down the book and shifted on the couch.

"Yeah. What's going on with you guys?"

"Oh, well, I like her."

"You like her?" Joy sounded skeptical.

He nodded. "Yeah. I like her. I like her a lot. Is that okay?"

"*Oh, Dad.*" She pushed out a long, disapproving breath.

"What?"

"It's just . . . Bianca is a good friend of mine."

"I know."

"Well, have you thought about what's going to happen when you break up?"

"When we break up?"

Nodding, she stared at him expectantly, waiting for his answer.

"Wow. Just go ahead and hammer that nail into the coffin containing my relationship, why don't you."

"Your *relationship*?"

"What's wrong with the word relationship?" he asked.

"Nothing. I've just never heard you say that word before."

"Relationship? I say that word all the time."

Her brow lifted. "Okay. What about your *relationship* with Uncle Enzo?"

His body stiffened. "What about it?"

"When are you going to fix things with him?"

"I don't know."

"Well, I know it's been bothering you. You haven't been the same since Christmas, and you didn't even tell Bianca about him."

He nodded, conceding the point. Of course, he was upset about Enzo, but he really wanted to talk to Joy about the secret. *Tell her*, a voice inside him whispered. *Just get it over with and tell her.*

"Look, Joy. We need to talk about something else."

"Okay, but if it's about Bianca, then I already know."

"What do you already know?"

"I know you've liked her for a long time, and I know you've been afraid to ask her out because of me. I appreciate that, but it's okay now. Just please don't hurt her."

"I'm not going to hurt her."

"Good."

"I'm serious," he said.

"I know."

He hesitated, feeling the need to reassure Joy that everything was going to be fine with Bianca. "Just so you know, Bianca and I are going to take things slow."

She laughed. "Slow? I saw you making out with her on the pergola swing."

Despite not wanting to be the kind of guy who blushed, heat burned Daniel's face. "Well, that's as far as it's going to go. I'm not going to sleep with her until—"

"*Dad!*" Joy's eyes widened. Sex wasn't something they discussed. Joy, thankfully, had Daniel's sister for topics like that.

Still, in a culture of easy hookups and disposable one-night stands, he wanted his daughter to know God had a better plan. At the same time, violating that plan had given him Joy, so he didn't want her to think he regretted her existence.

"Look, honey, I know it's uncomfortable to hear your old man talk about this, but there's a reason God wants us to preserve sex for marriage."

"*Dad. Please.* Just stop talking." She buried her face in her hands and shook her head.

"Okay, I will. But I want you to know I truly care about Bianca. I love her, and I can see a future with her."

"A future? Are you talking about marriage?" Joy stared at him with wide eyes. "Dad, isn't it too early to think about marrying Bianca?"

"Well, yes, but—"

"But what?"

He rocked back in the chair. "I don't know. I just . . . well, other than you, she's my favorite person in the world."

Joy's entire expression softened, and she smiled. "I know what you mean. Bianca's the best, and even though I'm giving you a hard time, I really am happy for you."

"Thanks, honey."

❧

THAT NIGHT, DANIEL couldn't sleep. Once again, he'd failed to tell Joy the truth she deserved to know.

If only he could talk to his brother about this. Despite Enzo's faults, he was surprisingly insightful when it came to parenting advice. Daniel figured it probably had something to do with being an eighth grade math teacher.

Picking up his phone, Daniel scrolled through his contacts until he found his brother's name. With a deep breath, he hit Enzo's number and waited until voicemail picked up. Slightly relieved, Daniel left a message. Then, he hung up and lay back in bed.

Even though he hadn't talked to his brother tonight, maybe it was a step in the right direction. Maybe his message was the spark that would reunite them. With that thought on his mind, he closed his eyes and fell asleep.

Chapter 24

Claudia

WHILE TRUDGING THROUGH the snow-covered sidewalk on campus the next day, Claudia heard Leland call her name. She spun around to see him running toward her with the biggest smile on his face.

"You look happy," she said, burrowing into her heavy coat.

"I am happy. We just finished the project, and they're going to air our commercial during the local news tonight at five. You're coming, right?"

"Coming? Where?"

"To our professor's house. The whole team is going to be there to watch it." He spoke as if she should already know this, but he'd barely said anything to her all week. He certainly hadn't invited her to watch his commercial with the rest of the team at their professor's house.

"I don't know," Claudia said.

His face fell. "Why not?"

"Well, you didn't invite me. This is the first I've heard about it."

"I'm sorry. I'm inviting you now. Can you come?"

Looking up at his expectant face, she sighed. He'd been so caught up in his own life that he had no idea she'd been upset this past week. Something in her expression must've clued him in because he frowned. "What's wrong? Is your dad okay?"

She nodded. *Way to put things into perspective, Leland.* "Yes, my dad's fine. Everything's fine. I just feel like I haven't talked to you in a long time."

"You didn't get my texts?"

She shrugged, wondering when she'd become that clingy girlfriend. "I got a few of them."

"I'm sorry," he said. "How about tomorrow we go see a movie? Just you and me."

"I'd like that."

"Yeah?"

She nodded. "I've got to get to class, but will you text me the details for tonight?"

"I'll pick you up," he said. "And I'll walk you to class right now." Reaching out, he took her violin case so she wouldn't have to carry it. It hardly weighed anything, but she appreciated the gentlemanly gesture.

They walked in silence for a beat, their feet crunching on the snow. "Leland, I've been thinking about what you said regarding driving down to your grandmother's house."

"Yeah?"

"I think I might want to meet her."

He stopped walking. "Are you talking about Mimi or your birth mom?"

She smiled. "Well, both of them. But yeah, I think I'd like to meet my birth mom. I just don't want you to film it, okay?"

"I won't. I know you were upset that I asked. I'm a filmmaker, so I'm always going to ask. You just have to tell me no, okay?"

"Okay."

They resumed walking, and Leland asked what had changed her mind. Claudia told him what Uncle Geoff had said about her not being part of the gene pool.

Leland swore. "That guy can be a little dense, can't he?"

Claudia laughed. "Yeah. I'm sure he was just trying to *bond* with me, but I didn't like hearing him say that."

"No, but I'm sure your parents don't feel that way."

"Probably not." Claudia opened her phone and found the picture of Bianca she had from the internet. "Do you really think we have the same smile?"

Leland peered down at the photo and nodded.

"I do."

"I do, too. I guess I'd like to see what else we have in common."

Chapter 25

Bianca

WHILE TALKING TO Daniel in my kitchen the next day, my phone rang with a call from an unfamiliar number. "Hello?" I said cheerfully.

"Is Bianca there?" I didn't recognize the young woman's voice and figured she was a new client calling on my personal cell number instead of the salon's.

"This is she," I said. "Or am I supposed to say this is her? I can never remember. Actually, I don't think I ever learned. Do you know?"

"This is she," she said without hesitating.

"Are you sure?"

"Positive. When a pronoun follows a linking verb, you use the nominative case."

"Oh, the *nominative* case," I said, sarcastically. "Well, there you go."

Daniel gave me an odd look like I was crazy for discussing grammar on the phone with a stranger. I laughed. "I'm sorry. I'm sure you didn't call to chat about the proper way to answer the phone. Were you needing to schedule an appointment?"

"An appointment? No, I . . ." A long silence followed, making me wonder if we'd lost the connection.

"Hello?" I said.

"Yes, sorry. It's just . . . I'm Claudia. Claudia Cavenaugh."

I froze. "Claudia?"

"Yes. You put your phone number on one of your emails. I hope it's okay I'm calling like this."

My heart began beating in my throat. This was Claudia, my daughter. Claudia, the beautiful young woman I'd watched play the violin on YouTube. Claudia, the baby I'd held in my arms all those years ago.

Daniel stopped what he was doing and stared at me. "It's Claudia," I whispered, shifting the phone in such a way that it slipped from my hand. My efforts to catch it failed, and I ended up knocking it across the kitchen. I scrambled to get it, but when I finally did, the line was dead.

Panic shot through me. "That was Claudia, my daughter. I hung up on her."

Daniel patted my shoulder. "It's okay. She'll call back, or you can call her."

"How can you be so calm?" I asked, fumbling with my phone to find the list of previous calls.

"She called you, Bianca. This is what you wanted, so it's a good thing. But you have to relax."

"I am relaxed," I shouted.

Thankfully, the phone rang with her number. I quickly hit the receive button. "Claudia?"

"Yes." She giggled nervously. "I guess we were disconnected."

"I know. I'm so sorry. It was entirely my fault. I'm just so excited to hear from you that I'm freaking out. How are you? How's your family? How's Leland? Tell me everything."

I turned away from Daniel so I wouldn't have to see him mouth the words *calm down.*

"Things are good," she said. "What about you? How are you?"

Tears filled my eyes. "Oh, honey, I couldn't be better. I'm just so happy you called. It's wonderful to hear your voice."

"It's nice to hear your voice, too."

Awkward silence fell, then I laughed because what exactly did one say the first time they spoke to the child they'd given up eighteen years ago and had dreamed of meeting forever?

"I must sound like a lunatic," I said. "I just can't

believe it's really you."

"Yes, well, it is. After I read Joy's email—"

"*Joy's* email?"

"Joy Serrano? The girl you've been teaching to drive. She said she knows you from Bible study?"

"Yes, of course. But . . ." I turned to face Daniel. "Joy emailed you?"

His brow lifted as Claudia said, "She did."

"Wow. What'd she say?"

"Oh, she just encouraged me to reach out to you. She said you're a wonderful person and I should contact you."

I pressed a hand to my heart, feeling incredibly grateful that Joy had done that for me. "I can't believe she wrote to you. I had no idea she was going to do that."

"Well, she did." Claudia giggled again, the sound like gold to me.

"I'm just so happy you called. And I'm amazed by your musical abilities. I've watched your video a million times. I have absolutely no musical talent, but my sister Vicki plays the piano. Well, she used to in middle school. She's probably forgotten everything by now.

"Anyway, you're tiny like she is and blonde as well. If you were able to look at any of the pictures I sent you in that email, you know, of course, that I'm the opposite of tiny and blonde."

"Yeah." Claudia was quiet as though overwhelmed by everything I just threw at her. I didn't blame her. I really did need to take Daniel's advice and calm down.

"I'm sorry," I said. "I know I'm talking too much. Daniel is here, and he keeps looking at me like I'm crazy, but I'm just so happy to hear from you."

"Daniel? Is that your boyfriend?"

"He's Joy's father. He's renovating my kitchen, but yes, I guess you could call him my boyfriend."

Daniel grinned at me, and I grinned back. "He was running a special," I continued. "Remodel your kitchen and get a free boyfriend."

At that, Daniel raised his brow. I probably sounded like such a dingbat. *Okay, Bianca. Stop talking about yourself and ask about her.*

"Tell me about you," I said. "I know you play the violin and you're studying French. Are you really planning on studying abroad next year?"

"I hope so. It will depend on my schedule and how my dad is doing."

"I bet he's so proud of you. And your mom, too. How long have you been playing the violin?"

"Since I was three."

"Three? That's so young. You must've had such a small violin."

"I did. Actually, I still have it."

"That's wonderful. I'd love to see it sometime."

"Oh, well, okay."

I cringed, knowing I was being too aggressive. She wasn't ready to meet me yet, so I needed to back off with those kinds of comments. "Sorry," I said.

"No, it's okay. Actually, Leland and I are driving down to Houston this week so I can meet his grandma. I was thinking we might come down to Rose Island to meet you. If you're available, that is."

"You're coming to Rose Island? This weekend?" My voice squeaked with excitement.

"If you're available. Is that okay?"

"Are you kidding? Of course, I'm available. When will you be here?"

"Friday around noon."

"Oh, that's great. I'm totally free Friday. I have an extra bedroom in my apartment and a comfortable pullout couch, so you can both stay here. Or my parents have plenty of room at the ranch. In fact, we should all stay at the ranch."

Claudia hesitated. "Oh, we weren't planning on spending the night. We were just thinking we could drive down for lunch or something."

"Yes, definitely. Lunch would be great. Lunch would be perfect." I spoke with an upbeat tone, all the time telling myself, *Keep it together, Bianca. Don't scare her away.*

"If you change your mind and decide to spend the night, we could have a big dinner at the ranch and you could meet your cousins."

"Matt and Drew?" she asked.

"Yes. I know they'd love to meet you as well as my parents and sisters. And you can meet Joy and Daniel." I'd told Claudia all about my family in one of my letters.

"Okay. I'll definitely be there on Friday, but I'll have to get back to you about spending the night, if that's okay?"

"Of course. Take your time. You can tell me later. You can even decide once you get here. Whatever you want is fine with me."

"Okay, thanks." She sounded relieved that I was so cool and laid-back. Ha! If only she knew how wound up I was at this moment. In fact, it took all my self-control not to invite myself up to Leland's grandmother's house in Houston.

"Well, I'll see you Friday," she said.

"See you Friday." I waited until she hung up, then I set down my phone on my new granite countertop and tried not to pass out again.

"Everything all right?" Daniel asked, eyeing me suspiciously.

Throwing my hands over my head, I gave a loud whoop of triumph. "Whooooo. Yes!"

Daniel laughed. "She's coming on Friday for lunch?"

"Yes! Can you believe it? She's coming here to the island with her boyfriend, Leland. I wanted her to spend the night, but lunch is good, too."

"Lunch is great. I'm really happy for you."

I gave another whoop, then I laughed. "Friday is going to be the best day of my life."

Daniel grinned. "Well, if she's coming on Friday, I guess I better get to work."

I glanced at him before taking in all that still needed to be done on my kitchen. "Do you think you'll be able to finish before Friday?"

"Definitely," he said.

Delirious with happiness, I flung myself into his arms and squeezed him tight. "Thank you, Daniel. Thank you so much."

He chuckled, the sound rumbling in his chest. "You're welcome."

Chapter 26

Daniel

*T*UESDAY AFTERNOON, KEITH called to ask if Daniel had a pump he could borrow to remove the excess water in his hallway. Apparently, the bathtub faucet had been left running all afternoon, creating a huge mess.

"I'll be right there." Daniel hung up the phone, collected his equipment, and headed over to Keith's place.

Pulling into the Fosters' driveway, Daniel noticed right away that Keith and Jillian were having an intense conversation near her minivan. The baby was in Keith's arms, screaming her head off, and Jillian looked like she was about to cry as well.

Feeling like he was intruding, Daniel reluctantly climbed out of his truck. Jillian kept her head down, but Keith acknowledged him by lifting his hand. "Thanks for coming, Daniel."

"No problem. I'll just let myself inside, okay?"

"Yes," Keith said, looking relieved. "Go right ahead.

Drew can show you everything."

Daniel grabbed what he needed and headed toward the house. Keith had his hand on his wife's back and was trying to comfort her, but she wasn't having any of it.

How many times in the few short years he'd been married had Daniel been the man in Keith's place, trying to calm his wife? Of course, Jillian seemed much more stable than Libby. Still, he didn't envy Keith's situation. Dealing with an emotional woman . . . well, Daniel could think of a lot of other things he'd rather do.

Inside the house, he found Drew attempting to scoop up the water with a bowl and a dustpan. Wet towels lay everywhere in a futile attempt to sop up the mess.

Drew gestured at the sump pump in Daniel's hand. "Is that to get rid of the water?"

"It is." Daniel set down the pump, opened the window, and threw the hose outside. "How do you get to the backyard?"

"This way." Drew sloshed down the hall, leading the way to the back door, which opened onto a wooden deck. Outside stood an old golden lab.

"Is your dog friendly?" Daniel asked.

"She is." Drew leaned over to pet the dog. "This is

Bella, the friendliest dog in the world."

Cautiously, Daniel stepped onto the porch. He'd been bitten before by a "friendly" dog protecting his property, and that wasn't an experience he wanted to repeat. Right away, the dog started barking.

"Hey," Drew scolded. "Daniel's here to help us."

As if understanding, the dog went silent and began wagging her tail. Hoping that was a good sign, Daniel offered his hand, which Bella sniffed before deciding he was safe.

With the dog situation taken care of, Daniel walked over to the discharge hose and dragged it away from the house. Back inside, he plugged in the pump.

"We're not going to get electrocuted, are we?" Drew asked, keeping his distance as the motor sprang to life. "Aren't you supposed to keep electricity away from water?"

"You are, but this is a submersible pump, so we don't have to worry."

"Oh, that's good."

Daniel nodded, then asked if the oven was on. "It smells like something is burning."

"Oh no! The cookies." Drew raced back down the hall, and Daniel followed just as the smoke detector went off.

In the kitchen, they removed the burnt cookies from

the oven, disabled the alarm, and opened a window to clear the smoke.

"I guess Mom forgot about the cookies, too," Drew said.

"I guess so."

The front door opened, and Keith entered the house with the baby, who'd thankfully stopped crying. "Is something burning?"

"The cookies." Drew poked at one of the blackened sweets. "I think they might still be good."

Keith shook his head in disbelief. "Daniel, thanks for coming to our chaotic home."

"No problem."

"Did Mom leave?" Drew asked.

"She did, but she'll be back." Looking down at the baby, he gave her a little jiggle. "Believe it or not, this precious baby girl is giving Mommy a hard time. Not to worry, though. Everything is going to be fine."

Drew walked over to his father and tickled his sister under her chin. "Why do you have to be so fussy all the time?" he asked, speaking in a high-pitched baby voice.

The baby looked at her brother with wide eyes. Then, she offered the biggest smile.

"Dad," Drew shouted. "She's smiling. Do you see it?"

"I do." Keith's smile matched his daughter's.

Daniel smiled too. There really was something powerful about an infant's smile.

"Well, there's your smile, baby girl," Keith said. "We were wondering when you were going to show it to us. Your mama was beginning to think you didn't like her."

"Mom is going to be so happy the baby finally smiled."

"She is," Keith agreed, "but you can't tell her."

Drew frowned. "Why not?"

"She needs to discover it for herself. If Mom finds out that Linda Faith smiled at us first, she's going to be disappointed."

"Oh." Drew mulled that over a second. "Can we tell Mom *after* she sees the baby smile?"

"I guess so. I don't want to encourage you to be dishonest, but I think Mom will be happier if she experiences the baby's first smile herself. What do you think?"

Drew nodded. "I get it. It's one of your 'wife whisperer' techniques. It's how you keep the ladies happy."

Keith chuckled and glanced at Daniel. "Drew and I have been talking about girls and dating and—"

"*Dad.*"

"Sorry." Keith shot a look of apology toward his son. "Anyway . . . you know I care about keeping just one woman happy."

"Mom?"

"Yep." His cell rang, and shifting the baby, he re-trieved the phone from his back pocket. When he saw it was his wife, he handed the baby to Drew who expertly propped his little sister on his shoulder.

"Hey, babe." Keith headed outside for some privacy.

As Drew patted the baby's back, he watched his fa-ther closely. "I don't think they're going to get another divorce," he said, more to himself than to Daniel. "Mom's just tired from the baby. Linda Faith can be a little monster sometimes."

Daniel nodded. He knew all about Jillian's divorce from Keith and their miraculous reconciliation. Hearing their story really emphasized the fact that they wor-shiped a God of second chances.

Because the kitchen window was open, Daniel caught snippets of Keith's conversation with his wife. "Baby, you could burn down the entire house, and I wouldn't care."

Keith chuckled at something Jillian must've said. "Okay, you're right. I'd care, but it wouldn't change how I felt about you. I love you. You're my sweetheart, and I'll always love you no matter how many faucets you forget to turn off."

Drew kissed the top of his sister's head. "See? I told

you everything was going to be okay."

As Daniel listened to Keith talk to his wife, he thought about how different this scenario would've played out between Libby and him. While Libby had some serious psychological issues, Daniel hadn't exactly been the most patient man. Maybe if he'd had a bit more "wife whisperer" skills, things would've turned out differently.

Then again, given what he'd learned about Libby this past Christmas, maybe there was nothing he could've done to save his marriage or his wife.

Chapter 27

Bianca

THE REST OF the week inched forward at a snail's pace. I couldn't concentrate on anything but what it would be like when I finally met Claudia.

Would things be awkward between us? Or would we easily fall into a relationship as effortless and enjoyable as the one I had with Joy?

When I told my mom the news about Claudia's visit over the phone, she was thrilled. She couldn't understand, however, why Claudia and Leland weren't staying longer.

"Maybe they have other plans," I suggested. "Or maybe she feels overwhelmed or uncomfortable. Her boyfriend is coming, too, you know."

"Yes, you told me, and it's not like I'm going to embarrass her in front of him."

"I know. She's probably just nervous about meeting us."

My mother scoffed. "She's part of our family. There's no need for her to be nervous."

I nodded. "True, but she's never met us before. She'll probably change her mind about staying longer once she sees we're normal."

"I hope so. Should I plan on them coming for dinner? We're having Jillian's fake birthday party that night."

"That's right." Part of the plan to surprise Jillian included celebrating her birthday with our family on Friday night. Then, when Keith took her out for dinner on Saturday, she wouldn't suspect they were really going to the Rose Museum for her party.

"I think you should plan on them staying for dinner," I said. "Better to have too much food than not enough."

"You're right. Please just tell me if things change."

"I will." With that, I hung up the phone and began puttering around my apartment, moving the vase from the mantle to the entry table, then deciding it looked better on the mantle.

What if Claudia's visit was a mess? What if she was disappointed in me and didn't even want to stay for lunch?

I knew I'd love her immediately. She was my own flesh and blood. I'd carried her inside me for nine months. I'd held her in my arms right after she was born. And I'd thought of her every day since telling her good-bye.

But what if she didn't feel the same way about me? What if she only viewed me as a stranger?

Alone in my apartment that night, I did my best to reassure myself everything would be fine. I even prayed the Abandonment Prayer, surrendering the visit to God.

Yet, the beast inside me that dealt with unease by eating reared its defiant head. I tried forever to resist, but finally I caved and marched downstairs to the break room. Vicki had left an entire strawberry cake, plus a plate of brownies and several chocolate chip cookies.

Standing at the counter in my nightgown, I shoved bite after bite into my mouth, desperate to calm the anxiety and negativity racing through me. Why was I doing this to myself? Why couldn't I stop?

I'd be mortified if Daniel caught me binging like this. He'd probably end things between us and never want to see me again.

After what seemed like forever, the switch in my head finally turned off, and I went back upstairs, defeated. All night, I tossed and turned. Feelings of shame plagued me. When was I going to stop doing this to myself? Why couldn't I have more control?

In the morning, I awoke to the sound of my phone

ringing. When I saw it was Daniel, I sent the call to voicemail, too ashamed to talk to him.

He texted a moment later. "Worried about you. Are you okay?"

"Sorry," I texted back. "Late night. Slept in. Have to skip the bike ride today."

"No problem. Do you want me to bring you breakfast from the bakery?"

Ugh, I thought, my stomach queasy. "No, thank you."

"Okay. See you tonight."

"See you tonight."

As I lay back in bed, I had to wonder what in the world Daniel saw in me. Yadira and I had talked a lot about Daniel during my last therapy session. She'd asked if being around him made me want to binge.

"Not at all," I'd said. "Daniel accepts me for who I am. I've never been with anyone like that. He actually thinks I'm beautiful."

"You are beautiful," Yadira had said. "But just remember that nobody can make you feel good or bad about yourself. Ultimately, it's your decision how you respond to a stressful situation."

Well, I hadn't exactly responded well last night, had I?

Getting out of bed, I declared it a new day. The past was the past. I wasn't going to let what happened yesterday define me. Not when I had such a good life.

Of course, post-binge declarations were easier said than done. Against my better judgment, I went into the bathroom and stepped on the scale.

"That can't be right," I said, horrified as I stared down at the massive number. Somehow, I'd managed to gain five pounds since last week.

Well, I just wouldn't eat today. I knew starving myself wasn't healthy or practical, but what else could I do?

Because I was actually hungry after my shower, I dug out the weight loss shakes I'd tried last year. Just the smell of the powder and the sound of the blender churned my stomach. Still, clinging to the promises advertised by the skinny lady on the package, I forced myself to choke down the shake before heading to work.

Despite feeling bloated, visions of the leftover cake, cookies, and brownies from the break room taunted me. How could it be that just the mention of the word "diet" sent my fat cells into protest mode, demanding nothing less than food loaded with sugar?

"You're fine," I said aloud, turning on the salon's lights and unlocking the door. I had to deprive myself by following the shake diet in order not to feel like a fat cow when Claudia arrived.

A kinder, gentler voice inside me whispered, *What about all those wonderful epiphanies you wrote in your journal the other day? What about accepting the body you have and making small changes?*

"No," said the skinny woman on the package of diet shakes. "Not today. Today, we need radical change."

Because I was motivated to stick to the program, the first morning on the shake diet was okay. As I was drinking my shake for lunch, Vicki came to the salon with a new peanut butter chocolate cheesecake she wanted us to try.

Insisting I was too full, I turned down the treat and raced upstairs to step on the scale. To my delight, I'd already lost two pounds. At this rate, I might be able to fit into my jeans by the time Claudia arrived.

By lunch the next day, I was down six pounds. While the weight loss thrilled me, my nerves were shot. Little things irritated me, and I felt light-headed. Worst of all, I couldn't stop obsessing over the delicious smells coming from the bakery.

In the afternoon, Daniel called to say he was running late but he'd be there as soon as he could. "I'm planning on finishing everything late tonight, so you might want to sleep at your parents' house."

"Fine," I said, my voice sharp.

There was a long pause on the other end of the line. "Bianca? Are you okay?"

"Yes." I pushed out a long breath, knowing I was

being snippy. "Sorry. I'm just busy."

"Okay, I'll let you go."

Hanging up the phone, I felt horrible over how I'd talked to Daniel. He didn't deserve that. When I saw him tonight, I'd be sure to apologize.

Unable to stand the thought of another shake, I scarfed down a banana. Didn't bananas contain some kind of ingredient that calmed your nerves? Apparently not, because by the time I closed the salon, I felt so cranky and out of control I could barely function.

Upstairs, I stepped on the scale, relieved to see I'd lost another pound. Maybe feeling edgy would be worth it if I could fit into my jeans. Immediately, I tried them on, relieved I could now zip them up.

When I looked in the mirror, however, disgusting rolls of fat spilled over the waistband. Ugh! Claudia would take one look at me and be horrified.

Tears filled my eyes. All I could think about was putting on my pajamas and sitting in front of the TV with a big bowl of buttery popcorn. Feeling worthless, I ripped off my jeans and flung them across the room.

The sound of the downstairs' doorbell caused me to groan. I quickly slipped on my most stretchy stretch pants and waddled to the intercom. "Hello?"

"Taco and plaster delivery," Daniel said, sounding cheerful.

Squeezing my eyes tight, I imagined my handsome boyfriend standing at the back door waiting for me to let him in. I swallowed the lump in my throat. "I'm sorry, but I can't tonight."

"You can't?"

"No, not tonight."

He hesitated. "What's wrong?"

Tears stung my eyes. I didn't deserve someone like Daniel. I bit down hard, not wanting him to hear me cry.

"What's wrong, sweetheart?"

His question and endearment caused my tears to overflow. "I'm sorry," I said sniffing. "I'm not doing so well. I just want to be by myself right now."

"Is it Claudia? Did she change her mind about coming?"

"No, she's still coming."

"Then what is it?"

"I don't know."

"Please let me in, Bianca. I'm worried about you."

I gave a derisive laugh. People didn't worry about me. It was my job to worry about them, but nobody worried about me. *Just give her a donut and she'll be fine.*

"Is it the wall?" Daniel's voice was gentle. "Do you want me to put it back up? I can do that if you want. It will take a couple of days, but it's no big deal."

"It's not the wall. Please, just go. I'll call you tomorrow."

"Are you sure?"

"Yes."

"Okay. Call me if you change your mind."

Part of me wanted to tell him I'd changed my mind. The other part of me, the part that had dealt with this issue for ages, felt relieved he was leaving and wouldn't have to see me like this.

Chapter 28

Daniel

WHEN BIANCA TOLD Daniel to leave, he almost listened to her. After all, he didn't want to barge into her life if she didn't want him there. Yet, he couldn't stand the thought of leaving when she was upset, especially not the night before Claudia arrived.

If he hadn't witnessed the interaction between Keith and his wife earlier this week, he might've actually left. Instead, he rang the bell again.

At first, Bianca didn't answer. When she finally did, her greeting was one word. "*Daniel.*"

"Will you please talk to me? I might not be able to fix everything, but I'm a good listener. And I have tacos."

Instead of laughing like usual, she gave a deep exhale. "That's part of the problem."

"Tacos are part of the problem?"

"Yes . . . no."

As he stood there confused, he heard the door unlock. "You can come up, but I'm warning you. I'm a mess."

"That's okay."

Relieved she was going to talk to him, Daniel climbed the stairs to Bianca's apartment where she met him at the door. Her makeup was smudged, and her eyes were red-rimmed, but she allowed him to come inside.

"What's going on?" he asked, setting the plaster on the ground and placing the bag of tacos on the coffee table.

She pushed out a slow breath. "You're going to think it's stupid."

"No, I'm not."

"Yes, you are. *I* think it's stupid."

Daniel studied her carefully. "It might be stupid, but it's upsetting you. I want to help, so please tell me what's going on."

She swiped at her eyes. "It's just that I have nothing to wear when Claudia comes. Nothing fits. My jeans are too tight, and everything else looks dumpy."

Dumpy was the last word he'd ever use to describe Bianca. He thought about how beautiful she looked, sitting on his backyard swing the other night. How beautiful she looked right now despite her tear-stained face.

"What about that black dress you wore when you came over for dinner?" he suggested.

"I wear that all the time."

"Do you?"

"Yeah."

He shrugged. "Well, you look great in that."

"No, I don't. And I can't wear the same thing I always wear when Claudia comes."

"Why? She's never seen that dress before. To her, it will be new."

Bianca groaned. "I knew you'd think it was stupid."

"I didn't say I thought it was stupid." Clenching his jaw, Daniel fought the urge to leave. Bianca was hurting, and she needed his compassion.

"Come here," he said, opening his arms.

Sniffing hard, she reluctantly walked into his embrace. He pressed her against him, wanting to take away her pain.

"I love you," he said, realizing he honestly meant it.

She pulled back and looked at him. "How can you say that?"

"Because it's true. I love you, and right now, I'd do anything to make you feel better."

She smiled sadly. "I love you, too, Daniel."

Brushing back her hair, he lowered his lips to hers.

As they kissed, Daniel remembered hearing that love was a decision. It would've been so much easier to leave tonight, but he'd made a decision to stay. As he kissed Bianca now, he knew there wasn't any other place he wanted to be.

"Better?" he asked when their kiss ended.

She nodded. "I just don't want Claudia to be ashamed of me, you know?"

"*Oh, sweetheart.*" Daniel pulled away so he could look into her eyes. With both hands, he held her beautiful face. "Listen to me. You gave birth to her. You gave her life. She's coming to see you through her own choosing. She's not going to be ashamed of you. She's going to love you."

"You think so?"

"I know so. I don't know how to explain it, but you have this glow that comes from inside you making you a very, very beautiful woman. You're beautiful without the glow, but the glow is where it's at. Claudia is going to see that."

Bianca swallowed hard. "Nobody's ever said that to me before."

"That's because the world is filled with idiots."

Bianca laughed, the sound filling Daniel with relief. They were going to be okay after all. Somehow, Daniel just knew it.

Chapter 29

Bianca

"Is Joy working?" I asked, tossing the weight loss shakes into the trash.

"She is, but she'll be here in a little bit to help me finish the project." Daniel gestured to the shakes. "What are those things?"

"Diet shakes. I was using them to lose weight so I wouldn't be so fat when Claudia arrived, but I'm done with them."

He picked up one of the packages and read the ingredients. "You haven't been drinking these, have you?"

"That's all I've had for the past few days. Well, I had a banana at lunch because I felt like I was going to pass out."

He shook his head. "No wonder why you're acting so crazy. These things are horrible for you. I could probably mix them with water and use them to plaster the wall."

"Be my guest," I said, smiling.

"No, just get rid of them."

"Are you sure?"

"Positive. Throw them away, then come outside with me to eat some real food."

I did as he said, and we sat side by side on the balcony sofa. As we ate, I told him how grateful Keith and Jillian were for his help with their flood the other day.

He shrugged. "I was happy to help."

"Jillian's been such a basket case since having the baby, but I think she's doing better. She told me Linda Faith smiled for the first time this morning."

"That's good." Daniel's phone dinged with a text, and he quickly typed out a response. "It's Joy. I assume you're okay with her sleeping on your couch tonight while I finish up the kitchen?"

"Sure, but she can sleep in my guest room. You can sleep there, too. I have twin beds, and I just cleaned the room for Claudia in case she changes her mind about spending the night. I'll be at the ranch with my parents tonight, so please, make yourself at home."

"Thanks. I don't think I'll sleep, but I'm sure Joy will appreciate that."

"You're going to stay up all night?"

He nodded. "I'm not going into work tomorrow, and I'm determined to finish your remodel so it will be ready for tomorrow's special guests."

I smiled. "Thank you, Daniel. That means a lot."

"I'm happy to do it."

I dipped a chip in the mango salsa I hadn't thought I'd like but was now considering eating with a spoon. "And you're still happy with our deal? You don't feel cheated or taken advantage of?"

"By you? Never." Leaning over, he kissed me, his lips tasting like salt, lime, and mango.

I rested my hand against his cheek, remembering what my sisters had said about Daniel's scruffy beard. As though reading my mind, he winked at me and kissed me again.

Chapter 30

Daniel

As Bianca and Daniel sat on the sofa, finishing dinner, she turned to him. "Do you mind if I ask you something about Joy's mom?"

Daniel's entire body tensed. "Go ahead."

"Well, you told me that Libby suffered from mental illness. Can I ask what it was? If that's too personal, you don't have to tell me. It's just something I've been wondering about."

"No, it's okay." He took a sip of his drink. "Basically, she was a pathological liar. It took me a while to figure that out because she was really good at lying. But her inability to tell the truth was her main issue."

"What kinds of things did she lie about?"

"Everything. Honestly, I still have no idea what was true and what was made up, so I probably don't even know half the lies she told."

Bianca was silent for a moment. "I'm sure it wasn't

easy being married to someone you couldn't trust."

"No, it wasn't."

"Did you ever think about leaving her?"

"Every day."

Bianca smiled sadly. "Why'd you stay?"

"Well, I kept thinking I could fix her. If I just confronted her with the evidence or found the perfect psychiatrist, she'd realize what she was doing and change."

"But that didn't happen?"

"No." Daniel looked down. "The day she died, we had a horrible fight over the phone. I'd caught her lying about some charges on the credit card. She denied them, of course. Then she went to pick up Joy from school and never made it home."

"Oh, Daniel."

"I've always regretted that last fight."

"I understand that, but you don't feel like the accident was your fault, do you?"

He shrugged. "I guess I just wish I would've handled things better. I've always felt guilty that I didn't find a way to reach her."

"You shouldn't feel guilty. It sounds like you tried."

"I did, but . . . I just didn't realize the extent she would go when protecting a lie."

"What do you mean?"

Daniel licked his lips. Maybe if he told Bianca his secret. . . No, he needed to tell Joy first. He owed that to his daughter.

"It was just tough," he said.

Bianca nodded. "I think the fact that you stayed in the marriage, trying to work it out and trying to help her, says a lot about your integrity."

Daniel smiled sadly. What would've happened to his integrity had he found out earlier the secret Libby had kept from him? The secret he couldn't seem to find the strength to tell Joy?

Chapter 31

Bianca

WHEN JOY CAME over after dinner, I made her drive me to the ranch. "I thought you could practice parallel parking in the driveway."

She groaned. "I'm horrible at that."

"I know, but the more you practice, the better you'll get."

"I don't know if that rule applies to me in regard to parking. Besides, I heard you can flunk that part of the test and still get your license."

"Really? I hadn't heard that, but I don't think that's the best attitude to have, do you?"

She laughed. "Probably not, but I did hear they're eventually going to eliminate parallel parking from the test since it's practically irrelevant these days."

"I guess that would make sense. I can't even tell you the last time I had to parallel park."

She shot me a sideways glance, before quickly returning her gaze to the road. "Do you still remember how?"

I grinned. "Of course, I remember how. I wouldn't exactly be the best driving instructor if I didn't remember."

She tapped her fingers on the steering wheel. "Be honest. How many YouTube videos did you watch this afternoon to refresh your memory?"

I laughed. "A lot, but that's beside the point."

She smiled and put on her blinker to turn into the ranch. After keying in the gate code, she drove toward the house. Right away, Lady and Duke came out to greet us, barking like crazy.

I unrolled the window so they could see it was me. In response, they wagged their tails and held their heads high as they escorted us down the driveway.

At the house, I climbed out of the truck and said hello to the dogs who returned the gesture by covering me with dog hair and slobber. "Where are Mom and Dad?" I asked, seeing only my dad's truck in the driveway. Maybe they'd driven my mom's car to go out to eat or something.

After setting up the garbage cans to act as markers for Joy, I climbed back in the passenger's seat and offered a few tips I'd learned from one of the videos I'd watched. "Are you ready?"

She nodded and pulled the car forward. At first, she was horrible, knocking over the garbage cans every time she backed up. Eventually, however, she improved.

When my dad came out of the house, Joy waved at him, and he waved back. I pushed open the truck door and told Joy to keep practicing.

"You're going to let me drive by myself?" she asked, sounding nervous.

"Yes. I want to talk to my dad. Plus, it'll be a good experience for you to park without me."

"Okay." She didn't sound too confident, but I told her she'd be fine. Then, I climbed out of the truck and joined my dad on the front porch.

"I was watching from upstairs," he said. "It looks like she's getting the hang of it."

"She is."

A beat of awkward silence fell between us. My dad and I hadn't really talked since I told him about deciding to look for Claudia.

Of course, I hadn't known Claudia's name until a few weeks ago. Now, she was coming to see me, and I was nervous about how my dad would act around her.

"Where's Mom?" I asked.

"She went out to eat with the mah-jongg ladies."

I nodded as Joy executed the most perfect parking maneuver in the history of parking maneuvers. "Oh, wow. That was great," I shouted, clapping.

"Bravo." My dad gave Joy the thumbs-up and grinned his special grin he reserved for people he really liked. Why couldn't he grin at me like that?

Maybe I hadn't always made the best choices in life, but I went to church and was a law-abiding citizen. I paid my taxes, ran a successful business, and led a Bible study. You'd think he could be a little more supportive of my desire to meet the daughter I'd given up for adoption.

My dad cleared his throat. "You've done a good job teaching Joy how to drive."

"Thank you," I said, surprised by the compliment.

A beat of silence followed before he said, "I watched the video of Claudia playing the violin again. I've never heard or seen anything more beautiful."

My heart lifted. "She's pretty amazing, isn't she?"

"She is." He turned to me and offered a sad smile. "It was my fault."

"What was your fault?"

"The reason you went to that party and got pregnant. The reason you had to go through the pain of giving away a child."

"What are you talking about?"

He swallowed hard. "I was supposed to take you out of town for a horse show that weekend, but I canceled because of work. You were so mad at me, and I get it. I'd promised to take you."

"*Dad.*"

He shook his head. "In hindsight, I should've kept my promise. If I had, you wouldn't have gone to that party and—"

"No, Dad. Getting pregnant was my fault. I was mad about that weekend, but I never blamed you for what happened. Never. And giving her away—"

"You wanted to keep her."

"I did, but I was young and didn't understand what that meant."

He looked down at his hands before lifting his face and meeting my gaze. "Did I do the right thing, insisting you give her up and not raise her on your own?"

"Yes," I said, and for the first time, I realized it was true. "I wanted to keep her, but if I had, she would've had a different life. *I* would've had a different life. We can't second-guess that decision, especially when she's obviously thriving where she is."

He nodded, then he said something so random that I didn't understand at first. "Your Aunt Wynona and I had an older sister."

"You did?"

"Yes. She drowned before I was born."

"*Oh, Dad.*"

"I don't think my mother ever got over it."

"Of course not." I thought about my own brother's death and how it continued to haunt my mother, especially on Marcus's birthday.

His hand slightly trembling, my dad reached into his pocket and pulled out a shiny silver, heart-shaped pendant on a chain. "My parents never talked about the daughter they lost, but after they passed away, Wynona and I found this in our mother's jewelry box."

I looked down at the delicate necklace in my father's beefy hand. He offered it to me, and as I examined it closer, I was shocked by the inscription. "*Claudia.*"

"That was her name," my dad explained. "Claudia."

"Oh, wow. No wonder you acted so strangely when I told you the Cavenaughs named her Claudia."

"It was a shock since it's not the most common name these days. Anyway, I don't know why I kept this necklace. Most of my mother's jewelry went to Wy or your mom. Some of it we sold, but I've kept this piece in my dresser drawer for years. Your mother even asked me last year if I was ready to let it go, but something told me I should hang on to it. I guess there was a reason for that."

"I guess so." I blinked hard, filled with emotion.

"I had the jewelry store replace the chain. I thought maybe you could give it to your Claudia when she comes tomorrow."

"I'd like that." Fighting back tears, I unfastened the necklace and put it around my neck.

Clasping the pendant, I smiled. "Thank you, Dad. Thank you so much."

He grinned his special grin. "You're welcome, sweetheart."

Chapter 32

Claudia

CLAUDIA HAD BEEN nervous about meeting Leland's grandmother, but it turned out that Mimi was wonderful. Yes, the older woman was hard of hearing and somewhat of a hoarder. Yes, the pot roast she served tasted like leather, but her shortbread cookies and lemonade were wonderful.

Plus, Mimi herself was so sweet and interesting. If Leland wanted inspiration for a film project, he needed to look no further than his own grandmother.

Every object in her home had major sentimental value and represented someone she loved or a major turning point in her life. Fascinated, Claudia followed her through the house, listening as Mimi told story after story.

At some point, Leland excused himself to lie down because he wasn't feeling well. An hour later, Claudia heard him throwing up in the bathroom.

"Are you okay?" she asked, standing on the other side of the closed door.

"Not really."

She waited until he finally emerged, his face red and sweaty. "I'm sick."

"I'll call the doctor," Mimi said.

Leland shook his head. "No, I'll be fine. It was probably something I ate. Let me sleep, and I'll be better in the morning."

Leland was planning on sleeping on the couch in the living room, but Claudia suggested he take the bed in the guest room so he could be more comfortable.

"No, that's okay." He staggered down the hallway, lay down on the couch, and immediately went to sleep.

In the guest room that night, Claudia scrolled through her phone as she lay in bed. If Leland didn't feel better in the morning, she'd probably have to cancel her trip to Rose Island. Leland drove a stick shift, something she'd never been able to master. No way could she navigate Houston traffic and make her way to Rose Island on her own.

If she were honest, part of her felt relieved. Her stomach had been in knots all day at the thought of meeting Bianca and the Morgan family. Maybe Leland's illness was a sign she shouldn't go right now.

Her phone rang with a call from her mother. While

she'd told her parents about driving down to Houston to meet Leland's grandmother, she'd left out the part about Bianca and Rose Island. Unable to face her mom right now, she sent the call straight to voicemail.

A few minutes later, Mom texted, "Just wanted to see how everything was going. Hope you had a good trip and arrived at Leland's grandmother's house safely. Have fun, and we'll see you soon. Love you."

Claudia swallowed hard and texted back the words, "Love you, too, Mom."

IN THE MORNING, Claudia awoke to the smell of bacon and pancakes. Hopefully that meant Leland was feeling better. Eager to start the day, she jumped in the shower and dressed before heading toward the kitchen.

To her relief, the blinds in the living room were open, and Leland wasn't on the couch. Expecting to find him eating breakfast, she wandered into the kitchen where Mimi was setting a plate of pancakes on the table.

"Well, good morning, dear," the older woman said. "Would you like a cup of coffee?"

"I'd love one." Claudia glanced outside, looking for Leland, but he wasn't anywhere among the garden trolls and hummingbird feeders.

"I sent him to sleep in my room," Mimi said, handing Claudia a cup of coffee. "I think he's really sick, and I'm worried. He told me about wanting to take you to Rose Island, but I think you'll have to reschedule. I don't see how he'll be able to do anything but lie in bed today."

After eating breakfast with Mimi, Claudia went into the dark master suite to check on Leland. He was sound asleep, but she sat on the bed beside him and pressed the back of her hand to his forehead.

"Hey," he murmured, opening his eyes.

"You're burning up."

"I'm so cold." He burrowed deeper in the covers. "I don't know what to do about today. I think I'm too sick to take you."

"I know. Mimi and I are going to drive her golf cart to the grocery store. Does anything sound good? Do you want me to bring you some ginger ale?"

He shook his head. "Just let me sleep, okay?"

"Okay."

She started to leave, but he reached out and patted her leg. "You should take my car to Rose Island though. I know you don't like to drive it, but you came all this way to meet your birth mother, so you should go."

"I don't know."

"You should." With that, he rolled away and went back to sleep.

Claudia sat in the dark until her phone dinged with a text from Bianca. "So excited to see you, I hardly slept last night! What time do you think you'll arrive? Feel free to come as early as you'd like! I'll be ready!"

Instead of answering, Claudia sighed and turned off her phone.

Chapter 33

Bianca

AFTER TEXTING CLAUDIA, I reread my message, hoping I didn't sound overly excited. Maybe I shouldn't have used so many exclamation marks.

When she didn't respond, I read my text again, knowing I'd come on too strong. Should I try again by sending a different message that said she could come whenever she wanted?

Reminding myself that Claudia was a busy teenager with a serious boyfriend, I decided to let it go. Who cared if she didn't return my text? She was coming to the island today, and that was all that mattered.

In my apartment, I found Daniel passed out on my couch. Seeing him sleeping so soundly stopped all the noise in my head. Mesmerized, I stood there, watching his chest rise and fall with each inhale and exhale.

He was such a good and handsome man. He had the kindest heart, and without a doubt, I was crazy in love with him. Regardless of what happened between the two of us, I only wanted the best for him.

"Hey." He opened his eyes and smiled at me.

I smiled back. "Hey, yourself."

He yawned and stretched, then he pushed off the blanket and sat up. "Joy's sleeping in the guest room."

"Good," I said.

Standing, he gestured toward the kitchen. "Well, what do you think?"

I'd been so enthralled with him that I'd forgotten about the project. Glancing at the kitchen, I sucked in a sharp breath. "It's amazing."

"Yeah?"

Clasping the Claudia necklace, I nodded. "I can't believe you finished."

"I told you I would."

"I know, but I never expected it to look so amazing." Striding into the kitchen, I marveled at everything from the new light fixture to the way he'd framed the opening where the wall used to be.

"You really like it?" he asked, coming up beside me.

"I love it." Throwing my arms around him, I hugged him tight. "Thank you so much. Everything is absolutely perfect."

"Perfect?" Joy said, coming into the kitchen. "There you go, talking about me again."

Laughing, I pulled away from Daniel and smiled at Joy. "You are perfect, my dear, but so is my kitchen. I'm so glad I took your advice about the cabinets and hiring your dad."

She grinned. "I love your guest room. Anytime you need someone to apartment sit, give me a call."

"I will, but you can spend the night any time. Just be forewarned that the bedroom isn't normally that clean. I picked up yesterday for Claudia."

"I thought she wasn't spending the night," Joy said.

"I'm hoping she'll change her mind."

AFTER JOY AND Daniel left, I jumped in the shower and got ready for work. Claudia and Leland were due to arrive around noon, so I'd kept my morning appointments, hoping staying busy would make the time pass quicker.

Around ten o'clock, a tall girl with short black hair came into the salon. "Claudia?" I asked, wondering why she'd decided to dye her hair black.

The girl offered an awkward smile. "No, I'm Emma. I have a ten o'clock appointment with Jenny."

"Of course." I shook my head, embarrassed by my foolishness. This girl didn't look anything like my family or the pictures I'd seen of Claudia.

"Jenny is in the back," I said. "I'll tell her you're here."

As I walked through the salon, I told myself to *settle down*. Getting all spun up wasn't going to hasten Claudia's arrival. She'd get here when she got here.

Still, I couldn't help but check my phone, wishing she'd reply to my message. Even though I desperately wanted to text her again, I didn't.

In the break room, I found Jenny sitting at the table, enjoying a cup of coffee and a piece of chocolate chip cake. Despite her sweet tooth, Jenny was one of those thin women who ate whatever she wanted, whenever she wanted. In fact, I was pretty sure she was responsible for eating most of the treats Vicki brought us.

"Your client, Emma, is here," I announced.

"Thank you." Jenny stood and covered the rest of her cake with a piece of plastic wrap. I'd seen her do this on numerous occasions. Instead of scarfing down the remaining three bites like I would do, she'd wrap it and save it for later.

"How are you doing?" Jenny asked.

"Not good. My ten o'clock just rescheduled for next week, so I don't know what to do with myself. I think I'm driving everyone crazy with my nervous energy."

"You think?" she teased.

"Sorry. I know I'm a basket case."

The back door opened, and I jumped. Seeing it was Joy, I laughed and pressed a hand to my heart.

"Did you think I was Claudia?" she asked, a twinkle in her eye.

"Yes." I buried my face in my hands. "How am I supposed to wait another two hours? I'm such a mess."

Joy laughed and gave me a hug. "Of course, you're a mess. This is a big day for you."

Jenny patted my arm as she headed up front to meet her client. I smiled at Joy. "I'm glad you're here. I don't have any more appointments, and I'm feeling a little restless. Do you want to squeeze in a quick driving lesson?"

"No, but I probably should since I'm taking my driving test this afternoon."

"You are?"

She nodded. "I wasn't supposed to take it until next week, but they had a cancellation, so my dad said to go for it."

"That's great."

"It will be if I pass. But first, I have to find my wallet."

"You lost your wallet?"

She nodded. "I usually carry it in my backpack with all my diabetes stuff, but it must've fallen out last night."

"I bet it's upstairs."

"I hope so."

Together, we hiked up to my apartment. Under one of the beds in the guest bedroom, we found her wallet.

As we were leaving the room, Joy stopped at the dresser where, this morning, I'd placed a new frame containing a copy of the photo of Claudia and me.

"Do you think it's too much?" I asked.

Joy shook her head. "It's such a great picture. I'm sure she'll love it."

"Thanks. I've always been so grateful to the nurse who gave it to me."

"I wish I had a picture like that. There aren't a lot of pictures of me as a baby."

"No?"

She shook her head. "No. I suppose all the other pictures I have make up for it."

"The other pictures?"

"When I was about one, my dad bought a new camera and took enough pictures of me to fill three huge albums."

"You'll have to show them to me next time I come over. I bet you were really cute."

She smiled. "Am I bragging if I said, yes, I was?"

I laughed. "No."

She set the photo back on the dresser. "So, what are

you going to do until Claudia and Leland arrive?"

"I don't know. What are you going to do until you take your test?"

She shrugged. "Maybe see if you're interested in watching one of my design shows with me."

"I'd love to. I have Brie and grapes in the fridge if you want something to eat."

"Actually, that'd be perfect. I was just about to test my blood sugar and have a snack when I noticed my wallet was missing."

"Great," I said, heading into the kitchen.

Ten minutes later, Joy and I were curled up on the couch with our snack, watching HGTV. Together, we laughed at all the outrageous things the designers thought would be simple to complete but ended up becoming a nightmare.

"Are you sure you don't want to wallpaper your cabinets?" she asked, teasing me.

I laughed, feeling happy beyond measure. The Lord had been so good to me. In addition to letting me meet my daughter, he'd blessed me with Joy and the other girls from Bible study. He'd also given me a hunky boyfriend who was a good man and an amazing father.

A text from Vicki interrupted my silent prayer. "Where are you?" she asked.

"In my apartment watching TV with Joy," I texted

back. "Why?"

"I'm coming up."

"Is that Claudia?" Joy asked.

I shook my head, hoping the fact that I hadn't heard from my daughter didn't mean she wasn't coming. I'd be heartbroken if she changed her mind. "That was Vicki. She's on her way up."

As we waited for Vicki to join us, a loud clap of thunder shook the building. Rain followed, smacking hard against the window.

I glanced outside, nervous about Leland and Claudia driving in the rain. Bad weather made Houston traffic even worse than usual, and the bridge connecting Rose Island to the mainland became slippery when it rained.

"I hope the weather's better when I take my test," Joy said.

"I do too, but if it's not, just keep your lights on, go slow, and make sure there's plenty of distance between you and the next car."

"You sound like my dad," she said.

I laughed. "Well, that's not necessarily a bad thing, is it?"

Vicki rapped on the door before turning the door-knob and entering the apartment. Behind her stood a young woman who looked vaguely familiar.

Like Vicki, the girl was petite and blonde. She had

glasses and wore jeans with a faded gray T-shirt. I knew I'd seen her before, but . . .

"Bianca, hi." The stranger adjusted the violin case in her hand.

For a moment, my brain stopped working. This girl knew me? Had I cut her hair? Was she the daughter of one of my clients?

"It's Claudia," Vicki said, stating something so obvious I should've figured it out myself.

"*Claudia?*" My heart made a loud thwacking sound as it slammed into my chest.

"Yes," my daughter said, nodding. "It's me."

Pulse racing, I leapt to my feet and threw my arms around her.

Chapter 34

Bianca

AS I HELD my daughter in my arms for the first time since that day long ago, I couldn't remember a time when I'd been more ecstatic. "I can't believe you're here," I said, my voice cracking.

"I can't believe I'm here either." Thankfully, Claudia didn't seem bothered by my exuberant show of affection. She was, however, the first one to pull away.

I reluctantly let her go and brushed back my tears. "I didn't think you'd ever get here."

She smiled. "I didn't think I'd ever get here either. I had to take the bus because Leland got sick and couldn't drive me. His car has a stick shift, and I'm hopeless when it comes to driving it. Anyway, even though I left pretty early, the bus took forever. You wouldn't believe how many stops we made."

"You took the bus? I would've driven up to get you."

"Oh, it's fine." She gave a good-natured smile that reminded me of my mother. "It was an adventure, that's for sure."

Studying her intently, I found myself amazed by everything about her. She really did have my smile. If my nose was cute like Daniel said, Claudia's was downright adorable.

Joy introduced herself, and the two exchanged pleasantries. I was happy they had a chance to meet in case I couldn't convince Claudia to stay for tonight's dinner with the family.

"Are you hungry?" I asked. "Can I get you something to eat or drink?"

Claudia shook her head. "No, thank you. I just had something at the bakery."

"That's how I found her," Vicki said. "She was sitting at one of the tables, eating a blueberry muffin, and I said, 'Hey, I know you.'"

Claudia gave me an apologetic look. "I was famished, and I didn't want to arrive on your doorstep starving."

"I wouldn't have minded," I said. "In fact, Joy and I were just having a little snack. If you'd like some—"

"No, I'm fine," Claudia said.

"Well, I should get back to work," Vicki said. "It was so nice meeting you, Claudia."

"You, too."

Joy's phone dinged with a text. "That's Kayla. She's giving me a ride home since it's raining."

"I can give you a ride," I said.

"That's okay." Joy grabbed her backpack and started to leave.

"You don't have to go, honey." I suddenly felt nervous and wanted Joy to stay. Maybe her presence would make things easier with Claudia.

"I need to go over a few things before I take my test," Joy explained, heading toward the door with Vicki. "Plus, Kayla is already here."

"Okay, I understand. Tell her I said hi. And when I see you tonight at the ranch, you'll be a licensed driver."

"I hope so."

"I know so."

After Vicki and Joy left, I turned to Claudia and heaved a big contented sigh. "Well, welcome to my home. I'm so sorry Leland's sick, but I'm thrilled you came."

She gave a bashful smile. I guess she was nervous, too.

I gestured toward my kitchen. "Joy and her father, Daniel, just finished renovating my kitchen last night. Actually, Daniel stayed up all night so he could finish it before you came. What do you think?"

"It's nice."

I stepped toward the opening that connected the kitchen to the living room. "There used to be a wall between the two rooms. Daniel took that down, painted the cabinets, and did a whole bunch of other work. Joy helped, too. She wants to study interior design when she goes to college, so she's always coming up with ideas on how to improve a room. She's the one who suggested we paint the cabinets. What do you think?"

"They're very nice." Claudia glanced around my apartment. "It's all very lovely, Bianca." She spoke with a formality I wasn't used to. Then again, I probably sounded like a country bumpkin realtor, listing off all the positive attributes of my home.

I gestured toward her bag. "Did you change your mind about spending the night?"

"Yes, if that's okay. There's a bus going back to Houston in an hour, but I thought maybe I'd spend the night and go back tomorrow."

"I'd love that."

She smiled. "Good."

"I need to call my mom and tell her you'll be here for dinner. We're having a fake celebration at the ranch house tonight for Jillian's birthday. Everyone will be thrilled you'll be here for that."

"A fake celebration?"

I nodded and explained about Jillian's surprise party. "I hope I can convince you to stay for that. It's going to be a lot of fun."

"Maybe." She offered a tentative smile.

I smiled back. "How about I show you the guest room so you can get settled?"

"Okay."

I led her down the hall, trying not to appear too excited, but how could I not be? Claudia, my daughter, was here in my home.

"Here it is," I said, striding into the guest room. "There's space in the closet if you want to hang up anything, and I have clean towels in the bathroom."

"Thank you." She glanced around the room before walking to the dresser and picking up the framed picture.

"That's us," I said. "One of the nurses in the hospital took it. Until recently, it's the only photo I've had of you. It's always meant the world to me."

Claudia stared down at the picture, not saying anything for a long time. Then, using her cell phone, she snapped a picture of it. "I want to send it to Leland."

"You can take this framed copy, too. I made it for you yesterday at the grocery store. They have a new photo department that has one of those photo scanning things, and they sell frames, too. Anyway, that's not important. My point is, the photo and the frame are yours."

"Thank you, Bianca."

"You're welcome." Happiness washed over me. *Thank you, Lord. Thank you.*

Suddenly, in a completely non-ominous way, a loud crack of thunder shook the building. Gasping, Claudia pressed a hand to her heart. "Is that normal?" Her eyes were wide, and she seemed terrified. "Don't you guys have hurricanes down here?"

"Oh, honey. Don't worry, okay? It's not a hurricane. I checked the weather earlier, and it's just a storm. It should pass in a few hours."

"Okay," she said, nodding.

I reached around to the back of my neck and unclasped the necklace my dad had given to me. "This is for you. It belonged to my dad's sister. Here, read it."

She took the necklace from me and read the inscription aloud before looking at me with confusion.

"Isn't that amazing?" I said. "You have the same name as my dad's sister."

"You have an Aunt Claudia?"

"Sort of. I never met her because she drowned before my dad was born, but he kept her necklace this whole time. He said I could give it to you."

Claudia stared down at the pendant. "This used to

belong to someone who drowned?"

"Yes." I suddenly felt stupid for being so excited. Claudia hadn't even been here ten minutes, and I was already making her uncomfortable by giving her some dead ancestor's jewelry.

"My dad put a new chain on it, but you don't have to wear it. And you don't have to keep it if you don't want to. I just thought . . ."

What? Had I actually thought she'd be as excited as me by the connection to my father's departed sister?

"Thank you." Claudia offered a polite smile as she set the necklace next to the framed picture of us.

WHILE WE ATE lunch and waited out the storm in my cozy apartment, Claudia and I talked about our lives. She also played the violin for me, which made me cry because she was even more beautiful in person.

"Hearing you play makes me wish I hadn't complained so much about piano lessons," I said. "It must be wonderful to play an instrument like that."

"Music is my passion. It's hard work as well, but I don't mind because I love it so much."

"Well, you're just amazing. Absolutely amazing."

She smiled. "Thank you. If you want, I could teach you how to play 'Twinkle, Twinkle Little Star.'"

"I'd love that."

For the next hour, Claudia tried to teach me the song. All I could say was playing the violin was much harder than I imagined. Every few minutes, I had to stop and rest because my fingers hurt from pressing down on the strings.

I'm sure by the end of our lesson Claudia wanted to poke her eyes out with the bow. Fortunately, her parents had taught her well, and she showed me nothing but kindness and patience.

"You're doing great, Bianca."

"You think so?"

"I do."

I almost believed her, then Vicki barged into my apartment to say I was scaring away all the customers in the bakery.

"You can't hear me from downstairs," I said.

"No, but I can hear you from my apartment, and it's giving me a headache."

"Well, I wouldn't want to give you a headache," I said, handing the violin back to Claudia.

AFTER THE STORM passed, Claudia and I went for a walk through town and down to the beach. She asked about her birth father, and I did my best to point out

Chad's better qualities, although it wasn't easy.

"Do you know where he lives or how I could find him?" she asked.

"I'm sorry, I don't. I might be able to put you in touch with one of his friends."

She bent over to pick up a seashell. "Maybe later. It doesn't sound like he's the kind of guy who would be interested in meeting me."

"I'm sorry. I wish I could tell you we'd been madly in love and getting pregnant was one of those things that happened in a moment of passion, but—"

"It's okay. I came here to meet you, so we don't have to talk about him if you don't want to."

I nodded, appreciating her sensitivity. Still, talk of Chad cast a dark shadow over the afternoon. Maybe I should track him down and tell him about the incredible child he'd fathered. The child he'd wanted me to get rid of.

I shuddered at the memory of how cruel he'd been when I told him about the pregnancy. Was he still selfish and self-centered like that?

IN THE EVENING, Claudia and I drove up the mountain to the ranch. I noticed she was wearing the necklace, and I wanted to tell her she didn't have to wear it if she didn't want to, but I didn't want to make things more awkward.

The storm had lifted, giving us the perfect view of the water and city below.

"It's incredible," she said, taking several pictures with her phone. "You never think about Texas as being pretty, but Rose Island is beautiful."

I didn't argue or take offense. Her statement was one I'd heard before from other visitors.

Still, I found it surprising the number of people who thought Texas only had desert terrain. While much of west Texas fit that description, the gulf coast was completely different.

At the ranch house, my heart lifted at the sight of Daniel's truck, pleased he and Joy had already arrived. I'd missed him today and was looking forward to introducing him to Claudia.

"That must be your mom," Claudia said.

I glanced at the wild woman waving madly from the porch. "Actually, I've never seen her before in my life."

Claudia raised her brow.

"Just joking. Yes, that's my mom. Prepare yourself to meet Luella Morgan. She can be a little high-strung. She's going to hug you and ask a million questions about your life. Hopefully, you'll survive and it won't be too bad."

"That's okay. My mom is the same way."

"Is she really?"

Claudia nodded. "She is. I about died of embarrassment the first time Leland came to the house. She asked him so many questions. My dad said she'd missed her calling as a CIA interrogator."

I smiled, imagining that Claudia would do just fine with my family.

Joy came onto the porch holding Linda Faith. "That's Jillian's baby," I explained.

"Zoey Rose?" Claudia asked.

I shook my head. "No, Zoey belongs to Nick and Anna who are still in Germany. Linda Faith is Jillian and Keith's baby."

She nodded. "That's right. Jillian's your oldest sister."

"Yes. I know it's a lot to keep track of." I pointed out everyone else—Jillian, Keith, Matt, Drew, and Vicki. "The pretty girl standing next to Matt is Hannah, Matt's girlfriend. She's in my Bible study."

Claudia nodded. "What about Daniel? Is he coming tonight?"

"His truck is here. He must be inside the house or out back with my dad." Turning off the engine, I took a deep breath. "Well, are you ready to meet my crazy family?"

"I am." Claudia pushed open the car door, and my mother charged down the porch steps toward us, her arms open wide.

Without waiting for an introduction or permission, my mom pressed Claudia to her bosom and squeezed tight. "Oh, honey. We're so happy you're here. So incredibly happy."

I worried it might be too much for this reserved daughter of mine. Nevertheless, tears blurred my vision as I realized how much my mother's words echoed my own feelings.

I, too, was so happy Claudia was here. So incredibly happy.

AFTER INTRODUCING CLAUDIA to everyone, my mother ushered us through the house to the garden where the long picnic table had been set with a new tablecloth and the best china. Although it wasn't dark yet, the garden lights were lit, casting a soft, magical light across the scene.

"Oh, Mom, it's beautiful. Thank you." I looped my arm through hers, touched she'd gone to such a great effort to make this dinner special.

My mother patted my hand. "In honor of Jillian's birthday and Claudia's visit, your father thought it'd be fun to eat out here like they do on all those cooking shows."

"This was Dad's idea?" I glanced ahead where my father was walking with Claudia, the two of them chatting away like old friends. My fear that things might be tense between my father and Claudia disappeared as soon as he saw the necklace around Claudia's neck.

"I thought setting the table out here wouldn't be worth the effort," my mother said, "but I'm happy how it turned out. Plus, Joy came early to help with everything."

I glanced behind me at Joy who was walking with Matt and Hannah. "That was nice of you to help."

She shrugged. "I wasn't doing anything. My dad said I could take the truck and—"

"Oh, that's right. Your test."

Her whole face lit up as she nodded. "I passed."

"Joy, that's fantastic." I gave her a huge hug. "I'm so proud of you."

She laughed. "Thanks."

"So you drove yourself here?"

"I did. My dad stayed home to help a neighbor with his roof that was damaged in the storm. If he can get a ride, he might come later, otherwise he said he'd stop by your place in the morning to meet Claudia."

I nodded, thinking it was just like Daniel to help

this neighbor. "Well, I'm so excited you passed your test. You should've called me earlier."

She shrugged and shot a quick glance at Claudia who'd taken a seat at the table next to Drew. "I thought about it, but I didn't want to disturb you."

I stopped walking and looked right at Joy. "You could never disturb me, honey. Please tell me you understand that."

She smiled. "I do."

"Good, because no matter what, you're very important and special to me."

"I know."

I gave her a quick hug, then we resumed walking and took our seats at the table with Claudia and the rest of my family. As soon as everyone was seated, my dad stood and cleared his throat. "I'd like to say a few words before we bless the food."

"What food?" Drew asked. "All we have out here are empty plates."

"The food's inside," Matt said, rolling his eyes at his younger brother.

Hannah nudged Matt with her elbow. "Be nice."

"Yes, ma'am."

Hannah nudged Matt again for good measure, and he laughed.

"Anyway," my father continued. "I'd like to welcome Claudia to our family. We're very happy you're here. If there's anything you need, just ask Luella. She has all the answers."

"Yes," my mother said, smiling, "we want you to feel at home, so please don't hesitate to ask for anything."

"I won't," Claudia said. "Thank you."

My dad nodded and turned his attention to Jillian. "Now, in regard to the birthday girl."

Jillian smiled, looking genuinely happy. The dark circles under her eyes seemed a little less noticeable today, and she was wearing a new outfit.

Reaching out, Keith took my sister's hand in his. Hopefully, he could see Jillian was going to be okay. And hopefully the surprise party would be as successful as he wanted it to be. I still had my doubts, but Keith was determined.

My dad smiled at Jillian. "It seems like a lifetime ago since your mother and I became parents. You were such a beautiful baby, and you've been a huge blessing to us. Watching you and Keith raise your family and rededicate yourselves to one another has been—"

My father shocked us by choking up. Tears filled his eyes, and overcome, he shook his head and fell silent.

"*Walter.*" The emotion in my mother's voice was palpable. With tears in her own eyes, she stood and walked to the other side of the table to console my father. Jillian stood as well, and my parents embraced their firstborn. Then, they all laughed and wiped their eyes.

"Okay," my father said, regaining control. "Enough of this sentimental business. Claudia, I promise, we're not normally like this."

My daughter smiled. "That's okay."

Raising his glass, my father said, "To Jillian on her birthday."

Everyone else chimed in, then we blessed the food and headed inside to fill our plates.

Chapter 35

Bianca

WHILE WE WERE having Jillian's birthday cake in the living room after dinner, Daniel arrived. I was thrilled to see him and introduce him to Claudia.

"What do you think about the island so far?" he asked.

"I like it." Claudia told him about the dolphins we'd seen while walking on the beach this afternoon and some of the shops we'd visited. They talked about the used bookstore down by the harbor and Viktoria Mullova, a famous violinist I'd never heard of.

At one point, my mother offered to make a dinner plate for Daniel if he hadn't eaten yet.

"That'd be great," he said. "I'm actually starving."

"Come on." I watched as she led him into the kitchen, remembering that corny line, "I hate to see you go, but I love to watch you leave."

"You okay?" Keith quietly asked, coming over to

stand next to me.

Embarrassed I'd been caught staring at Daniel, I laughed. "I'm great. What about you?"

He glanced across the room where Jillian sat on the couch, nursing the baby and talking to Joy. Lowering his voice, he said, "Everything is all set for tomorrow. She thinks we're going to dinner in Galveston."

I nodded. "Good."

Turning to Claudia, Keith asked if she would be here tomorrow night. "We're having a surprise party for my wife up at the Rose Museum, and we'd love to have you join us."

Claudia nodded. "Bianca told me about the party. It sounds like fun, but it will depend on how my boyfriend is feeling."

"Well, he can come too," Keith said. "The more the merrier."

"Thank you. I'll see what he says."

"Claudia," Drew said, coming over, "Matt, Joy, Hannah, and I are going upstairs to play ping-pong. Do you want to come?"

"Sure." She glanced at me as if asking permission.

"Have fun," I said. "And watch out for Matt's backhand. He'll slam the ball down your throat if you give him the opportunity."

"*Aunt Bianca*," Matt whined, pretending to be up-

"I wouldn't dare." I winked at him.

He laughed and led the others upstairs. It made me happy to see Claudia fitting in as well as Joy did with our family.

Spending time with her this afternoon had been wonderful, but it'd also been a little awkward. I chalked it up to the fact that we were both just nervous. Hopefully, the more time we spent together, the easier things would be.

My mother winked at me as she came out of the kitchen by herself. Striding across the living room, she said something to my father who was talking to Vicki.

"You should probably go check on Daniel in the kitchen," Keith said. "Your mom left him all alone. He might need help finding the salt or using the microwave."

I smiled. "Good idea. And you should go check on your wife." Jillian had taken the baby into the other room, probably to change her diaper.

Leaving the living room, I wandered into the kitchen where I found Daniel rinsing his dish in the sink. "Hey, you," he said, smiling at me. "I was hoping you'd come find me."

"Yeah?"

Nodding, he set his dish on the counter and turned

to face me. Then, he opened his arms, and I walked into them as if it were the most natural thing in the world.

He'd recently showered, and I could smell the scent of his shampoo. When he kissed me, I couldn't imagine feeling any happier than I felt right now.

Tightening his arms around my waist, he shocked me by lifting me into the air. Then, he started spinning me around like I was a dainty heroine on the cover of a romance novel.

"Daniel," I said, mortified, "put me down. I'm going to crush you."

Assuming I was joking, he shook his head and laughed. "You're not going to crush me."

"I am," I insisted, my voice tight. "I weigh like a thousand pounds."

"You don't, but even if you did, I could still lift you."

"Daniel, *please*."

Responding to the seriousness in my voice, he set me on the ground and released me. "Sorry."

I took a step back, my stomach heavy. "It's fine. I just don't want to hurt you."

He kept his eyes locked on mine. "I'm a strong guy, Bianca. Lifting you in the air isn't going to hurt me. But if you don't want me to do that, I won't."

I swallowed, suddenly on the verge of tears. "You

have no idea how much I weigh."

"I don't, but I know I can lift you."

When I didn't respond, he took a deep breath. "I wish you could see yourself like I see you."

I blinked. "What do you mean?"

"You're kind and generous with everyone but yourself. When I hear you make these horrible comments about your weight or how you look . . ." He shook his head. "You don't need to do that. I don't care how much you weigh. You're perfect just the way you are."

I lifted my chin, uncomfortable with the vulnerability surging through me. "You know that's a line from a popular romantic comedy."

"Well, it's true. To me, you're perfect just the way you are."

I clenched my jaw, wanting to believe he really felt that way about me. "I love you, Daniel."

"I know. And I love you, too. That's why it's hard to hear you say negative things about yourself."

I stepped toward him and we embraced, but thankfully, he didn't try to lift me again. Maybe he was strong, and maybe he didn't really care how much I weighed, but being lifted in the air like that wasn't something I could handle right now.

The sound of the piano playing drifted from the other room. "Who is that?" he asked.

"It must be Claudia. She's the only one I can imagine playing the piano like that."

We went back to the living room to find Claudia sitting at our neglected piano, playing a duet with Drew. Well, Drew was basically pressing the same chord over and over while Claudia's fingers flew up and down the keyboard.

I pressed a hand to my heart, overcome with love and tenderness for my talented daughter. Daniel slipped his arm across my shoulders, and I rested my head against his chest.

My thoughts drifted back to that horrible night when I'd told my parents I was pregnant. They'd been devastated and extremely disappointed. For me, it felt like I'd ruined my life and theirs.

Nevertheless, nobody dared suggest I terminate the pregnancy. Our faith taught us that every baby was a gift from God. Regardless of circumstances, every child deserved a chance.

Now, my life had come full circle. I'm not saying it was God's will for me to get pregnant in high school, but once again, the Lord had transformed an imperfect situation into something incredible.

Glancing around the room, I took in the sight of my family, captivated by the music. My parents sat on the couch, holding hands. Vicki stood off to the side by herself, watching Claudia.

I didn't know where Keith and Jillian were, but Matt and Hannah sat on the love seat, looking at their phones. Hannah leaned over to show Matt something on her screen, and he nodded.

In my father's recliner sat Joy holding the baby who was sound asleep. Joy was so good with Linda Faith. It was way too early to entertain thoughts like this, but I imagined Joy would be a very good big sister if the need ever arose.

As though reading my mind, Daniel pulled me closer, causing my heart to nearly burst. I'd only known this man a few weeks, but already I couldn't imagine my future without him.

⁓∞⁓

THE NEXT MORNING, Keith called me in a state of panic. He and the boys were having a hard time figuring out how to set up everything in the banquet hall for Jillian's birthday party tonight. Vicki was supposed to help, but she'd gotten caught up with some issue at the bakery.

"We'll be right there," I said as a baby in the background began crying. "Do you have Linda Faith with you?"

"I do. She's been fussy all morning. I thought it'd be

nice for Jillian to have some time to go shopping on her own before our big date tonight, but I can't get anything done holding the baby all day. Plus, I thought—"

I couldn't hear anything else my brother-in-law said because his daughter let out an earth-shattering scream. "Keith, if you can hear me, I'm on my way, okay?"

I hung up the phone and explained the situation to Claudia.

"I heard," she said. "Well, I heard the baby screaming."

"Yes, my niece isn't shy about expressing her dissatisfaction, that's for sure."

Claudia smiled. "My mother said I cried a lot when I was a baby. The only thing that soothed me was one of those battery-operated swings and the shower."

I frowned. "She put the swing in the shower?"

"No, she set it outside the shower. I guess I liked listening to the sound of running water. Eventually, they bought me one of those sound machines with a rain setting so they wouldn't have to run the shower all day. Now, I have a rain app on my phone, and it really works when I can't sleep."

"I have that same app," I said, my heart warming at this shared connection between us. "And you're right, listening to the sound of rain is the perfect cure for insomnia."

After getting ready, Claudia and I jumped in my car and took off. Her bus back to Houston didn't leave until after lunch, so she still had a few more hours on the island with me. My hope was she'd change her mind and stay for Jillian's party tonight.

On the way up the mountain, her phone dinged with a text, and she smiled. "It's Leland. He's feeling a lot better and is driving down to Rose Island this morning."

"That's wonderful. I can't wait to meet him. He knows he's invited to the party, right?"

"I told him."

"Well, I hope y'all will stay."

She shrugged. "I guess it will just depend on how he feels once he gets here."

I nodded, not wanting to pressure her. "Whatever you decide is perfectly fine. I'm just so happy we were able to have this time together."

"Me, too."

Outside the museum, Claudia and I found Keith, pacing the sidewalk with the baby on his shoulder. "She's finally asleep," he whispered.

"Okay, we'll be quiet," I whispered back.

He gestured toward the banquet hall. "Your boyfriend is inside hanging the strobe light."

I smiled at the word *boyfriend*. I, Bianca Morgan,

had a boyfriend, something I'd almost given up on.

Claudia and I went inside where Daniel stood on a ladder, adjusting the light that reflected off the disco mirror ball.

"What do you think?" he asked.

"It looks great," we both said.

"Good. Let's turn off the overhead lights and see what it looks like in the dark."

Matt hit the switch, and the effect was enchanting. Bits of light flickered across Daniel's face and hair as he climbed down the ladder and came toward me. I sucked in a sharp breath, daring to believe this handsome man actually cared about me as much as I cared about him.

❦

FOR THE REST of the morning, everyone worked hard arranging the tables and decorating for the party. As I ironed the wrinkle-free tablecloths, Joy and Claudia worked together to come up with the perfect solution for the centerpieces—a combination of wild daisies, cedar branches, and roses.

While Keith had purchased the daisies and roses from the flower shop, the girls had collected the greenery from the woods surrounding the museum. Listening to the two of them chat as they corroborated together warmed my heart. It felt as though God had given me two daughters instead of just the one I'd asked for.

When everything was all set, Keith took the baby home while the rest of us wandered through the museum. I wanted to show Claudia some of the exhibits; plus, I was determined to find the plastic horse Joy had talked about in the Urgent Care the other day.

The horse must've been moved, however, because the place where I'd last seen it had been taken over by dozens of enlarged photographs displayed on easels. According to a sign, all the pictures had once appeared in the local newspaper.

"That girl looks like Vicki," Claudia said, pointing to one of the photographs.

I followed her gaze and laughed at the picture of my sister wearing a tiara and cape. "It is her. That's the night she was crowned homecoming queen."

"I didn't know she was homecoming queen," Matt said.

"She was."

"Is that Seth Watson?" Daniel asked, pointing at someone in the background of the picture.

"It is, and . . ."

"That's your brother standing next to him," Joy finished for me.

"Wow," Drew said, "that is Uncle Marcus, isn't it?"

I nodded, the lump in my throat aching as it often

did whenever I unexpectedly came across a photo of Marcus. Daniel rested a hand on my shoulder and gave it a squeeze.

Matt pulled out his phone and took a picture of the photograph. "I'm going to send it to Aunt Vicki."

"Let's go see if we can find any more pictures of people we know," Drew said. He took off, wandering through the exhibit with Joy, Claudia, and Matt.

Daniel and I trailed behind, taking our time. "Are you okay?" Daniel asked.

"Yes, I'm fine. Sometimes it's just really hard to see pictures of Marcus looking so happy and full of life."

"I imagine so." His tone was somber. "I wish I could say the same thing about Libby, but things were so tense in our marriage, especially at the end, that I don't have a lot of good memories of her."

"I'm sorry."

He nodded and glanced across the room at Joy who was laughing with Claudia. "My dad made a comment when he was here at Christmas. Enzo had said some-thing similar when Joy was younger, so—"

"Aunt Bianca," Drew shouted from the other side of the exhibit, "come here. I want to show you something."

I pulled my gaze from Daniel and glanced at Drew. "Give me just a minute, okay?"

When I turned back to Daniel, he was staring down

at his phone. "Sorry, I've got to get this." Without further explanation, he headed toward the exit door and left.

I stared after him, desperate to know what he'd been about to tell me. What had his dad and brother said?

"Aunt Bianca, are you coming?"

"Yes." I strode over to Drew and the others who were studying a photo taken on the old Ferris wheel that used to be down by the pier.

"It's Grandma and Grandpa," Drew said.

"Oh, wow. It is." I smiled at the sight of my mom and dad who both looked so happy. My parents had definitely experienced their share of marital problems, but for the most part, they had a loving relationship I admired.

"I think I remember riding that Ferris wheel," Joy said.

I nodded. "You probably did. Until it was destroyed by a hurricane a few years ago, it was one of the most popular things to do on Rose Island."

Matt, who was standing behind me, said, "Joy, is that you?"

I turned to see that Matt was looking at another picture taken of the Ferris wheel. This one showed a little girl and her mother.

"Oh my gosh, it is me." Joy stepped toward Matt to

get a better view of the photo. "I can't believe it, but that's me and my mom."

"You were so cute," Claudia said. "Look at your pigtails and that little dress. And your purse. I had a purse just like that."

"My mother gave me that purse for my birthday." Joy's voice held a note of melancholy.

I glanced at the image of Joy before turning my attention to her mom. For some inexplicable reason, my heart began pounding and I struggled to breathe. I must've made a gasping sound or something because everyone turned to stare at me.

"Bianca?" Joy asked. "Are you okay?"

I pressed a hand to my chest. Was I having a heart attack? No, it was more like a panic attack. A feeling of dread that something wasn't right.

Leaning closer to the photograph, I studied Joy's mom. A ragged scar ran from the corner of her eye down to her lip. I'd seen that scar before. Seen it turn red with anger.

Taking a deep breath, I looked at Joy. "Did your mom ever work as a nurse in South Carolina?"

Joy shook her head. "No, I don't think so. Why?"

"It's just . . . well, she looks like the nurse from the hospital when Claudia was born. The one who took that picture of us."

Joy frowned. "My mom worked as a preschool teacher in El Paso. We never lived in South Carolina."

"That nurse's name was Tiffany Jackson," I continued. "Did your mom ever go by the name Tiffany Jackson?"

"No." Joy folded her arms across her chest. Something wasn't right, but what was it?

"It's probably just the scar," Drew said. "Not a lot of people have a scar like that."

"Drew," Matt scolded. "Don't be rude."

Drew shot Joy a look of apology. "Sorry. I wasn't making fun of your mom's scar, it's just really noticeable."

"My mother hated that scar," Joy said. "She used to say it was proof that the gods despised her."

"The gods?" Drew said.

Joy nodded as my stomach roiled. Then I remembered. Tiffany had used the exact same words to describe her scar. The exact same words.

Chapter 36

Daniel

STANDING OUTSIDE THE museum, Daniel answered his phone. "Enzo?"

"Yeah," his brother said.

"Oh, hey."

"Hey," Enzo said. "I got your message about calling you back. It sounded important. Is Joy okay?"

"Yeah, she's fine."

"Her numbers have been good?"

Daniel nodded. "They've been really good lately."

A deep silence fell between them. Although Daniel had rehearsed what he'd say if his brother actually returned his call, he found himself unable to speak.

"So, what is it? Why'd you call?" Enzo's voice held the same measure of anger it had during their fight at Christmas.

Daniel continued walking away from the museum. "I wanted to talk to you about . . . well, about everything. About—"

"About betraying me by cozying up to Dad behind my back?"

Enzo's words hit him hard. "I should've told you he was on the island," Daniel conceded.

"Yeah, you should've. And maybe you should've remembered what he did to us. What he did to Mom."

"I remember."

"Do you? Is that why you invited him to Christmas? Is that why you were playing *Happy Family* with him like nothing had happened?"

Daniel took a deep breath. "I didn't invite him to Christmas, and I wasn't playing *Happy Family* with him. He just showed up. I was just trying to deal with it the best I knew how."

"You didn't think about dealing with it by telling him to leave?"

"Of course, I thought about that." Daniel shoved a hand through his hair. He wanted to shout back at Enzo and say this was why he'd been afraid to say anything in the first place. He'd known his brother wouldn't understand.

"Look, I gotta go," Enzo said.

"Please don't."

Without a word, his brother hung up the phone. Frustrated, Daniel kept walking. After a while, he turned and headed back to the museum.

Sinking onto a bench, Daniel placed his ankle across his knee and tapped his foot. Why had he listened to Bianca about calling his brother? He couldn't make Enzo see his side of things any more than he could cure Joy's diabetes or erase his father's mistakes.

Sometimes things were just out of your control.

Father, I abandon myself into your hands. Do with me what you will—

"Daniel?"

Looking up, he found Bianca, staring at him with concern. "Are you praying?"

"Sort of." He motioned for her to join him on the bench. "That was my brother on the phone. I left a message for him last night, and he was calling me back."

"What did he say?"

Daniel just shook his head, discouraged.

Bianca sat beside him, uncharacteristically quiet. He glanced at her, worried by how pale she looked. "Are you okay?"

She shrugged. "I don't know. There's this photograph inside."

"A photograph?"

She nodded. "It's of Joy and her mom on the Ferris wheel when you came to the island."

"Oh, wow. What'd Joy say about it?"

"Not much, but Daniel . . . I think I met Joy's mom before."

An ominous feeling slithered up his spine. "Where?"

"At the hospital in South Carolina when I had Claudia. Did you and Libby live there when Joy was a baby? Did Libby ever work as a nurse or use the name Tiffany Jackson?"

Daniel's head pounded. "I don't know."

Bianca frowned. "What do you mean you don't know? Joy's birthday is a month before Claudia's. This nurse told me she had a newborn at home, so if it was Libby, Joy would've been her baby."

Wiping his hands on his jeans, he took a deep breath. He'd never told anyone this. Not Enzo, not his sister, and not even Joy.

"Daniel." Bianca placed a hand on his arm. "What is it?"

He studied her carefully. "I don't know if Libby ever worked as a nurse in South Carolina when Joy was a baby."

The furrow between Bianca's brows deepened. "I don't understand."

"I wasn't there. I didn't meet Joy until she was almost a year old."

"You didn't?"

"No. I've never told anyone that. Not even Joy."

"I won't say anything, but why didn't you meet her until then?"

He sighed. "It's a long story. You have to understand I was a different person back then. Before I found God, I slept around a lot. I'm not proud of it, but I was just your typical guy who didn't think it was a big deal. If the girl was willing, why not?

"Anyway, Libby and I hooked up a few times. Then, she moved away, and I didn't see her for a while. After my mom died, Libby just showed up on my doorstep, claiming Joy was my daughter. She even showed me the birth certificate, which had my name on it."

Bianca's eyes widened. "That must've been a huge shock."

"It was. I didn't think Joy was mine, regardless of what the birth certificate said, but Libby insisted. She told me she'd lost her job and didn't have anywhere else to go. I felt sorry for her, so I agreed to let them stay with me while we waited for the results of the paternity test."

Bianca nodded. "The test obviously came back positive."

"Why do you say that?"

"Because Joy looks just like you."

"Does she?"

"Definitely. She has your laugh, and you both have

this funky way of saying the word tomorrow."

"Tomorrow?"

"Yes, just like that. Joy says tomorrow just like you do."

Daniel offered a sad smile. "Well, like I said before, blood isn't always thicker than water."

"What do you mean?"

He pushed out a deep breath. "The paternity test came back positive, but this past January, I learned that Libby had falsified the test results. She'd also lied on Joy's birth certificate. Any characteristics Joy and I share are because of nurture, not nature."

"I don't understand. Are you saying you're not Joy's biological father?"

"That's right. I'm not."

"Are you sure?"

He nodded. "A long time ago, Enzo told me he didn't believe Joy was mine. I insisted he was crazy, but when my father came down at Christmas, he made the same comment. Hearing that really bothered me, so I decided to do another paternity test. This time it came back negative."

"It was probably a mistake."

Daniel shook his head. "No, I ordered it three times from three different labs, and the results were the same. I know it doesn't matter. Joy's my daughter. She'll always be my daughter, but I feel like she should know the truth."

Bianca sat back hard. "Wow. When are you going to tell her?"

"I don't know."

"Well, given what you told me, it's possible that Libby was the nurse in the hospital."

"Yes, it's possible."

"I'm sure Joy's going to tell you what I said about recognizing her mother, so you should probably say something sooner rather than later."

"I know," he said, feeling cornered by the accusation in Bianca's voice. "I'm going to tell her. I just have to figure out how."

"How what?" a voice behind them said.

Spinning around, Daniel's heart sank at the sight of Joy staring at him. "*Joy.*"

"What are you talking about, Dad? What do you need to tell me?"

Swallowing hard, Daniel formed his words carefully, knowing what he was about to say would impact his daughter for the rest of her life.

Chapter 37

Claudia

*L*OOKING OUT THE window, Claudia watched as Bianca and Daniel talked to Joy. Something was going on with the three of them, and it didn't look good.

Claudia assumed their conversation had to do with Bianca's belief that Joy's mom was the nurse from South Carolina, but she had no idea why that would be a big deal.

The sound of her phone ringing caused her to jump. Glancing down, she saw it was her mother. "Mom?"

"It's Clark," her brother said, his voice small. "I'm calling you on Mom's phone."

"Hey, Clark. How's it going?" She turned from the window, happy to hear his voice. Even though she'd only been gone a few days, she missed him. For that matter, she missed her entire family.

"When are you coming home?" he asked.

"I don't know."

"Oh. We're at the hospital. Did Mom tell you?"

Claudia's heart plummeted. "No, what's going on? Is it Dad?"

"No. It's Clay. He broke his arm because of me. I was the one who told him to do it." Clark started crying so hard she could barely understand him. "He didn't want to do it, but I told him he was a baby for not trying."

"What did he do?"

"He tried jumping onto the ceiling fan when it was moving. We both did. I missed and landed on the bed, but when Clay went, he landed on the ground and broke his arm."

"Oh, Clark."

Her brother sniffed hard. "Please don't be mad at me, Claudia. Dad said I was grounded for a year, and Clay said he was never speaking to me again. I think even Mom—" He heaved a giant sob. "I didn't mean for him to get hurt."

"I know you didn't."

"What if he gets cancer and loses his hair like Dad?"

"What?"

"Because of the hospital. Dad went to the hospital and came home without any hair. What if that happens to Clay? Then he'll really hate me."

Her brother was crying hysterically now. "And tomorrow's our birthday, but you're not even going to be here. You're going to miss our party and everything."

"I'm going to be there, okay?" The words left her mouth before she could think them through.

He stopped crying and sniffed hard. "You are? Mom said you weren't getting home until after our party."

"No, I'll be home for it. What time is your party?"

"After church at two."

"Okay. I can make that."

"You promise?"

Claudia sighed. She didn't want to promise in case it turned out she couldn't make it. But if she and Leland left as soon as he got here, they could definitely be home in time.

Bianca would be upset she wasn't staying for Jillian's party, but from the looks of it, Bianca had other issues to deal with. Plus, there was Joy who was more like a daughter to Bianca than Claudia could ever be.

Not that Claudia minded. She already had a mother. Joy didn't.

"You promise you'll be here?" Clark asked again.

"I promise."

"Okay. I'll tell Clay. Maybe that will make him not so mad at me."

"Good luck. Just remember that sometimes people

have to be mad for a little bit before they can get over it."

"Okay, I'll remember."

With that, she said good-bye to her little brother and called Leland. Hopefully, he hadn't changed his mind about driving down this morning.

"Hey, there," he said, picking up on the first ring. "I'm at Vicki's Bakery. Have you tried this coffee? It's amazing."

Relief washed over Claudia. "I'm so happy you're here."

"Me, too. The island is beautiful. Are you next door at the salon?"

"No, we're here at the Rose Museum. It's on the top of the mountain."

"I think I saw a sign for it. I'll plug it into my phone and come up there."

"Okay, but Leland . . ."

"You want to stay longer?"

"No. Just the opposite. I'm actually ready to go home. I know you just got here, but can you take me home?"

Chapter 38

Daniel

"*D*AD?" JOY STARED at Daniel, her eyes wide with fear.

Blood pounded against his skull. "We need to talk, honey. There are some things I need to tell you."

"Is it about the picture? Was Mom the nurse in the hospital like Bianca said?"

He hesitated. "I don't know."

"What do you mean you don't know?" Joy looked at him expectantly. She'd always trusted him to be honest. "Dad?"

"The reason I don't know whether or not your mom was Bianca's nurse is because I wasn't around your first year of life."

"You weren't?"

He shook his head. "No. I didn't even know about you until you turned one."

Joy blinked. "But Mom said you were there when I

was born. She said you cut the umbilical cord."

"I know she said that, but it wasn't true. The first time I saw you, you could already walk. I wanted to tell you, but you were so young when you came to live with me that I didn't think it mattered."

"It shouldn't." Joy's voice wobbled. "I don't remember, so I don't know why I'm upset. I guess I just always thought of you being there when I was born."

"I know. And I'm sorry. I didn't want to contradict your mother for something that seemed harmless like that. And I guess I wanted it to be true."

"But it wasn't."

"No."

A beat of silence fell, then Joy said, "You're not my biological dad, are you?"

Her question pierced his soul. "*Joy.*"

"Just answer my question. Please."

He nodded. "You're right. I'm not, but I didn't know that until recently."

"How'd you find out?"

"My dad said something at Christmas about us not looking anything alike, so I had your DNA tested with mine. It wasn't a match."

Joy blinked. "You've known since Christmas?"

"Since January." He swallowed the lump in his throat. "I've been trying to figure out how to tell you. I wrote you a letter, but . . ."

Joy wrapped her arms around her waist. "I heard your dad say that, but I thought you'd tell me if it was true."

Daniel's heart split right down the middle. "Oh, Joy."

"I can't believe you've known since January and you haven't said anything." Anger thickened her voice as she swiped at her tears.

"I know, but this is hard for me, too."

"Is it?"

"Yes, of course. I don't feel any differently toward you, but it's still hard."

"Why didn't you tell me about not being there when I was born?"

He shrugged. "I guess I was ashamed."

"Ashamed of me?"

"No, ashamed of my behavior. Ashamed I didn't even know I'd fathered a kid until she was almost a year old."

Joy sniffed hard. "I know Mom lied and did crazy things, but I always expected you to tell me the truth."

"I know, and I'm sorry. I messed up by not telling you earlier. I just—"

"Daniel," Drew shouted, running toward the group with Claudia behind him. "Daniel."

"Not now," Bianca said.

"But Matt turned on the mirror ball with the remote, and it's spinning really fast. We can't get it to turn off. I think it's going to fall and bust someone's head open."

"Did you try turning it off at the switch?" Daniel asked.

"Yeah, but it didn't work."

"Okay." Daniel glanced at Joy who turned from him and started walking away. "Joy, don't go."

She shook her head and picked up her pace. "I just need to be alone for a minute."

"*Joy*," Bianca said.

"Is she crying?" Drew asked as Joy strode further and further away.

"I'll check on the strobe light," Bianca said, taking charge. "Daniel, you go talk to Joy, okay?"

The condescending way Bianca spoke frustrated Daniel. "No. I don't want that strobe light injuring anybody. I'll talk to Joy after I sort out things inside."

"Daniel," Bianca said, "you can't just let her run off like that."

"She'll be okay." He headed toward the museum, hoping he was right.

"Fine, I'll go talk to her," Bianca said.

Something inside Daniel snapped. "No. Don't. Just

let her go. This is how she deals with things."

"This is how *you* deal with things. Not everyone ignores things until they become a crisis. I'm going to go talk to her."

All of Daniel's protecting instincts kicked in, and he spoke more harshly than intended. "No. She's my daughter, and I need you to back off. I'm going to take care of the strobe light, then I'll talk to her. So, please, just respect my decision."

Without waiting for Bianca's response, Daniel turned and marched toward the museum. Everything inside him told him he was making a big mistake, but he did it anyway, not knowing what else to do.

Chapter 39

Bianca

*A*NGER FILLED ME as Daniel walked away. What a stubborn, stubborn man. Pushing out a deep breath, I glanced across the lawn at Joy who was rounding the hedge that led to the Rose Garden. Was she going to be okay? Should I ignore what her father said and go after her?

"Bianca?" Claudia asked. "What's going on?"

I shook my head, then because she was going to find out soon enough, I told her everything.

Claudia's eyes widened. "So, Joy's mom might actually be the nurse who took our picture?"

"It's possible."

"Wow. That's crazy."

"I know. It's almost too much to believe."

Claudia nodded. "When Joy and I were gathering the cedar branches for the centerpieces, she told me that her mom was a pathological liar, so I guess it's not too far-fetched to imagine her using a different name."

"No, but it does make me wonder if she had a nursing license."

"Oh, wow. That's scary to think about her in the nursery with all those babies if she wasn't a real nurse."

"I know." I glanced back at the garden, worried about Joy. "Do you think I should go talk to her?"

"I don't know."

"I don't know either. And I don't want to interfere, especially if Daniel's right about Joy needing time alone to process everything. I don't want to make things worse."

Claudia's phone dinged with a text, and she typed back a quick response. Then, she looked at me, her expression guilty.

"What?" I asked.

"I'm really sorry, Bianca, but Leland's here."

"He's here at the museum?"

"In the parking lot." She gestured toward a green Toyota pulling into a parking spot.

"Well, that's okay. I'm sorry he's arriving when everything is so tense, but I'm glad he's here."

Telling myself everything was going to be fine, I followed Claudia to the parking lot to meet her boyfriend. As we approached, a tall, thin kid with a man bun climbed out of the car.

"Hi, Leland. I'm Bianca."

"Hi." He held out his hand, but I pushed past it and gave him a big hug instead.

"Oh, okay." He awkwardly hugged me back.

"I'm so glad you came. You're going to stay for the party, right?"

His body stiffened, and when I pulled away, I caught him shooting Claudia a nervous look. Was I missing something? Turning, I met my daughter's gaze.

"I'm sorry," she said, "but we're not staying."

"You're not?"

She shook her head. "I'm really sorry. My brothers have their birthday party and Clay broke his arm and I just need to go home."

Tears stung my eyes. I knew I was overreacting, but between Claudia leaving, Daniel being mad at me, and Joy upset, I felt crushed.

"I'm really sorry," she repeated.

Blinking back tears, I shook my head. "No, I understand. I wish you weren't leaving, but I get it."

"You do?"

"Of course." I forced a smile, determined to tamp down my disappointment. "Do you want to come inside and say good-bye to everybody before you go? I know things are a little uncomfortable right now . . ."

Claudia glanced at Leland, then back at me. "I guess

I'm anxious to get on the road. Maybe we could video chat later?"

"Okay," I said, trying to sound cheerful and understanding. I glanced over my shoulder, wishing to see Joy headed toward me, but the lawn was empty.

She'll be okay, I told myself. Turning back to Claudia and Leland, I forced a smile. "I left my keys and purse under my seat in the car, so we can drive back to my apartment right now and you can get your things."

"That'd be great," Claudia said.

Nodding, I headed toward my car, hoping she'd follow so we could spend the last few minutes of her time on the island together. Instead, she announced that she was going to ride with Leland. "I want to make sure he doesn't miss the view and all the other sites."

"Sure," I said, quickening my pace to the car so she wouldn't see my tears.

Chapter 40

Daniel

AFTER SECURING THE strobe light and making sure everything was fixed, Daniel went outside looking for Joy. A light rain had begun to fall, bringing with it a cold front.

Hopefully, Joy hadn't gone far. He just wanted to find her and go home where they could talk about all this in private.

Later, he'd find Bianca and apologize for lashing out. He hadn't meant to take his anger out on her. He'd just been so frustrated with himself and the situation. He never should've waited so long to tell Joy the truth.

Heading toward the Rose Garden, he pulled out his phone and called his daughter. To his relief, she answered on the first ring.

"Honey, I'm sorry," he said.

She was quiet for a minute, then she choked back a sob. "Why didn't you tell me?"

He didn't know what part she was talking about, but it didn't matter. "I should've. I wanted to, but I didn't know how."

"You didn't know how?" Anger thickened her voice. "How about, hey, by the way, not only was your mother a pathological liar, but I haven't been honest with you either. That's right, Joy, I didn't even know about you until you were a year old, and guess what? I'm not even your real dad."

His jaw clenched. "I *am* your real dad."

She sniffed hard. "A real dad wouldn't keep something like this from his daughter."

His heart cracked wide open. "You're right. I should've told you."

She exhaled. "Do you even know who my real father is?"

He refrained from repeating that he was her real father. "I don't. If you want, I'll help you find him."

"You'd do that?"

A ray of sunshine filtered through the dark clouds. "Of course."

She started crying softly then. Maybe Bianca had been right. Maybe he shouldn't have let her run away like that.

"Will you meet me at the truck so we can go home and talk about this?" he asked.

"I can't."

"Come on, Joy. It's raining, and I just want to go home."

"I want to go home, too, but . . . I'm lost, Dad."

"What do you mean?"

"I walked through the garden to the viewing area and took one of the trails, but I'm all turned around. I can't figure out how to get back to the museum. I keep thinking if I take the trail that goes uphill, I'll get back to the viewing area, but it just keeps sending me in circles."

"Do you have your backpack with you?" That was his first thought because low blood sugar could cause confusion.

"I left it on the bench in the museum," she said, panicking.

"Okay, honey. Take a deep breath. It's going to be okay. I'll come find you. Do you remember which trail you took?"

"No."

Jogging toward the viewing area, he picked up his pace. "Did the trail go off to the right or the left?"

"I don't remember."

"When did you last eat?" he asked.

When she didn't answer, he freaked out. "Joy?"

No response.

"*Joy.*"

The line was dead. Trying to stay calm, he hung up the phone and called her number again.

She didn't pick up. Had her phone died? Had she passed out?

If her blood sugar was low enough to cause her to lose consciousness, then she was in danger of slipping into a diabetic coma, something that could have grave consequences.

Terrified, Daniel bolted down the path, calling her name and praying with every footstep. *Please, Lord, keep her safe. Let me find her.*

In hindsight, he should've prayed for his own safety as well because somehow he lost his footing. One second he was charging down the trail, and the next he was tumbling down the mountain, swept away in an avalanche of mud, rock, and debris.

Save me, Lord, he called. *Save me.*

Chapter 41

Bianca

AS RAIN POUNDED on the roof of my apartment, I crawled into bed and sobbed. Claudia had left with Leland, Daniel wasn't returning my phone calls, and Joy's life had just been turned upside down. How in the world had things become such a mess?

I should've handled the situation better. I should've taken some time to think about the consequences of telling everyone I thought Joy's mom was my nurse.

Why was I always blurting out the first thing that came to mind? What did it matter if Tiffany/Libby had lied about her name? She probably wasn't even a real nurse, but still, I should've kept my mouth shut.

At some point, I must've fallen asleep. When I awoke, it was dark outside and the rain had stopped. Glancing at the clock on my phone, I realized I was going to be late for Jillian's party if I didn't get moving.

Dressing up for a party was the last thing I wanted

to do, but Jillian was my sister, and I needed to be there. Plus, I'd told Keith I'd come early to help greet the guests. Maybe Joy and Daniel would be there as well, and we could make amends.

For a moment, I thought about calling them, but something stopped me. What if they didn't want to talk to me?

My mind went to the box of Thin Mints sitting in my freezer. I'd bought them for Claudia, but we'd never gotten around to eating them. Everything inside me wanted to scarf down the entire box while getting ready.

And then what? Feel fat and gross the whole night long? I didn't want to feel like that anymore. I didn't want to count calories and be on a diet for the rest of my life, but I also didn't want to keep trying to solve my problems with food.

Oh, Lord. Can you fix me and everything else that's messed up in my life? I know I sure can't.

The words of the Abandonment Prayer came to me then, and I prayed what I remembered as I got ready for the party.

Let only your will be done in me and in all your creatures. I wish no more than this, O Lord.

On the way up the mountain, Jillian called. I answered, determined to play it cool and not ruin her surprise. "Hey, sis."

"*Bianca?*" Her voice was tight.

"What's wrong?"

She inhaled sharply. "I think Keith is having an affair."

The statement was so absurd and so far from the truth that it brought me out of my pity party. Unable to help myself, I burst out laughing.

"You think this is funny?" she said, outraged.

"Oh, Jillian. Your husband is *not* having an affair. Why would you say something like that?"

"He's been acting so strange."

"Strange? Strange how?"

"Secretive. Something is going on. Every time I ask him about it, he gets this glimmer in his eye and tells me it's nothing."

"Hmmm." Despite the huge smile on my face, I tried to sound serious, like I had no idea why Keith was acting strange. "Aren't y'all supposed to go to dinner tonight for your birthday?"

"We are, but he's not home. He's been gone all day. Well, he had the baby this morning, but after bringing her home, he left again. He promised to be back at seven, but he's still not here. I'm about to cancel the babysitter."

"No, don't do that. He'll be there." I imagined Keith had gotten caught up in some party planning detail. Maybe Daniel hadn't been able to fix the strobe light and they were still working on it. Or maybe Vicki never showed up with the desserts. Regardless, hadn't I told Keith his plan to surprise Jillian would backfire?

"I just don't understand," she said, sniffing hard. "Things were going so well, but now . . . I checked the location of his phone, and he's at the Rose Museum."

"Are you sure? Why would he be there? That doesn't make sense. I bet the location system on his phone is messed up."

"I don't know. What if he's having a secret rendezvous up there?"

"He's not having a secret rendezvous. Trust me, if he was going to have an affair, he wouldn't go to the Rose Museum. The rooms there are way too expensive."

"Bianca, that's not helping."

My in-car hands-free phone buzzed with an incoming call from Keith. "Jillian, listen to me. I'm one hundred percent positive your husband is *not* seeing someone else. I have another call I have to take, but I'm sure you'll be hearing from him real soon."

Without saying good-bye, I switched over to Keith's call. "Your wife thinks you're having an affair. Where are you?"

"I'm at the museum."

"Well, call her now and go home. Otherwise, you're

going to have serious problems."

"Bianca—"

"I know, I know. I'm running late, but I'm almost there."

"Is Joy with you?"

"No."

"Have you heard from her?"

The alarm in Keith's voice caused the hair on the back of my neck to prickle. "No. What's going on?"

Before he could respond, I turned into the museum's parking lot and gasped at the sight of several emergency vehicles, their lights flashing.

"*Keith.*"

"I see you. I'm walking toward your car. Just park, and I'll explain everything."

Hands shaking, I pulled into a parking spot and cut the engine. Then, I pushed open the car door and ran to Keith. One look at his stricken face told me something was horribly wrong.

Chapter 42

Daniel

WHITE-HOT PAIN SEIZED Daniel's ankle as he awoke in darkness. He knew he'd slipped and fallen down the mountain, but he had no idea where he was or how long he'd been lying in the mud.

Automatically, he reached into his pocket for his phone. It wasn't there of course. Most likely, it'd been swept away by the river of mud that'd brought him down here.

Joy.

Was she okay? Had she found her way back to the museum?

Sitting up, pure agony shot up his leg. He fumbled in the dark to discover his ankle was trapped beneath a log.

Using his good foot, he tried to free himself, but the log wouldn't budge. Again and again he tried to pull himself free without success.

"Help! Help! Joy!" His frantic voice echoed off the cliffs, taunting him and reminding him he was all alone. Nobody was coming to save him. Nobody knew where he was. Nobody even knew Joy was missing.

Father, I abandon myself into your hands, do with me what you will. Whatever you may do, I thank you.

I *thank you?* Were those really the words of the prayer he prayed every day? How was he supposed to be thankful for something like this? It was one thing to be stuck down here, but not knowing about Joy? How was he supposed to just sit here knowing his daughter was in trouble?

Lord, I want to be grateful for everything that happens to me, but I don't know if my daughter is okay or not. Please keep her safe. Please protect her. Please let her know that I love her.

In the silence, he listened, desperate to hear an answer, desperate to hear the voice of God or his daughter or a hiker calling out to him.

"Help!" he screamed again. "Help!"

Nothing.

He swallowed hard, bile burning the back of his raw throat. *Lord, is this your will for me? To be trapped under this stupid log while Joy needs me? What am I supposed to do?*

God's answer was to send sheets of rain, pelting

down so hard he had to throw his arms over his head for protection.

His thoughts turned to Bianca and the rainstorm they'd been caught in last week during their morning bike ride. Laughing, they'd sped through the streets to the safety of Keith and Jillian's house.

The other couple had welcomed them onto the front porch where they'd been sitting with their baby, watching the storm. Keith went inside and brought each of them a cup of coffee and one of those enormous, plush bath towels that took weeks to dry.

As thunder shook the house, Daniel had cozied up on the outdoor sofa with Bianca, thinking there wasn't any other place he wanted to be. This afternoon, he'd treated her unfairly, snapping at her for something that wasn't her fault. She'd only been trying to help. Only been trying to encourage him to do the right thing.

If he ever got out of here, he'd beg both Joy and Bianca for forgiveness. He'd confront his brother in person and talk to him until Enzo finally forgave him.

Then, he'd do his best to make up for everything. And he'd try to be grateful for this moment that led him to that conclusion.

Chapter 43

Bianca

*H*EART IN MY throat, I ran to Keith. "What happened?"

"Daniel was spotted at the bottom of a ravine by a hiker. They think he fell and is trapped beneath a log."

"Is he okay?" I asked.

"He's moving. At least, that's what the hiker said."

"And what about Joy?"

Keith shook his head. "Nobody knows where she is. Matt, Drew, Hannah, and Kayla have been trying to get ahold of her, but she's not answering her phone."

My stomach sank. "What about her backpack?"

"Her backpack?"

"Her diabetes backpack. She's supposed to have it with her at all times. I can't remember if she had it when she ran off."

"She ran off?"

I nodded.

Keith's phone rang, and he picked up immediately. "Keith Foster... yes... that's great news... no, nobody has heard from her... Yes, Bianca is here now... okay, on our way."

He hung up the phone. "That was the sheriff. He wants to talk to you."

"What's going on?" I asked.

Keith explained as we headed across the parking lot. "They reached Daniel, and he's going to be okay. His ankle is broken, but other than scratches and bruises, he's fine."

"What about Joy?"

Keith shook his head. "Daniel doesn't know where she is, and her phone isn't on. Apparently, she went walking in the woods and got turned around. Daniel's afraid her low blood sugar caused her to get confused."

My stomach sank. "Oh no."

The sheriff looked up as Keith and I approached him. "Bianca Morgan?" he asked.

"Yes."

"I'm Sheriff Strickland. Daniel talked to one of my deputies about Joy. He's hoping she might've found her way back to the museum and you might know where she is."

I swallowed the lump in my throat and shook my head. "I don't. The last time I saw her was several hours ago. She was headed toward the Rose Garden."

"And you haven't heard from her since?"

"No."

A deputy joined us, carrying Joy's backpack. "Here it is, Sheriff."

"That's her diabetes backpack," I said. "If she doesn't have it . . ."

"I know," the sheriff said. "We're sending out a team to look for her right now."

"Everyone who goes looking needs to have a piece of candy or juice," I said. "If her blood sugar is low, she's going to need sugar to bring it back up."

"I understand."

I glanced around the parking lot, which was beginning to fill with guests for the party. Dr. Jacobs, the psychologist who'd worked with Keith last year, strode toward us.

Keith explained the situation, and Dr. Jacobs gave a decisive nod. "I'll put a crew together from the other guests. We'll start from the bottom of the mountain and work our way up."

"Thank you," I said, grateful for his plan of action.

"I'll go with you," Keith said.

Dr. Jacobs nodded, and the two of them left. I turned to the sheriff and told him I was going to check Camp Windham.

Sheriff Strickland frowned. "Do you really think she could make it that far with this rain?"

"I know it sounds crazy, but I just have this feeling she's there."

"Okay," he said. "Keep in touch and tell me what you find."

Heading back to my car, I glanced at the party guests standing outside the museum. Someone else would have to tell them what was going on because I was driving down to Camp Windham right now. I couldn't explain it, but like I'd told the sheriff, I just felt Joy was there.

A car pulled up beside me. As the driver's side window came down, I realized it was Jillian.

"What's going on?" she asked.

As quickly as I could, I explained everything.

"Get in," she said. "I'll drive you to the camp."

I climbed into my sister's van, and we flew down the mountain, making it to the turnoff in record time. Although Jillian's brights were on, it was almost too dark to see the dirt road leading to the camp.

A couple of times, the van got stuck in the mud. Powered by prayer and sheer will, we finally made it.

Using the hidden key, we let ourselves into the main cabin and turned on all the lights. Then, we ran outside, calling Joy's name. I waited, expecting to hear her voice, but she didn't respond.

Where is she, Lord? Where is she?

"We should ring the bell," Jillian said.

"Yes, good idea."

We raced to the chapel, and Jillian climbed the ladder to let down the heavy rope. Pulling together, we rang the bell until our arms felt like they were going to fall off. Then, we rang it some more.

Exhaustion forced us to stop, but we walked back through the camp, yelling Joy's name. When it started to rain again, Jillian stepped under the covered porch and pulled out her cell phone.

I held my breath as she called both the sheriff's department and Keith. Hopefully, someone had found Joy.

Chapter 44

Daniel

*L*YING IN THE hospital bed, unable to do anything but wait for news of his daughter was the hardest thing Daniel had ever done. Because he'd lost his phone, he couldn't even call to see if she'd been found. Instead, he was at the mercy of everyone looking for her.

Over and over, he pleaded endlessly with God. And he'd prayed the Abandonment Prayer, desperate to align his will with the Lord's.

Defeated, he leaned back in bed and closed his eyes. What else could he do?

His greatest fear had come true. He'd lost his daughter, and he was powerless to find her.

The door opened, and for a moment, Daniel's heart lifted. Had they found Joy?

"Hi, Daniel," a salt-and-pepper-haired woman in her forties said. "I'm Dr. Martin, and I'll be performing your surgery tomorrow."

Daniel nodded and did his best to pay attention as the doctor explained tomorrow's procedure. Given Joy's unknown whereabouts, however, he hardly heard a single word Dr. Martin said. When she finished, she asked if he had any questions.

"No, I don't."

"Okay. I want you to know we're all praying for your daughter."

"Thank you."

Dr. Martin reached into her coat pocket and handed Daniel a business card. "Here's my personal cell phone number. Please don't hesitate to call if you have any questions."

"Thank you," Daniel repeated, unable to say anything else.

She started to leave, then she stopped. "Daniel, is there anything I can get you? Something to eat or—" A text interrupted her, and she glanced down at her phone before firing off a reply. "I'm sorry. They need me in the ER."

"It's not Joy, is it?"

"No, it's a ninety-year-old woman who fell, but if I hear anything about your daughter, I'll tell you."

"Thank you."

With a nod, Dr. Martin turned and strode out the door, leaving Daniel lying there, completely helpless and alone.

Chapter 45

Bianca

RAIN BEAT AGAINST the metal roof as I stood under the covered porch at Camp Windham. "I can't believe she's not here," I told Jillian, feeling discouraged. "I know logically it doesn't make sense that Joy would come this way, but I just had this gut feeling she'd be here."

Jillian nodded. "Did I ever tell you about the time I lost Matt at the Target in the Woodlands?"

"No."

"It was horrible. The manager locked all the doors and wouldn't let anyone leave. Christmas was just a few days away, so the store was packed. Everyone was calling Matt's name and looking for him, but it was like he'd vanished. One minute he was riding on the edge of the cart like little kids do, and the next minute he was gone."

"Jillian," I snapped. "This isn't helping. You found

Matt. Matt is perfectly fine. Joy could be anywhere. And she's diabetic. If her blood sugar gets too low, she could die."

Jillian reached out and clasped my hand. "I know, but there's a point to my story."

"Well, get to it."

She nodded and released my hand. "After praying and pleading with God to let us find him, this female cop told me to close my eyes and think about where he could be. She said the connection between mothers and their children is so powerful that I might be able to find him just by thinking about him.

"So, I did what she said. I closed my eyes, and I thought about where he could be. And I saw him. Just like that, I saw him sleeping in one of the cribs underneath a blanket. I opened my eyes and rushed over to the baby furniture department where he was sleeping in a crib just as I'd pictured him."

"That's great," I said, frustrated, "but I still don't get your point."

"My point is you should close your eyes and see if you can feel where Joy is. I know you're not her mother, but you two have a special connection. It might just work."

Desperate to do anything to find Joy, I did as Jillian suggested. I closed my eyes and tried to picture where she could be.

"Anything?" Jillian asked.

Opening my eyes, I shook my head. "It just feels like she's here. It feels like any minute she's going to come strolling into the camp."

"Then we'll wait."

I paced the floor. "I can't just stay here doing nothing. Maybe we can take one of the paths."

I peered into the darkness, helpless. Even if it was light enough to take one of the paths, which one would we take?

Lord, you alone have the power to find her. Find her, please. Find her.

"Bianca?" a small voice said.

"Joy?" My heart pounding, I waited to hear her voice again.

"Did you hear her?" Jillian asked.

Ignoring my sister, I screamed Joy's name over and over and over. She was out there, I knew it.

"Let's go ring the bell again," I said.

Jillian nodded, and we raced back to the chapel. Grasping the rope, we pulled and pulled. The blister on my palm split open, but I kept ringing the bell, knowing Joy would hear it and find her way to me.

And then, there she was, standing less than ten feet from me. There was a horrible gash on her arm, and blood soaked her shirt, but she was here, and she was safe.

Rushing toward her, I threw my arms around her. "Oh, Joy! Honey!"

"I got lost and couldn't find my way back to the museum," she said. "My phone died and—"

Tears streamed down my face as I held her tight. "I know, but we found you, and everything is going to be okay."

Chapter 46

Daniel

THE FIRST TIME Joy called Daniel "Daddy" was amazing. For the longest time, she called him Daniel, which was adorable because she pronounced it "Dan-wul."

Then, one evening he was pushing her on the swing at the park. "Higher, Daddy, higher," she yelled.

His heart filled with so much love it felt like it would burst. "What'd you say?" he asked, wanting to hear it again.

"Higher, Daddy. Please."

Needless to say, he obliged. In return, Joy threw her head back, laughing like she'd never had so much fun. He laughed as well, wondering how he'd ever lived his life without her.

As they walked home that night, Joy slipped her hand in his and looked up at him with pure admiration. "I love you, Daddy."

"I love you, too," he said, hardly able to speak.

This was the memory he was thinking about when the door to his hospital room opened. He feared it was another nurse, coming to take his blood pressure or tell him he needed to get some rest.

Instead, it was Joy.

"Dad!" she shouted, racing across the room.

"*Joy.*" Tears stung his eyes as he opened his arms to embrace his sweet and precious daughter. "Oh, Joy. Are you okay?"

She nodded. "I'm fine. I got lost and my phone died, but Bianca and Jillian found me. Bianca had some candy, which was good because I was feeling low. When we got back to the museum, I checked my numbers and I'm okay."

"You're okay? Are you sure?"

"Yes. I'll check my numbers again in a minute, but they weren't bad. I promise."

"What about your arm?"

Joy smiled. "I cut it on a branch. Bianca washed it out with an unopened bottle of water and bandaged it up for me. A doctor's going to look at it in a minute to see if I need stitches, but I wanted to see you first."

He breathed a sigh of relief. "You're really okay?"

She nodded. "I am."

He held her tight. "Bianca washed out your cut?"

"She did. Jillian volunteered to do it, but Bianca made her drive so we could get to the hospital faster."

"You said there was blood. Bianca didn't pass out?"

Joy laughed. "No, she was like this commando, telling Jillian to drive and me to hold still so she could take care of my wound."

Smiling at Joy's description, Daniel gave his daughter another hug. "You're really fine?"

She nodded. "Yeah, I'm really fine."

He studied her carefully, looking for any signs of distress. She actually looked amazing. Her hair was damp from the rain, and her clothes were dirty, but she seemed healthy and happy.

"I'm sorry I ran off," she said. "I didn't mean to cause so much drama. I just needed a minute to wrap my head around everything. And then I got lost, and my phone died."

"I know. And I'm sorry that I didn't tell you about the paternity test or the first time I met you. I love you so much, honey. I'd never intentionally do anything to hurt you. You know that, right?"

She nodded. "I love you, too."

Overcome with emotion, a tear slid down Daniel's face. He hastily brushed it away and blinked hard. He'd never cried in front of Joy. Never really cried in front of anyone.

"Dad," Joy said, smiling. "I'm fine. Really."

"I know." He wiped his eyes and gave an embarrassed laugh. "Lying here, not knowing if you were okay or not, was torture. I don't know what I'd do if anything happened to you."

"You're one to talk. You had to be carted off in an ambulance."

"And I'm having surgery tomorrow," he added.

"I heard."

A beat of silence fell between them, then he asked about her rescue. "You said Bianca and Jillian found you?"

"Yeah, it was crazy. All these people were looking for me, but Bianca said she had this feeling I was at Camp Windham. I don't know how I got there. It was so dark after my phone died. I kept walking along the trail, thinking it'd lead me back to the museum. Somehow, I eventually came close enough to see the camp lights and hear the bell."

"The bell?"

She nodded. "Bianca and Jillian rang this church bell at the camp. That's how I found them."

"Where's Bianca now?"

"She's in the waiting room with Jillian."

He swallowed. "Will you go get her for me? I need to see her."

Joy nodded. "I'll be right back."

Chapter 47

Bianca

"So, I guess Keith's not having an affair after all," Jillian said as the two of us sat in the hospital waiting room.

I laughed. "Now you understand why I thought you were crazy."

She nodded. "I can't believe I didn't figure out Keith was planning a surprise party for me. All his secrecy and suspicious behavior makes sense now."

I smiled. "He loves you. He's worried about you, but he loves you so much. He'd never do anything to hurt you."

"He's worried about me? Why?"

I chose my words carefully, not wanting to cause any more problems today. "You're not sleeping, you're folding laundry in the middle of the night, and you're trying to do everything yourself."

"He told you that?" She made a scoffing sound. "It's

just been so hard keeping up with everything. I had all this energy when Matt and Drew were babies, but now I'm exhausted, and the house is a wreck."

"You had the boys years ago. You're a little older now. Don't you think your *advanced maternal age* makes a big difference?"

She gave me a loving elbow to the stomach. "Thanks a lot."

I laughed and nudged her back. "It's true."

"I know, but you don't have to remind me."

I shrugged. "Linda Faith is a difficult baby, too. Don't get me wrong. She's delightful and I adore her, but I don't remember the boys being so demanding."

My sister stiffened, making me fear I'd gone too far. "I'm sorry," I said, quickly apologizing. "I shouldn't have said that."

"No, I'm really happy to hear you say that."

"You are?"

"Yes. I thought it was just me. Mom thinks Linda Faith is perfect. She said I've just forgotten how hard it was with the boys. Keith thinks the baby's crying is cute. To me, her shrieks set me on edge. It makes me feel like a bad mother."

"You're not a bad mother, Jillian. Just the opposite."

"Thanks."

"And she has to grow out of it, right? Eventually?

She's not going to be fussy her whole life."

Jillian sighed. "I hope not."

I glanced outside, noticing the rain had finally stopped. "Has seeing her smile made a difference?"

"Yes." For the first time since our conversation, Jillian relaxed. "I was so relieved when she finally smiled."

"Relieved?"

She nodded. "I was beginning to think she didn't like me."

I laughed. "How can someone as intelligent as you believe your own baby didn't like you?"

"I don't know. I probably sound crazy and irrational."

"You do, but lack of sleep and a crying baby can make a person crazy and irrational."

"True. Speaking of crazy and irrational ideas . . . the other day, Keith asked me what I thought about not going back to work."

"What'd you say?"

"I said I didn't know. I love being a nurse, and I worked hard to get where I am in my career. Plus, it took us forever to find someone to take care of the baby."

I nodded, understanding her struggle. "Maybe, after everything you've been through, staying home to take care of your family full time might be a good thing."

"Maybe." She glanced across the waiting room as the emergency room doors opened and Keith strode toward us.

Immediately, Jillian shot to her feet and raced to her husband. They embraced, and Keith kissed the top of her head. "You found Joy? She's doing okay?"

Jillian nodded. "We did. She's back with her father right now."

"I can't believe she made it all the way to the camp in the dark. Even the sheriff didn't think she'd go that way."

Jillian gestured toward me. "Bianca was the one who found her. I just drove the car."

I shook my head. "Had you not told me the story about Matt, we might've missed her."

Keith frowned. "What story about Matt?"

"I'll tell you later." Jillian shot me a warning look that said I needed to keep my big mouth shut.

Keith started to press her about Matt, but Jillian cut him off. "I can't believe you've been planning a surprise party for me this whole time. I was worried you might be having an affair."

Keith stared into his wife's eyes and shook his head. "Never."

My sister swallowed hard. "I just can't believe you went to all that effort for my birthday."

Keith grinned. "We wanted to surprise you, didn't we, Bianca?"

I nodded and refrained from adding that I hadn't been part of the "we" until much later. And the person who'd been part of the "we" all along, Vicki, had been too busy with work to help today.

"So, what's going on with the party now?" Jillian asked. "Are people still there?"

"They are. Half the guests joined the search party in looking for Joy," Keith explained. "Once she was found, they went home to shower and change. The other half have been up at the museum with Matt and Drew the whole time."

Jillian glanced down at her muddy clothes, then looked at me with a guilty expression.

"You should go," I said, reading her mind. "I'm going to wait for Joy and make sure Daniel's okay, but you should go to your party."

"Are you sure?"

"Positive."

Jillian looked at Keith who said, "It's up to you, but I think your sister is right."

"Of course, I'm right. I'll come a little later if I can."

"Well, don't come too late," Keith said. "You're going to want to be there for the big surprise."

"The big surprise?" I asked.

Keith grinned. "Yeah, it's a good one. You'll never guess what it is." He glanced at his clock. "It should be arriving in an hour, so try to make it by then, okay?"

"What is it?" Jillian and I asked at the same time.

Shaking his head, Keith chuckled. "Sorry, ladies. You're going to have to see this one for yourself."

Looking at my sister, I mouthed, "Text me as soon as you find out, okay?"

Keith just laughed. "I promise, neither one of you will ever guess. Even your parents and Vicki don't know. All I can say is it's big, and everyone is going to be blown away."

"Now you have to tell us," I insisted as Jillian nodded in agreement.

Keith shook his head. "No way."

Jillian glanced at me. "Don't worry. I know what his weakness is, so I'll get him to tell me."

Keith just laughed.

Joy came into the waiting room then and apologized. "I'm sorry I caused so much trouble. I shouldn't have run off like that. It was just such a shock. Then I couldn't find my way back to the museum, and you know the rest."

I slipped an arm around her shoulders. "It's okay, honey. The most important thing is you're safe now."

Both Keith and Jillian nodded.

"What about your dad?" Keith asked. "How's he doing?"

"He's okay. He's having surgery on his ankle tomorrow."

"I bet he was happy to see you," I said.

Joy smiled. "He cried."

"Of course, he did," Jillian said. "He was worried sick about you. We all were."

Joy nodded. "I know. Right now, he's worried about messing up your party. Please tell me it's still on."

"It is. Keith and I are headed up there now."

"Good. Will you tell everyone thank you for helping me and my dad tonight?"

"We will," Keith said. "And if you're up to it, you should come, too. Like I told Jillian and Bianca, there's going to be a big surprise."

"What is it?" Joy asked.

Keith just grinned. Then, he took his wife's hand and led her out the door.

After they left, Joy told me her dad wanted to see me.

"Oh, okay." I suddenly felt anxious as I ran a hand through my tangled hair. I'd tried brushing it in the hospital bathroom, but it was no use.

"You look fine," Joy said, smiling at me.

"No, I don't."

She laughed. "My dad's not going to care what you look like. He's just going to be happy to see you."

I hope so. Nervous about seeing Daniel, I walked down the hall to his room. At the door, Joy paused. "I'm supposed to see the doctor about the cut on my arm."

"Do you want me to come with you?"

She shook her head. "No, you go see my dad, and I'll catch up with you later."

I stared at her a beat. "If the doctor says you need a stitch, let's see if we can get a plastic surgeon to do it so it won't leave a scar."

She smiled. "Okay."

"Good luck, honey, and I'll come find you in a minute."

She nodded and headed back to the ER, giving me a chance to talk to her father in private. I needed to apologize to him for my role in all this drama.

Knocking on the door, I pushed it open. "Daniel?"

"Hey." His voice was gravelly, but he smiled.

"Daniel, I just want to say that I'm so sorry. My timing was horrible and—"

He patted the bed beside him. "Come here. You didn't do anything wrong. I'm the one who needs to apologize to you. Do you think you could forgive me?"

I sighed. "Oh, Daniel. There's nothing to forgive."

Blinking back tears, I gave him a huge hug.

He wrapped his arms around me. "I love you."

"I love you, too." He kissed me then, and everything inside me melted. There wasn't any other place I wanted to be than right here, right now, with this man.

When our kiss ended, he took my hand and smiled. "Let's not do that again, okay?"

"What? Make out in a hospital room?"

He laughed. "No, get in a fight that leads to me tumbling down a mountain."

I laughed, and we talked a little more about everything that'd happened. He told me about his upcoming surgery and asked if Joy could stay at my place while he was in the hospital.

"Of course. I'd love to have her."

When Joy returned with news that she didn't need a stitch for her arm, we told her the plan, and she seemed pleased. Then, she asked if she could go to the party. "Kayla said everyone is there, and the DJ is really good."

"You want to leave me so you can go to the party?" Daniel asked, feigning mock outrage.

She nodded. "I know you could've died out there in the woods trying to rescue me and all, but yeah. I want to go to Jillian's party. There's supposed to be a big surprise and fabulous food. Plus, you're probably going to sleep anyway."

Stifling a yawn, he laughed. "You're probably right."

"Does that mean I can go?"

He nodded. "Yes, you and Bianca should definitely go. Just promise you'll come back in the morning before my surgery."

"We promise," Joy said as I nodded in agreement.

"Good. Now, let me get some rest, okay?"

"Okay." Joy gave her dad a quick hug, then headed out the door.

The hug I gave Daniel before leaving wasn't so quick, but eventually, I left with Joy as well.

Chapter 48

Bianca

AFTER SHOWERING AND changing, Joy and I arrived at the party just as Keith offered a toast to his beautiful bride. I'd always thought it pretentious and annoying when a man referred to his wife as his bride, but my handsome brother-in-law managed to pull it off.

By the time he finished speaking, there wasn't a dry eye in sight, mine included. After that, the band played the happy couple's song, "Do I" by Luke Bryan. Keith and Jillian opened up the dance floor, followed by several other couples, including my parents.

I thought about Daniel back in the hospital by himself and said a little prayer he was sleeping well. Tomorrow, he'd have surgery, then he'd begin the road to recovery. I imagined it would take a while for his ankle to fully heal, but thankfully his injuries hadn't been more extensive.

I thought about Claudia and had a moment of sadness that she wasn't here. Hopefully, she and Leland would make it home safely.

Maybe Daniel was right. Maybe blood wasn't thicker than water, and maybe I'd never feel as close to Claudia as I felt to Joy. But I was so grateful to have met her and learn how wonderful she was. And I was so grateful for the healing between my father and me.

As for whether or not Joy's mom was the nurse in South Carolina, maybe we'd never know. I suppose I could do an internet search for the name Tiffany Jackson, but that wasn't happening tonight, not when I was surrounded by friends and family at this beautiful party.

"They look good together," Joy said, gesturing across the room at Vicki who was dancing with a tall, broad-shouldered, military man.

"That's Mac Baumguard, a friend of Keith's. He was engaged last year, but it didn't work out."

"Do you think Vicki's interested in him?"

I shrugged. "Who knows. Vicki's a heartbreaker with the attention span the size of a gnat when it comes to guys. She talks about wanting to get married, but she doesn't seem to be able to stay with anyone long enough for that to happen."

Joy smiled, and we continued watching Vicki and Mac dance. Joy was right in that they did look good together. Then again, Vicki was so cute she looked good with every guy.

When the song ended, Keith took Jillian's hand, and they returned to the stage. "My wife just told me she's ready for her surprise, so without further ado, let's get started."

He clicked a button and a large screen behind them descended. *Great*, I thought, *the surprise is a photo and video montage to my perfect older sister. Prepare yourself, Bianca. You're about to see several unflattering pictures of yourself standing next to your gorgeous sisters.*

Joy leaned over and whispered, "Please tell me the surprise isn't a slideshow."

I shrugged. "I know just as much as you do, but hopefully, there will be more to it."

"*Hopefully.*" Her voice matched the sarcasm I felt.

Speaking into the microphone, Keith said, "I started planning this party a few hours after we opened Christmas presents. Jillian gave me a beautiful photo album filled with pictures, showing all our years together. That album meant the world to me, and I wanted to give my beautiful bride something in return that might mean a fraction as much. So, Jills, sit back, relax, and enjoy the show."

Soft background music played. Then, the crowd sighed as pictures and video clips of Jillian as a child appeared on the screen. Just as I expected, there were several cringe-worthy photos of myself with Jillian. There were also several pictures showing me laughing with my family. I had to blink back tears at the sight of Marcus, riding horses with Jillian, Vicki, and me. What a heartthrob.

Joy must've noticed my emotion in the darkness because she gave me a little side hug. "I wish I could've met your brother."

"Me, too. You would've loved him."

The slideshow continued until it reached a video clip of Anna, Nick, and their kids. I smiled as my sister-in-law and her family wished Jillian a very happy birthday.

In a voice that seemed coached, Travis, my brother's son, turned to his mom. "If only there was a way we could go to Rose Island and wish Aunt Jillian happy birthday in person."

"If only," Hailey said.

The way Travis and Hailey spoke caused the hair on my arms to stand up. *No, this wasn't the surprise, was it?*

Anna spoke next. "That would be pretty amazing. I'd love to see Aunt Jillian and everyone else in person. I miss Rose Island so much."

"Me, too," Gabby, the toddler, said.

Then, Nick looked right at the camera with a gleam

in his eye. "You know what? I think we should go to Rose Island. We've been gone way too long. What do y'all think?"

Anna and the kids leapt to their feet, cheering as the video screen faded to black. The overhead lights turned on and murmurs of excitement spread through the crowd as everyone looked around to see if Nick and Anna were actually here. At first, it seemed like a cruel joke.

Suddenly, a side door opened and my beloved sister-in-law, her gorgeous husband, and their adorable children entered the banquet hall. I joined everyone in clapping and hollering at the sight of them.

"It's them," Joy said, squeezing my hand as we both jumped up and down with excitement. "It's really them."

Laughing, I grabbed her hand, and we raced forward to greet the rest of our family.

⚭

AFTER THE PARTY, Joy and I drove back to my apartment. I desperately wanted to stop by the hospital and tell Daniel all that'd happened tonight, but I didn't want to risk waking him. After everything he'd been through, the man needed his sleep.

Because Joy and I were too wound up to sleep, I

made us each a cup of herbal tea. We settled ourselves on the couch and rehashed the day.

"How are you feeling about everything your dad told you?" I asked. "Is it okay for me to ask that?"

"Of course, it's okay for you to ask that." She shifted the pillows on the couch and relaxed against them. "I'm okay. I think more than anything I was just so shocked. My dad has always been my dad. To find out he isn't my biological father and wasn't there when I was born . . . well, it felt like a betrayal at first."

I nodded, thinking I'd never associate the word "betrayal" with Daniel. While I understood Joy's feelings, her father had only been trying to protect her.

"I get why he didn't tell me. The thing is . . . my dad has always been my rock. Finding out we weren't biologically related was a huge shock."

"I'm sure it was."

She nodded. "Getting lost in the woods, however, put things in perspective for me."

"How so?"

"Well, I kept thinking about all those dorky Father's Day cards and birthday cards I've made for him throughout the years. Can you believe he's actually saved all of them?"

"I believe it."

"They're in this wooden box I made at Diabetes

Camp. Anyway, each Father's Day, he takes them out and looks through all of them. Most of the cards talk about him being the best dad in the world, and here's the thing, he is the best dad in the world. What he told me today doesn't change that. He's still my dad."

I nodded, completely agreeing with her.

"Claudia asked me if I was going to look for my biological father, but I don't think so. At least, not right now."

"You talked to Claudia about this?"

Joy nodded. "We texted when I was waiting for the doctor at the ER. I told her everything, and she said she was sorry she missed all the excitement."

A strange mixture of sadness and happiness filled me. Claudia had texted Joy, but she didn't bother to text me? While I was definitely happy Claudia and Joy had become friends, I felt a little left out.

"She said to tell you 'hi.'"

I nodded and tried not to take it personally. "Did she and Leland make it home yet?"

"Not yet. They were almost there when she texted."

"That's good."

We both finished our tea and yawned at the same time. "Well, we have to be up early to see your dad before his surgery, so we should probably go to bed."

"We probably should," she said, making no effort to

get up. "I never did find out . . . are Nick and Anna back on the island for good or just here for a visit?"

"Well, they're back for as long as the Army says they're back. Anna said they'll be here at least six months, maybe longer depending on Nick's orders."

"Everyone seems really happy about that. Especially your parents."

"They're thrilled. I am, too. I've really missed them."

"Matt and Drew and the other cousins are lucky to grow up with so much family. I wish my cousins didn't live so far away."

The wistfulness in Joy's voice made me sad. "Joy, honey, is there anyone we should call before your dad's surgery tomorrow? I know things have been rough between your dad and your uncle, but what about your aunt or your grandfather?"

She nodded. "Actually, that might be a good idea."

Chapter 49

Claudia

AFTER DRIVING ALL afternoon and most of the night, Leland finally pulled into Claudia's driveway early Sunday morning. "You must be exhausted from all that driving," she said.

He shrugged. "I'm okay. I slept all day Friday and most of Saturday morning, so I'm all right."

"Well, thank you for driving. I really need to learn how to drive a stick shift."

He grinned. "Maybe I just need to buy a new car."

"That would be helpful. But seriously, Leland, thank you for taking me. I'm so glad I met Bianca and the Morgans. I'm glad to be home, too. There's nothing like your own family."

He nodded before letting out an enormous yawn. "All right. Let's get you inside so I can go home."

They both climbed out of the car, and Leland opened the trunk so Claudia could retrieve her things.

She kissed him on the cheek. "See you at school Monday."

He grinned. "You'll see me at two today for the party."

"Oh, you don't have to come. I'm sure the boys will understand."

He shook his head. "I promised I'd film the party. Unlike you, your brothers love being the center of attention and don't mind me capturing their every event on film."

She smiled. "That's true. Okay. I'll see you in a few hours."

"See you in a few hours."

Quietly, so as not to wake anyone, Claudia crept inside and up the stairs to her room. She set her things on the ground, then she slipped off the "Claudia" necklace and put it in her jewelry box. Exhausted, she climbed into bed and slept until Clark woke her up a few hours later.

"You're here," he said, wrapping his arms around her neck and giving her a big hug.

"Of course, I'm here. I promised, didn't I?"

He laughed. "You did, but I didn't know if that was a real promise or a fake one."

"It was a real one."

He grabbed her stuffed elephant and held it against

his chest. "Clay's home, but he's sleeping with Mom and Dad."

"Yeah?"

"Yeah, he has to keep his arm elevated, so Mom and Dad thought it would be easier that way."

"Well, that doesn't sound like fun."

He frowned. "I don't think it's supposed to be fun. Although Nona came over and said she'd teach him how to play canasta when he was feeling better."

"Nona's the best, isn't she?"

Clark nodded.

"Are Mom and Dad still sleeping?"

"Yeah. They didn't get home until late last night."

"Well, how about you and I go downstairs and cook everyone breakfast?"

"Crepes?"

"Of course. It's your birthday, isn't it?"

Despite being tired, Claudia went downstairs with her brother, happy to be home. While she didn't regret going down to Rose Island to meet Bianca, this is where she belonged, especially today on her brothers' birthday.

"How do you make crepes again?" Clark asked.

Claudia listed off the ingredients and helped her brother gather everything before mixing the batter. When it was ready, she heated the skillet, and they began cooking.

A little later, Mom came into the kitchen. "I thought I heard your voice."

"Mom." Claudia crossed the room and hugged her mother. "Leland drove all night so I could be here."

"That doesn't sound very safe. I wish he wouldn't have done that."

"I know, but he did, and now I'm home. How's Clay?"

"Sound asleep, just like your dad. Me? I tossed and turned, worried about you, worried about Clay, and worried about Clark."

"Why were you worried about me?" Clark asked.

"That's just what moms do. They worry about their kids."

"You don't have to worry about me. I'm fine now that Claudia is home."

Mom smiled. "I'm fine, too, now that Claudia is home."

Claudia felt the same way.

Chapter 50

Daniel

*G*ETTING A GOOD night's sleep in the hospital before surgery had to be the biggest joke in the world. All the noises and people coming in and out of Daniel's room made sleeping impossible.

Still, he must've dozed off at some point because he awoke in the morning to find his brother sitting beside his bed. "Enzo?"

"Hey." Enzo came to his feet. "How are you feeling?"

Daniel studied his brother carefully. "I've been better."

"I'm sure."

"What are you doing here?"

Enzo shrugged. "I wanted to see you before the surgery in case . . ."

"In case I died like Mom did?"

Enzo looked away, obviously just as uncomfortable

as Daniel when it came to talking about their mother's unexpected death during what was supposed to be minor surgery. Daniel pushed himself up in bed. "I'm not going to die."

Enzo shrugged. "Good to know. I guess I'll go then."

A slight smile tugged at the corner of Daniel's lips. "You don't have to."

"No?"

Daniel shook his head. "How'd you even know I was here anyway?"

"Your girlfriend called me last night."

"Bianca?"

Enzo nodded. "Unless you have more than one girlfriend."

"No, just Bianca."

"Well, Joy gave her my number. Apparently, she called Miriam and Dad, too."

"Oh. Are they coming?"

"No. Dad's on a fishing trip, and Miriam is too busy with the kids, so it's just me. Is that okay?"

Daniel nodded. "Yeah. I'm glad you're here."

Enzo looked down at the ground and shifted from one foot to the other. "Daniel?"

"Yeah?"

"Maybe now that you're dating a hairdresser she can

do something about all that gray in your hair."

Daniel grinned and ran a hand over his head. "You ever look in the mirror, little brother?"

Enzo shook his head. "Not if I can help it."

WHILE ENZO AND Daniel were rehashing old memories and laughing about the time Enzo fell off the roof while hanging the Christmas lights, Joy and Bianca arrived. Joy rushed across the room and hugged her uncle.

"Who's this girl all grown up?" Enzo asked.

Joy laughed. "It's good to see you, Uncle Enzo."

"It's good to see you, too."

Daniel introduced Bianca to his brother, noticing that Enzo's eyes lingered a little too long on Bianca's face. His brother better not get any ideas because reconciling next time might not be so easy.

"How was the party last night?" Daniel asked.

Joy and Bianca filled him in on all the details. While he'd missed them last night, he was glad they went and were able to see Keith's surprise firsthand.

All too soon, the surgeon entered the room. She greeted everyone and asked if Daniel had any questions.

"No." Daniel tried to sound braver than he felt. He was having a simple surgery. Nothing to worry about. His mother had been a smoker and had had all sorts of health issues that Daniel didn't have. He was going to be fine.

Dr. Martin smiled at Enzo before turning her attention to Bianca. "I heard about your aversion to blood, so we'll make sure to cover up Daniel's incision before you see him."

Bianca gave a hearty laugh. "Thank you, Dr. Martin."

"My pleasure." The surgeon grinned. "Well, it was nice meeting all of you. Daniel, someone will be here shortly to wheel you to surgery."

"Thanks, Doc."

She left, and immediately Enzo made up some excuse about needing to grab breakfast from the cafeteria. "I'll see you after the surgery," he told Daniel.

Daniel nodded, wondering if Enzo remembered those had been the last words he'd said to their mother.

"You're gonna be fine," Enzo said, stepping toward the bed and shocking Daniel by leaning over to hug him.

Daniel was so stunned by the gesture that all he could do was return his brother's hug. When Enzo pulled away, he gave Daniel one last nod before walking out the door.

"That was weird," Joy said.

Daniel shrugged. "You know your uncle. He can be

a little weird."

"No kidding." She giggled, putting Daniel at ease. "Are you doing okay, Dad?"

"Yeah, I'm fine. I don't like hospitals, and I'm ready to get the surgery over with, but I'm fine."

She groaned. "I don't like hospitals either."

"Of course, you don't." Daniel smiled at her, realizing she'd been through so much more than him when it came to medical issues. He seriously needed to stop making this operation into a bigger deal than it was. Still, there were some things he needed to set straight.

"Joy, would you mind giving me a minute to talk to Bianca?"

"Sure." She came over and hugged him one last time. "Good luck, Dad. I love you."

"I love you, too, sweetheart." Daniel tried to keep the waver out of his voice. This *wasn't* the last time he'd see her. Everything was going to be fine.

After Joy left, Bianca sat beside him, entwining her fingers with his. "You seem nervous. Are you feeling okay?"

He nodded. "Look, I know we haven't been together long, but I don't want to go under the knife without telling you something."

"You love me?"

He grinned at her and squeezed her hand. "I've already told you that, but yes, I do love you."

"I love you, too." Her tone was serious, and he wished he didn't have to say what he needed to say. "Look, my mother died during surgery. She went in for something minor and didn't make it."

Bianca's eyes widened. "*Daniel.*"

"I know. It's scary, but I'm much healthier than my mother was. Still, her death was unexpected and left a huge mark."

"I'm so sorry. I'm sure that makes you anxious about this surgery, but Dr. Martin is well respected. I went to high school with her brother."

"Of course, you did."

Bianca gave a little laugh, filling Daniel with love and hope. "Don't worry, okay?" she said. "I'll be praying for you the whole time and so will my family."

"I appreciate that, but just in case I don't make it—"

"You're going to make it."

"I know, but just in case I don't, I need you to do me a favor."

"Anything."

He pushed out a deep breath. "Will you take care of Joy? I realize she's legally an adult, but she needs a mother. Especially if something happens to me."

Tears filled Bianca's eyes. "Joy is like a daughter to me. I promise I'll be there for her. In fact, I'm planning on being in her life until she kicks me out of it. Which will hopefully be never."

"What about my life?"

She smiled. "If it's okay with you, I'd like to stay in your life for a long time, too."

"So that's a yes?"

"A yes?"

Daniel nodded. "A yes that you'll marry me."

"*Daniel.*"

He put up a hand to stop her protest. "This isn't an official proposal, and I don't mean to put you on the spot, but I love you, Bianca. I'm not just saying that because I'm scared or under the influence of these painkillers. I know we haven't been dating very long, but I want to spend the rest of my life with you."

"Oh, Daniel." Her eyes filled. "Are you sure?"

He nodded. "I've never been more sure of anything in my entire life."

"What about kids?" she asked.

"What about them?"

"If it's not too late, I want to have kids. How do you feel about that?"

He grinned so hard his cheeks hurt. "I can't think of anything more I'd like to do than have a baby with you."

"Really?"

"Really. But first, maybe we could get married? Maybe go to Hawaii or Fiji for the honeymoon?"

She laughed. "Yes, but you have to ask my dad for permission first. That's really important to him."

"I already have."

Her eyes nearly popped out of her head. "You have?"

"No. Just joking. But I will. I promise."

She gave him a light smack on the arm. "You're horrible."

"Hey, careful of the IV, woman."

The door opened, and two men dressed in scrubs entered. "Mr. Serrano? Are you ready for surgery?"

"I am." Daniel gave Bianca a wink. "We'll finish this discussion later, okay?"

She nodded, then she brushed her lips across his. "I love you, Daniel."

"I love you, too."

Chapter 51

Bianca

GIVEN WHAT DANIEL told me about his mother dying during surgery, it was difficult waiting for news that the operation was successful. Fortunately, Joy, Enzo, and I had lots of visitors including my parents, Jillian, Vicki, and Anna.

Vicki brought muffins and coffee for everyone in the waiting room as well as the hospital staff. Anna filled us in on their temporary orders to leave Germany for Rose Island.

"Does that mean you'll be asking for your old job at the salon?" I teased. "All the booths are filled, but I could probably find you another station."

She shook her head. "No. My days at the salon are over. Between flying and taking care of my family, I don't really have time to cut hair."

"Of course, you don't," my mother said, squeezing her hand.

I winked at Vicki and Jillian. "Guess who just moved into the role of favorite daughter?"

My mother scoffed. "You're all my favorite daughters. Every last one of you."

I rolled my eyes, and everyone laughed, even Jillian. She seemed especially happy today. I guess Keith knew what he was doing when he planned the surprise party, certain it would boost her spirits.

My mom inquired about Joy's health, meaning her diabetes. "I'm doing really well," Joy said, not appearing to be bothered by the question.

My mom heaved a sigh of relief. "That's good. That's really good."

Thankfully, Joy was saved from further scrutiny when Claudia called me via video chat. The connection was perfect, and I was able to introduce her to Anna as well as Daniel's brother, Enzo.

Enzo was a funny character. While he and Daniel were identical twins, Daniel had taken better care of himself over the years. Plus, Daniel had a sweetness about him that Enzo seemed to lack.

Not that Enzo wasn't nice. In fact, when everyone but the two of us went to get coffee, he told me I was good for his brother.

"Thanks," I said. "I think he's good for me as well."

"So, how did you two meet?"

I told him about meeting Joy and Daniel at church four years ago and how being stiffed by my first contractor had led to Daniel renovating my kitchen. Enzo listened intently, then he told me about his girlfriend, Wilma.

"How long have you been dating?" I asked.

"About seven years. She wants to get married, but I don't know."

I stared at him, incredulous. "You don't know?"

He shrugged. "I imagine we'll eventually get married. Just not right now, you know?"

"Oh, I know all right," I said, recalling all the women from the salon who'd dated his type.

"Excuse me?"

"You're never going to marry that poor girl."

"That's not true."

"It is true. You may love her, but if you've dated her for seven years and still don't know if you want to marry her, then the answer is no."

"How can you say that? You don't know me."

"Maybe not, but I do know that you need to let this woman go so she can find someone else."

"But I love her."

"Then marry her. But stop making her wait. It's not fair to let her waste her best years on you."

He stared out the window. "Well, Bianca, why don't

you tell me what you really think?"

I laughed. "Sorry. I'm not trying to run your life, but the older a woman gets, the harder it is for her to find someone. Trust me. And if she wants kids, well, that window of opportunity isn't open forever, you know."

He studied me closely to the point that I felt uneasy. He must've sensed my discomfort because he apologized. "Sorry, you just remind me of someone I know."

"Who?"

He shook his head and didn't answer my question. "You may be right about Wilma, but—"

"Of course, I'm right."

He laced his fingers together, placed them on top of his head, and leaned back in his seat. "I like you, Bianca. You speak your mind, which is probably why Daniel's so crazy about you."

A thrill skittered through me. "You think Daniel's crazy about me?"

"Yeah, I can tell by the way he looks at you."

I grinned, feeling happy and secure that everything was going to work out. As if to prove my point, the surgeon entered the waiting room with a huge smile on her face.

Chapter 52

Claudia

ALTHOUGH CLAUDIA ENJOYED video chatting with Bianca and Joy, she didn't regret coming home early. Not only had she been able to help her mother with the party, but Clark had said she was the best sister in the world. Clay had given her the privilege of being the first person to sign his cast, and Nona said she was proud of her.

That night, after the boys fell asleep, Claudia went into her parents' room where they were both reading in bed. "Hey, sweetheart," her mom said, looking up from her book.

"Can I talk to you?" Claudia asked.

"Of course."

She sat at the foot of their bed, remembering how she used to crawl in between them when she was a little kid. She'd long since outgrown that childhood practice, but she had fond memories of falling asleep while they read long into the night.

"What's on your mind?" her father asked, closing the cover of his iPad. "Is everything okay?"

She nodded and looked down at the quilt Mom had made during her short-lived quilting phase. "I should've told you, but one of the reasons I went to Houston this weekend with Leland . . . well, besides meeting his grandmother . . ."

"Please don't tell me you eloped," Dad said.

Claudia groaned. "No, it's nothing like that."

"Good because I'd be very disappointed if I didn't get to walk my only daughter down the aisle."

She smiled. "I promise I won't get married without telling you first."

"Okay, then whatever you did is probably fine."

Claudia blinked, suddenly overcome with emotion. "It's just that—"

"What is it?" her mother asked, concerned.

"I found my birth mother. Well, she found me. I wasn't looking for her. On my birthday, she sent me a letter saying she wanted to meet me. She lives on Rose Island, which is about an hour's drive from Leland's grandmother's house."

"How was it?" Mom asked, her voice calm.

"It was fine. She's nice. Her name is Bianca Morgan, and she owns a hair salon called The Last Tangle."

"Cute name for a salon," Mom said.

Dad didn't say anything, and the pain in his eyes made Claudia feel guilty. "I wanted to tell you, but I was afraid of hurting your feelings."

Dad shook his head. "Wanting to know where you came from is normal. I'm not hurt by the fact that you went to meet your birth mom. I just wish you would've told us that was the reason for the trip."

Mom nodded in agreement. "We always said we'd help you find her when you turned eighteen. In fact, Dad and I were talking about it the other day. We didn't know whether or not to mention it to you first or wait until you came to us."

"I should've come to you. The whole time I was there I felt bad you didn't know."

Dad shook his head. "Don't feel bad. You're an adult now, and being an adult means making choices, questioning those choices, and ultimately living with the choices you make. Honestly, sometimes being an adult is highly overrated."

Mom smiled. "Dad wants to buy a boat, but we discussed the budget tonight, and he's a little disappointed."

Dad shrugged. "Like I said, sometimes being an adult is highly overrated."

Claudia smiled. Mom was all about the budget,

something she'd never appreciated until Dad got sick and money became an issue. Thanks to Mom, they'd been okay.

"So, what is your birth mom like?" Dad asked. "Is she kind and wonderful like you?"

Claudia swallowed hard, then she told her parents about Bianca and the Morgan family. At first, she was guarded, but eventually her words gained momentum, and she told them everything—teaching Bianca how to play the violin, walking on the beach, dinner at the ranch, and helping decorate for the party at the Rose Museum.

At some point, she slipped in between her parents on the bed so she could show them her pictures, including the one she'd snapped of the framed photo taken by the nurse who may or may not have been Joy's mom.

"You changed so much once we got you home from the hospital," Mom said, studying the picture closely.

"That's right," Dad said. "We were concerned about how much weight you lost at first, remember?"

"I remember." Mom's voice sounded wistful. "I had this idea that I'd try to breastfeed you, but when that turned out harder than I imagined, I put you on formula. And despite my guilt, you thrived."

"Why did you feel guilty?"

Mom grinned and smoothed back Claudia's bangs.

"I just wanted the best for you. All the literature says breastfeeding is best, and it's entirely possible for adoptive mothers to do it, but I couldn't figure it out. I felt like a huge failure."

Claudia leaned her head against her mom's shoulder. "It's really okay, Mom."

"I know. It just felt like such a big deal at the time."

The three of them lapsed into silence, then Dad asked, "So, are you glad you went?"

Claudia nodded. "The trip was nice, and the Morgans are great, but I'm happy to be home. Besides, it kind of got awkward at the end."

"Awkward how?" Dad asked. "They weren't rude to you or anything, were they?"

"No." Claudia explained about Daniel having to reveal he wasn't Joy's biological father after Bianca thought that Joy's mom was the nurse from the hospital.

"Was she?" Dad asked.

"I don't know. Apparently, Joy's mom was a pathological liar, so it's entirely possible."

"Yikes," Dad said. "I've only encountered one pathological liar in my life, but it was rough because she literally lied about everything. Trying to figure out what was true and what she'd made up was nearly impossible."

"Well, Joy's mom was such a skilled liar that she

even falsified the paternity test Daniel took when Joy was a baby. That's why Daniel didn't know he wasn't Joy's biological father until this year when he took another test."

"That's horrible," Mom said.

Claudia nodded. "When we saw the photograph of Joy and her mom, and Bianca said something about recognizing Joy's mom as the nurse from the hospital, Daniel was kind of forced to tell Joy right then. I think he would've rather told her under different circumstances."

"Of course," Dad said. "Secrets are always best revealed in private, but most people don't confront them until they're forced to do so."

"You picked me up from the hospital in South Carolina, right?" Claudia asked.

"That's right," her parents said.

"Did you ever meet the nurse Bianca was talking about?" Claudia scrolled through her phone until she found the picture she'd taken of the photograph of Joy and her mom. "Here, this is her."

Mom took Claudia's phone and enlarged the image. Then, she showed it to Dad, whose eyes grew wide. "That's the nurse the police questioned us about after the kidnapping."

"The kidnapping?" Claudia stared at Dad. "What

are you talking about?"

Dad glanced at Mom before explaining. "The day after we brought you home, we learned that a baby had been kidnapped from the hospital. The police questioned us, but we didn't have any information for them. This nurse, Tiffany Johnson or Jackson or something like that—"

"Jackson," Claudia said. "At least that's what Bianca said."

"Okay. Tiffany Jackson. Well, she was one of the suspects because she was working in the nursery at the time the baby went missing. Police thought she was involved because she had a baby, but her baby's blood type turned out to be different from the missing one."

"Did they ever find the missing baby?" Claudia asked.

"I don't know," Dad said. "One of the janitors came under suspicion because he'd lied on his application about having a prior arrest, but I don't think anything came out of that. Honestly, I stopped following the story because it was so heartbreaking thinking about those poor parents when your mother and I finally had a child of our own."

Mom scrolled through her phone and shook her head. "I just looked up the case, and this article doesn't say anything about the baby being found, but it shows a picture of the nurse. I'm pretty sure it's the same woman as Joy's mom."

They placed the phones side by side, and after comparing the pictures, Claudia and her parents agreed that Joy's mom and the nurse were the same person.

"Given what you said about her being a pathological liar," Mom said, "it's hard not to jump to the conclusion that she was somehow involved."

"But why would she kidnap a baby if she already had Joy?" Claudia asked.

"Sex, power, money, or mental illness," Dad said. "Those are four common motivations for people to choose evil over good."

"Well, according to Joy, her mother was definitely mentally ill, but it still doesn't prove that she had anything to do with the kidnapping."

Mom shuddered. "It's just so horrible. I can't imagine losing a child, but not knowing where they are or what happened to them . . ."

"I know," Claudia agreed.

Dad glanced at the article on Mom's phone and typed something into his iPad. "Oh, whoa," he said, staring at the screen.

"What?" Claudia and Mom said together.

When Dad didn't answer, a sickening feeling took up residence in Claudia's gut. Leaning over, she saw that her father was looking at a picture of a young girl with her parents.

"She looks just like our Claudia," Mom said, her voice tight.

The little girl did look just like Claudia. "I don't understand."

"It's the Klines," Dad said. "The family whose baby was kidnapped."

Claudia pointed to the daughter. "But she looks just like me. At least, that's what I used to look like when I was her age. How can that be?"

Dad's Adam's apple bobbed up and down. "I think it's because—"

"Do you think I'm the baby who was kidnapped?" Claudia's heart pounded so hard her chest hurt. "But you adopted me. You didn't kidnap me."

"No, of course not," Mom said. "We adopted you from a legitimate agency. We didn't take you from the Klines."

Nobody spoke for a minute, then Dad said, "Do you think maybe the babies got switched? Do you think that somehow we got the Klines' baby and Bianca's baby is the one that's missing?"

Claudia shuddered, thinking that was the only logical explanation.

Chapter 53

Bianca

*A*FTER DINNER AT Daniel's house, I helped Joy clean the kitchen while Daniel sat in the living room, looking for a movie for us to watch. His ankle was propped on the coffee table, elevated and packed with ice per Dr. Martin's instructions.

When the doorbell rang, Joy went to answer it. As I dried the last dish, I could hear her talking to Kate Tate.

"I've been out of town," Kate said, coming into the house. "I came as soon as I heard. Daniel, you poor thing."

"It's not too bad," Daniel said.

"You should've called me. I would've come directly from the airport."

"Oh, that wouldn't have been necessary. Between Joy and Bianca—"

"Bianca?" Kate said my name as if it were a joke.

Smoothing down my shirt, I stepped around the

counter, trying not to feel self-conscious about my appearance. "Hi, Kate. Is that tater tot casserole? Do you want me to put it in the refrigerator for you?"

Her grip seemed to tighten on the dish as though she was afraid I might steal it and eat it on the spot. For a brief moment, my stomach knotted, filled with all the passive-aggressive insults Kate had ever tossed my way.

Then, I let it go. I literally let it all go.

Just like Yadira had told me, I couldn't change the way Kate felt about me. I couldn't even change the way she treated me.

No, all I could do was be myself and try to love her. Regardless of her attitude toward me, God had called me to love my enemies, even Kate.

"That's so nice of you to bring Daniel dinner," I said, sincerely meaning it. Or at least, trying to mean it. "I know tater tot casserole is one of his favorites. I'm not the best cook, so I'm sure he appreciates it."

She relaxed, realizing she had the upper hand. "Yes, everyone loves my cooking."

"I know they do." I smiled as she reluctantly handed me the casserole dish.

"Let Joy take it," Daniel said, patting the seat beside him. "Come sit down, Bianca, and put up your feet. I'm sure you're worn out from taking care of me all day."

"I'm tired, too," Joy said.

Daniel chuckled. "Okay, princess. Once you put away the casserole, you can take a break, too."

Joy took the dish into the kitchen, and I sat beside Daniel who took my hand and smiled up at Kate. "Bianca and Joy have done everything for me today. Joy obviously has no choice on account that she's my daughter, but I guess this is what Bianca signed up for."

"There's a sign-up?" Kate asked.

Daniel laughed. "No, I meant when she signed up to be my . . ."

Daniel didn't say *future fiancée*, but that's what he'd been calling me in private. It wasn't official yet, but we'd made plans to go ring shopping as soon as he was up to it.

"Your girlfriend?" Kate asked, finishing Daniel's sentence.

Daniel squeezed my hand. "Yes, my girlfriend."

"Oh, I didn't realize you two were dating, although that makes sense. You two are perfect for each other."

I didn't think Kate was sincere, but I chose to give her the benefit of the doubt.

"Well, I should probably get going," Kate said, heading toward the door.

I suddenly remembered that Kate's kids had gone out of town for spring break this week. I imagined not having them home would make life lonely for her.

"Kate, do you want to stay and watch a movie with us?" I asked, surprising myself.

For a moment, I thought she might say yes. Then, she offered an amused smile. "No, thank you, Bianca. I'm afraid I have more important things to do than watch TV, but you go ahead."

Instead of feeling judged, I leaned back against the couch cushions. "You know what? I think I will."

After she left, Joy joined Daniel and me on the couch, and the three of us watched the movie *I Can Only Imagine*. Just when Amy Grant made her appearance on screen, there was another knock on the door.

"I'll get it." I strode across the room, and when I opened the door, I found a clean-cut man dressed in a suit, holding a leather briefcase.

"Bianca Morgan?"

"Yes?"

"I'm Special Agent Banks." He showed me his badge and explained he was with the FBI. "I need to speak to you and Daniel Serrano regarding Tiffany Jackson."

I glanced at Daniel before turning my attention back to the man. "Daniel is recovering from surgery."

"Yes, Ms. Morgan. I'm aware of that. I'll try to make my visit as brief as possible."

"Come in," Daniel called from the couch, pausing the movie.

Despite my apprehension, I stepped back and allowed the agent to come inside. Daniel beckoned from the couch. "I'd stand to welcome you, but—"

"I understand." The agent smiled like this was just a regular visit from your local FBI agent. No big deal.

"Do we need a lawyer?" I asked, remembering my father had told me to always seek counsel before talking to the police. I supposed the same advice applied to the FBI, but I didn't know. I'd never interacted with an FBI agent before.

"You don't need a lawyer," the agent said. "I'm just here to ask a few questions and provide you with some information."

What kind of information? I wondered.

"Joy," Daniel said. "Would you mind giving us a minute? Maybe you could go check on the garden or—"

"Actually, this concerns Joy as well," the agent said.

My stomach twisted. Had Joy done something wrong? No, the agent had said this was regarding Tiffany Jackson. He probably just wanted to follow up on my belief that Joy's mom had worked as a nurse in South Carolina under a different name.

I'd meant to do a search for Tiffany online to compare her photo with the one in the museum, but with Claudia leaving, Daniel's accident, Joy missing, Jillian's party, Daniel's talk of marriage, his surgery, and everything else that'd followed since seeing the picture, I hadn't gotten around to it.

"Please, have a seat," Daniel said, gesturing to the chair opposite the couch. The agent sat while Joy and I resumed our previous spots.

"I'll get right to the point," Special Agent Banks said. "Ms. Morgan, I understand that you recognized Tiffany Jackson from the photograph of Joy and Libby Serrano in the museum."

I nodded. "I thought Libby and Tiffany were the same person, but I don't know for sure. They may have just had the same scar."

The agent pulled a photograph from his briefcase and placed it on the coffee table. "Can you identify this woman?"

I studied the photo that showed Tiffany dressed in nurse's scrubs, carrying a large purse. The quality wasn't the best, and I imagined the photo had been taken from a hospital security camera.

"That's Libby," Daniel said before I could speak.

"Are you certain?" the agent asked.

"Positive. But what's this all about?" Daniel asked.

The agent turned his attention to me. "Ms. Morgan, were you aware that a baby was kidnapped from the hospital the day after you were discharged?"

"What?"

The agent nodded. "The FBI spoke to Wynona Morgan, your aunt, after the baby went missing. While you were out of the residence, her home was searched."

"Why?" I said, shocked and confused. "Did you think my Aunt Wynona stole the baby?"

"All leads had to be checked, but after a thorough investigation, you, your aunt, and your mother were removed from our list of suspects."

"Of course, we were removed from the list of suspects. I gave my baby away; I didn't try to steal another one."

The agent nodded and started to speak, but I interrupted him. "Why didn't I know about this?"

"You'll have to ask your aunt and mother. Perhaps they didn't want to cause you unnecessary worry."

I sat back, shocked. The days after I left the hospital were a complete blur. I mostly slept, but at some point, my mother had woken me and forced me to go next door to visit the retired librarian because Aunt Wynona's house was being sprayed for bugs. I remembered thinking it was such a random event. Now, I understood they needed me out of the house while the police searched for the missing infant.

"Your mother and aunt were concerned about your baby," the older agent continued. "The FBI assured them that your child was safe with the family who adopted her."

"Yes, I recently met Claudia, so I know she's fine. But what about the missing baby? Was she ever found?"

Something shifted in the agent's demeanor. From his briefcase, he withdrew two photos and set one of them on the coffee table. I stared down at the young couple, thinking there was something familiar about the woman, but I couldn't quite place her.

"This is Giselle and Charlie Kline, the couple whose baby was kidnapped," the agent explained. "The photo was taken eighteen years ago, but here's a more recent one that shows them with their ten year-old-daughter, Paulette."

"Paulette," I said, happy that the Klines had been able to have another child. Not that one child could replace another. Still, I didn't even know these people, and it broke my heart to think about what they'd been through. Maybe this second child had brought them some comfort.

"When was this photo taken?" Joy asked, leaning closer to get a better look.

"Just a few months ago," the agent said.

I stared down at the photo, confused. "But she looks—"

"Paulette looks just like Claudia," Joy said.

My heart leapt to my throat. Joy was right. The

Klines' daughter did look just like Claudia. And even more unsettling was the fact that Paulette and her parents were all holding violins.

"They own a music studio," Special Agent Banks said. "They're a very musical family."

"Like Claudia." My heart was beating so hard I could barely think.

"Are you saying Claudia was the baby kidnapped from the Klines?" Daniel asked.

The agent nodded, and had I not been sitting down, my knees would've buckled.

"But what about my baby?" I asked. "If Claudia belongs to the Klines . . ." I couldn't breathe. *Oh, Lord, what happened to my baby? Who took her and where is she?*

My stomach roiled, and I thought I might be sick. Daniel took my hand and held it tight.

"We've developed a theory," the agent said as if he hadn't just delivered the worst news of my life. How was I supposed to care about his theory when my baby was missing?

Oh, Lord, where is she? Where is she?

"While working at the hospital," the agent continued, "Tiffany told several people that she had a newborn at home. We believe that was a lie. Our theory is she switched the Klines' baby with yours and then stole your baby to raise the child as her own."

Joy sucked in a sharp breath. "You think my mother kidnapped me?"

The agent nodded. "When the Klines' baby was reported missing, Tiffany was questioned, but for some reason, authorities believed her claim that the child was hers. According to the report, agents took a sample of blood from Tiffany's baby, but that blood type didn't match the Klines because—"

"Because I wasn't the Klines' baby," Joy said, piecing it all together. "I was Bianca's baby. I *am* Bianca's baby." Joy turned and stared at me with wide eyes. "You're my mother, Bianca."

"That's our theory," the FBI agent said. "We'll have to confirm it with DNA testing."

My body shook as all the pieces of this jumbled puzzle slid into place. I didn't need a DNA test. I knew with every fiber of my being that Joy was my daughter.

Her eyes filled. "Of course, you're my mother. It all makes sense. All of it."

Daniel started to speak, but his voice cracked. Without a word, he wrapped his arms around Joy and me and pulled us close. I clung to him, and I clung to Joy, overwhelmed by a mixture of confusion, terror, understanding, and jubilation.

Tears streaming down my face, I didn't know whether to be happy, sad, mad, or just relieved. In the end, I chose to be happy that, through a miracle, I'd been reunited with my daughter.

In the end, I chose joy.

Chapter 54

Bianca

*F*INDING OUT THAT Joy was the daughter I'd carried for nine months, given birth to, and had held in my arms all those years ago was unbelievable. They say that truth is stranger than fiction, and honestly, the whole thing was surreal.

Looking back, I should've known it all along. While Joy and I didn't look like twins, there was a similarity between us I couldn't believe I'd missed.

Daniel's brother claimed he'd seen the resemblance the first time he met me. My mother said the same thing about Joy, although neither one of them had voiced their opinion until after the truth was revealed.

As wonderful as this discovery was, part of me felt a loss. After all, for a brief time, I'd thought of Claudia as my daughter. In many ways, I still did even though I knew that between the Cavenaughs and the Klines Claudia had enough people to love her.

A few weeks after Claudia returned from meeting the Klines, she called while I was blow-drying my hair. We'd exchanged a few texts, and I'd learned that her biological mother was originally from France. She'd met Claudia's biological father while studying music in Charleston, South Carolina. They now owned a music studio just outside of Charleston.

After talking for a few minutes, Claudia told me she was going to return the "Claudia" necklace. "It's part of your family history," she explained. "I wouldn't feel right keeping it."

"*You're* part of our family history," I said. "I want you to have it, and I'm sure my dad feels the same way. In many ways, it's because of you that my dad and I were able to reconcile."

She grew quiet, and I asked what she was thinking.

"I'm thinking that after everything that's happened, hearing you say that is one of the nicest things anybody could've said to me." Her voice wavered, and she sniffed hard.

"Oh, Claudia, honey. Are you okay? I'm sure this has been really hard."

"It has. The Klines want me to come live with them in South Carolina and my parents . . . well, they're trying to be understanding and supportive, but all this is breaking their hearts."

"I can't imagine."

She pushed out an exasperated breath. "Maybe I'll just move to Rose Island and go to community college with Joy. She told me she's staying on the island after high school graduation so she can continue working with the interior designer while she takes a few classes."

"She is, and we would love to have you here on Rose Island. You could even stay in the guest room in my apartment."

She sighed. "I know I can't really do that, but maybe I could bring both my families down for a visit."

"You're welcome anytime. I mean that."

"I know you do."

Claudia and I ended our call with promises to talk soon, but I imagined she'd be pretty busy over the next few months with finals and sorting out her life. My prayer for her was that she and both her families would be able to make peace with what happened to them.

Picking up my mascara, I resumed getting ready. Tonight, Vicki and I were babysitting Anna and Nick's kids so they could attend some military event on post. Twelve-year-old Hailey had asked Vicki and me to dress up so she could practice taking pictures of us on the beach with her new camera.

In the past, I would've shied away from having my picture taken, but I was getting better at that. As instructed by Hailey, I was wearing my blue and white dress with pearl earrings.

Glancing at myself in the mirror, I thought, *Not bad.* I turned to the side and placed a hand on my stomach, which had gone down a little bit due to the small amount of weight I'd lost. I hadn't been dieting, I'd just been trying to embrace the idea that I didn't need to punish myself for being overweight. And I didn't need to punish myself for wanting a piece of cake or for even eating that piece of cake.

At the same time, I'd finally demanded that Vicki stop filling my break room with all sorts of tempting sweets. While I understood her heart was in the right place, sugar was a real problem for me. The less I consumed, the better I felt. And that meant limiting the number of sweets that surrounded my personal space.

Right on time, Vicki pounded on my door. As usual, she barged into my apartment without an invitation, claiming that we were going to be late.

"I'm ready," I said, coming down the hall.

"Hello, hot mama!" She grinned at me, and I laughed.

"Hello yourself," I said. "You're looking very pretty."

"Maybe, but Bianca . . . you look gorgeous." Her voice held so much emotion I wondered if something was wrong.

"Are you okay?"

She nodded. "We better go."

"Vicki? What is it?"

She blinked hard. "Nothing. At least, nothing I want to talk about, okay?"

"Okay."

Giving my sister her privacy, I said nothing as we drove out to Nick and Anna's house. Something was obviously going on with my little sister. She'd been acting strange the last few days, and I wondered if she was just jealous that things were going so well between Daniel and me.

Although Daniel and I were still planning on getting married, we'd decided to wait until this fall to get engaged. Given everything that'd happened, I was perfectly fine with that. In fact, now that I had my daughter, I was perfectly fine with anything.

At Nick and Anna's house, I knocked on the front door, but nobody answered. Vicki stepped right past me and walked into the house. "Hello?"

"Do you think they forgot or had a change of plans?"

"They're probably down at the beach." Vicki marched through the kitchen and opened the back door, leading to the porch.

I followed her, awed as usual at the incredible view of the ocean from Nick and Anna's house. Down on the beach were several lit lanterns arranged in the shape of a large heart. A group of people stood nearby, including a man dressed in a black tux.

"Oh look, Vicki. I think someone's going to propose. I wonder if we know who it is."

My little sister gave me a blank stare.

"What?" I said. "Have you become so jaded about love and marriage that you don't think a beachside proposal is romantic?"

She gave me the biggest eye roll of her life, then she laughed, the sound filling me with relief that she was okay. "Oh, Bianca. Are you that dense? Look again."

"What?"

"Just look, okay?"

I glanced back down at the beach, and after a beat, I realized the group of people was our family. And the man in the tux was Daniel.

My Daniel!

My hands shot to my face. "What's going on?"

"What do you think is going on?"

"Daniel's proposing? Tonight?"

She nodded.

"I don't believe it."

"I guess not," she said, laughing again. "Thank

goodness I'm here, otherwise the poor man might've been left standing on the beach all night waiting for you to clue in."

"So we're not babysitting?"

She shook her head. "No, we're not babysitting. That was just a distraction to get you here tonight."

"Oh, Vicki." I gave her a huge hug. "Thank you. Thank you so much."

"Don't thank me. All I did was drive you here. And track down the lanterns for Daniel. But all this was his idea."

From the dunes below came the sound of a cell phone. I glanced down to see Joy striding toward us. "Yes, she's here . . . I think so . . . okay . . . see you in a minute."

Joy hung up the phone and bolted up the stairs. "That was my dad. He was wondering if you were going to come down to the beach. You still want to marry him, right?"

I nodded. "Of course, I still want to marry him."

"Good because he's a nervous wreck."

I smiled at Daniel, then looked at my daughter. "Are you okay with all this, Joy? With your dad and me getting married?"

"Of course, I am." She smiled. "I'm really happy for both of you."

I glanced at Vicki who nodded. "I'm happy for you, too. Now, go get your ring."

"Okay." Giddy beyond belief, I looped my arm through my daughter's, and together we descended the steps.

Oh, Lord. Is this really happening for me? A daughter and a husband? Thank you. Thank you.

Joy and I took the path through the dunes. When we reached the beach, my mother shouted, "She's here. She's finally here."

As though the whole scene had been well rehearsed, my entire family moved away from Daniel, giving him space. He looked at me, and our eyes locked as though we were the only two people in the world.

"I love you, Mom," Joy said, leaning in for another hug.

She'd recently started calling me mom every now and then, and each time she did, it felt like my heart would explode with pure elation. I hugged her back. "Oh, honey. I love you, too. I love you and your father with all my heart."

"I know you do. Now, go say yes and put my dad out of his misery."

I laughed. "You got it."

My heart pounding, I kicked off my shoes, then I followed the rose-petaled path through the sand to

Daniel. With tears streaming down my face, I stopped in front of him and smiled. "Hey."

"Hey yourself," he said, grinning.

Before he could speak, I said, "Can I ask you a question?"

His expression faltered. "What is it?"

"Well . . . I was just wondering if you knew where the bathroom was."

"The bathroom?" He hesitated for just a brief second, then he threw his head back and laughed. I laughed, too, my heart overflowing with endless love for this man who'd once asked me the same question.

When we stopped laughing, his face grew serious. "You don't really have to go to the bathroom right now, do you?"

I shook my head. "No."

"Good because I have something I want to ask you."

"Yeah?"

He nodded, then he knelt on one knee. "Bianca Grace Morgan, I've loved you for the past four years, and even though it took me almost that long to make you realize it, I promise if you marry me I'll spend every day of my life showing you how much I love you. I'll always cherish you and take care of you. And I'll never leave you. Will you marry me?"

Swallowing the lump in my throat, I nodded. "Yes.

Yes, Daniel. I'll marry you."

Leaning over, I kissed this man who'd come to mean the world to me. Daniel came to his feet and pulled me closer as my family clapped and hollered.

"Lift me up," I said.

"What?"

"You heard me. Lift me up . . . unless you're not strong enough."

He grinned. Then he lifted me in the air and spun me around. This time, I threw my head back and laughed, feeling not like that dainty heroine from the cover of a romance novel, but like me. Like Bianca Grace Morgan, the full-figured woman who'd just agreed to marry the man of her dreams.

When Daniel set me on the ground, he kissed me again. "I love you, Bianca."

"I love you, too."

For a brief moment, we gazed into each other's eyes, then we were joined by my mom, my dad, Enzo, Jillian, Keith, Matt, Drew, Linda Faith, Anna, Nick, Travis, Hailey, Gabby, and Zoey Rose—all of them offering their congratulations with hugs and kisses.

When things settled down, I glanced back at the house, noticing Vicki standing by herself on the porch. I waved, and she waved back.

Would love happen for her? It'd happened to me, so

I had to believe that she too would find her soul mate.

My mother interrupted my thoughts by taking Daniel and me by the hand. "You proposed, and she said yes."

My *fiancé* slipped an arm around my waist. "I did, and thank goodness she said yes. I don't deserve her, but—"

"You do. You're a good man, and Bianca is—" Tenderness filled my mother's eyes. "Bianca is my precious daughter whom I love beyond measure. The two of you will have beautiful babies. Lots and lots of beautiful grandchildren for me, right?"

"Yes, that's right," Daniel said, smiling.

Heat warmed my face, and I laughed. But deep down, I hoped it was true. I hoped with all my heart that one day Daniel and I would tell our children, *Yes, angels, just when Mommy thought there was no hope for her, God sent Daddy and your big sister, Joy.*

As though reading my thoughts, Daniel leaned over and whispered, "I can't wait to get started."

I laughed and gently nudged him in the gut. Then I threw my arms around him. I couldn't wait to get started either.

THE END

Dear Reader,

Thank you so much for reading *Bianca's Joy*! This book is dear to my heart, and I am grateful to be able to donate a portion of every sale to the search for a diabetes cure. Before writing this book, I really didn't know anything about type one diabetes. My research was both heartbreaking and inspiring.

I am so thankful to my readers and everyone who encouraged me to continue writing the Rose Island series. If you enjoyed *Bianca's Joy*, please consider leaving a review wherever you purchased this book. The review doesn't have to be long. Just one or two sentences giving your honest opinion would really help me out by allowing other readers to find me.

The best way to keep up with me is by subscribing to my Newsletter. Go to www.KristinNoel.com and subscribe.

I love connecting with readers! You can join me on **Facebook** (facebook.com/KristinNoelFischer) or contact me through my website.

Again, thank you for reading my book!

Love,

Kristin

Acknowledgments

A huge thanks to everyone who helped bring Bianca's story to life! I'm incredibly blessed to be supported by so many wonderful people.

First of all, thank you to all my readers who have bought my books, left reviews, or written me an encouraging note. Your support and love mean the world to me. Without you, I wouldn't have this wonderful career.

Thank you to The Dale Tribe and their YouTube channel. Your videos showing life with type one diabetes were so informative and well done. Aspen, you are incredible!

A huge thanks to Michelle Lord and her YouTube channel! I love your honesty and wonderful personality, Michelle.

As always, thank you to my husband and family! I know living with a writer can be challenging at times. Thank you for always loving me, believing in me, and keeping me well fed and educated. I love you guys with all my heart! Joe, you are the true love of my life, and I'm so grateful to have you as we go through this crazy life together.

A special thanks to the best editor in the world,

Chrissy Wolfe at EFC Services, LLC. You are amazing! I don't know what I'd do without you. Thank you for all your help, corrections, encouragement, and suggestions. And thank you especially for helping me with all the type one diabetes information.

Thanks to my beta readers: Juanita Spaulding Jones, Chris Campillo, and Cerrissa Kim. Your feedback is immeasurable, and I couldn't have written this book without you.

Thank you to Kat at Blurbwriter.com who helped me with the back cover copy.

Thank you to Lyndsey Lewellen who created my beautiful cover and Paul Salvette who formatted the book.

Finally, thank you to my parents, Jeanne and Phil Smith. I'm so lucky to be your daughter.

Happy Reading to all of you!

Love,
Kristin

Have you read my first book, "A Mother's Choice?"

A Mother's Choice

By Kristin Noel Fischer

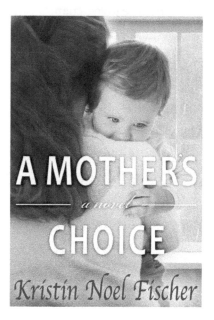

Chapter 1

Seattle – 1961

*I*T WAS RAINING *the day I fell in love with Jude Kingsley, and whenever it rains I can't help but think about that February day in 1961, my junior year of high school.*

My best friend Ruby dashed across the parking lot as a light drizzle escalated to a downpour. I scrambled to keep up but found running impossible in the high heels I'd bought for the Valentine's dance. I despised my freakishly large feet, so I was willing to sacrifice comfort for shoes that made me feel pretty and sophisticated.

Ruby and I joined the other girls in the bathroom and crowded around a single foggy mirror, where we attempted to fix our hair and makeup before venturing out to the stuffy gymnasium. On the stage, a local band played an old Frank Sinatra song, but nobody danced. Rock 'n' roll had been outlawed at our little private school after the archbishop of Chicago had publicly condemned it. My parents, especially my ultraconservative father, agreed with the decision, insisting school dances should be kept innocent and pure.

Ruby scanned the gym. She'd been distracted all week, and while I suspected it had to do with my seventeenth birthday, I didn't know for sure.

I tugged on her sleeve. "Why are you acting so strange?"

She twirled around and gave me an innocent look. "I'm not."

One of our teachers passed by and wished me happy birthday. I thanked him, then placed a hand on my hip and grinned at Ruby. "And how did he know it was my birthday?"

A sly smile played on her lips. "I don't know. School records?"

"Oh, school records," I repeated, with a smile of my own that called her bluff. Ruby and I were close like that. We always knew what the other person was thinking, and we never kept secrets.

All that changed after the accident, of course, but I'm getting ahead of myself.

Ruby had befriended me in the second grade when I'd moved to Seattle from Texas. All the kids had made fun of my southern accent, especially pesky Tim O'Connor who always tried to imitate me. Ruby, however, had brought me into her fold, insisting she'd have her father arrest anyone who bothered me.

"Okay," Ruby said, threading her elbow through mine. "If you wouldn't mind closing your eyes for a moment—"

"Closing my eyes? What's going on?"

Ignoring my question, she covered my eyes with her hand. "Come on. You'll find out soon enough."

She guided me across the gym where voices erupted with

shouts of "Happy Birthday, Nadine!" I opened my eyes to see all our friends gathered around a table that held a small pink and white cake with seventeen candles.

"For me?" I said, feigning surprise.

Ruby hugged me. "You knew, didn't you?"

"No, of course not. This was completely unexpected."

We laughed at the absurdity that either one of us could keep a secret from the other. "Attached at the hip" was what people used to say about us.

Annoying Tim O'Connor sidled up beside me. "How about a birthday kiss, sweetheart?" He waggled his thick brow and puckered his lips.

I smacked him on the arm. "In your dreams."

Everyone laughed except Tim, who rubbed his arm, offended. Over the years, I'd grown fond of him. He was funny, although many people didn't like him because he often went too far with his teasing. Nevertheless, he had a good heart and had become somewhat of a friend. Part of me even thought he was kind of cute with his curly red hair, bushy eyebrows, and ruddy Irish complexion.

Ruby lit the birthday cake and led everyone in singing Happy Birthday. Before blowing out the candles, I looked around the room, taking it all in. Nobody had ever given me a surprise party before, and I was overwhelmed. Smiling, I blew out the candles, making a wish that every birthday would be just as memorable.

When I looked up to thank Ruby, I found her talking

to Jude Kingsley, an absolutely divine boy with intense green eyes and thick black hair that swept across his forehead. Jude sat next to Ruby in art class and behind me in world history. He'd just moved here from Boston, and both Ruby and I thought he was gorgeous, although until now neither one of us had worked up the courage to talk to him.

Tim grabbed my arm. "Come on, Nadine. Dance with me."

I pulled away, my eyes glued to Ruby and Jude. Something odd settled in my throat. Jealousy? A premonition that everything was about to change? Or maybe just a desire to reach up and brush Jude's hair off his brow.

My stomach clenched as Ruby took Jude's hand and led him toward me.

"Nadine," Tim said.

"Not now. I'll save you a dance when they play Elvis."

"Elvis! That's never going to happen. Elvis is a horrible dancer, and according to Sister Hildegard, the devil incarnate."

I scowled at Tim. "Elvis is the greatest musician in the world, and he served in the Army, which is more than you can say, Tim O'Connor."

He batted the air and shook his head. "That's it, Nadine Greene. I'm crossing you off my list." Although he was joking, he turned abruptly and headed toward another girl.

Ruby nudged my shoulder. "He's such a dweeb."

I shrugged. "He's okay."

Jude stared at me with his beautiful green eyes, and I felt a thrill skitter up my spine.

"You like Elvis, Nadine?" he asked.

My stomach did a little flip flop. Jude Kingsley knew my name?

Ruby answered for both of us. "We love Elvis." Although she was no longer holding Jude's hand, she continued standing close to him.

Jude nodded approvingly. "I'm going to sing Jailhouse Rock *at the talent show next month."*

I laughed, convinced he was joking. "Sister Hildegard has outlawed rock 'n' roll. I'm certain she won't allow you to perform a song by Elvis."

Jude's gaze didn't waver from mine. His lips tugged upward in a conspiratorial smile. "True, but I have a plan, and if you'll help me—"

"Me?" Heat burned my face. For the first time, I allowed myself to really study his eyes. In addition to being the most incredible shade of forest green, they contained shards of amber that caught the light as he spoke. I'd never noticed that detail before, not that sparkling shards of amber were something easily noticed during fifth period when our history teacher was droning on about the Bolshevik Revolution.

"So, will you help me?" Jude asked.

I wet my bottom lip. "Sure. What do I have to do?"

"Just play the piano. You can sing if you want, but Tim said you're a talented pianist."

Nervous laughter squeaked out of my mouth. Ruby gave me a disapproving glare, but Jude didn't seem to mind. He reached his hand toward me. "Come dance with me, and I'll tell you about my plan."

I hesitated a moment, too shocked to move. I liked Jude. Really liked him, but so did Ruby, and I wasn't going to let a boy—even a boy as cute as Jude Kingsley—get in the way of our friendship.

Ruby shrugged. "Go ahead. You're the birthday girl, after all."

Her tone held a layer of irritability, but before I could address it, Jude clasped my hand and led me to the dance floor. I glanced back at Ruby, relieved to see her talking with another boy. Maybe she didn't like Jude as much as I thought.

Jude smiled and gestured toward my heels. "Can you dance in those things?"

"I don't know. I've never tried."

He chuckled, the sound rumbling in his chest. Then he pulled me close, and I ignored everything except my body against his. I closed my eyes and rested my head on his solid chest. My insides tingled from my toes to the top of my head.

Lowering his hand, he pressed it to the small of my back. "Is this okay?"

I nodded and held onto the moment. The band played Earth Angel, *and my heart burst with elation because from that moment on, I knew I would love Jude Kingsley forever. I just wasn't prepared for what that love would cost me.*

A Mother's Choice is available

CPSIA information can be obtained
at www.ICGtesting.com
Printed in the USA
FSHW021740100719
59888FS